POISONED BONDS

THE HIGH COUNCIL WITCH CHRONICLES

JULIE CATHERINE

POISONED BONDS

THE HIGH COUNCIL WITCH CHRONICLES

JULIE CATHERINE

Edited by
KATIE WOLF

For Bub and Little Bub.

"*Each year, the High Council chooses seven potential bonds, then whittles them down. The strongest five, the five couples with the most potential, are welcomed inside. This year, through a very messy reaping period, the High Council welcomed fourteen candidates to its front doors. With the mandate, like always, that only the ten most worthy would one day enter, we built the strongest tests the Council could think of to allow your truest energies to shine. Then fate made its selections.*" *Lady Gray took a deep breath. Her eyes shone. So proud.* "*Congratulations to the ten of you. This is the first time in the history of the High Council that we can claim each of you has parabonded through earth, wind, water, and fire.*"

The two women waved their arms.

They swung their hands over the pool and the motel and the property.

As their fingers danced by, the grounds began to change before our very eyes. The pool became a magnificent fountain with jets of water shooting spouts of waterfalls. Behind the fountain, the motel transformed into a magnificent castle on epic grounds of lush green plants. The magnificent home looked both ancient in beauty and slickly modern, with turrets and dormers rising several stories from the grounds where we stood. On its southern face were a thousand windows. Delicate stonework with expressive balconies dotted each floor. And in the center of the estate, an impressive, oversized atrium of bay windows extended up and up, three floors into the air. It was stately and noble.

Then they gestured to the right, and a cold wind blew in from the north.

The fall season returned all at once, and I realized the ladies had been holding the warmer weather until the end of limbo. I slipped on the little jacket I'd been carrying. The breeze was chilly. We gathered closer together. Winter was coming. The summer was gone.

I snuck a glance at Beck and discovered he was also looking in my direction.

Instead of dodging my eyeline or becoming shy, he playfully raised an eyebrow.

I smiled and wiggled mine as well. We shared a private smile.

Big changes were coming.

"Ladies and gentlemen..." Lady Mauve regained our attention.

The illusion around us was fully dissipated.
She threw our focus back to the expansive castle.
"Welcome to the High Council."

ONE

THE GRAND TOUR

WHEN THE HIGH Council grounds appeared before us, they were even better than I imagined.

"Holy snot balls," Greg said.

"Whoa," Hilde murmured beside me.

"You got that right," Tej agreed.

We stared up at the beautiful country estate that looked part elegant French manor, part modern, sleek hotel. It was one of the most stunning castles I had ever seen. The building was at least four or five stories tall with an atrium made entirely of windows. Wings stretched out on either side, with wraparound balconies and decadent pillars holding up their structures. The fountain in front of its doors sprung to life, gurgling at first, then creating a majestic cascade of water. We took it all in, a ragtag group of teens on the front lawn. This was the place we had been battling to enter. Our new home. The doors were opened to us now. It was more spectacular than I had ever dreamed.

And so was my parabond.

I snuck a look at Beck.

His head was tilted back, eyes wide, taking in all the details. He raked a hand through his sideswept hair. He was tall, sturdy, athletic. He must have sensed my looking because his glance flashed in my direction.

I quickly looked away. Wouldn't want him to think I was staring.

"Is it everything you thought it would be?" Sloane asked, her tone respectfully hushed.

"And more," I agreed.

"I meant the building." She winked.

We both grinned, but I rolled my eyes. I guess she noticed my wandering view. I blushed and prepared for more teasing, but she didn't engage in a second round of banter. She let me off the hook. My attraction to Beck was hard fought for. Instead, she gave my hand a little squeeze. I smiled, grateful. Sloane always saw everything.

"A-whoooo!" Greg howled like a wolf. "Well, don't just stand there, come on!" He grabbed Marcy's hand, and the two of them left our stoic half-circle and ran forward towards the castle.

Lady Mauve and Lady Gray approved, dramatically waving us ahead.

We had officially arrived. It was time to explore. The real property, the building... the *real* High Council. Our five parabond partnerships and the two teachers closed in on the front doors.

Greg and Marcy ran up to the grand entrance,

swerving back and forth in childlike formations, running, jumping, touching every stone and surface as they went. I knew how they felt. The energy buzzed inside each of our chests. We felt like young kids again. Hilde, really only a child herself, joined them, climbing up on curbs and hopping off, releasing her pent-up energy. Nicolette spun around joyfully in the driveway until she caught Vince's disapproving frown. Quickly, she fell back into line with the rest of the crowd.

Beck floated to my side.

"Welcome to the rest of your life," he said.

Did he mean with him?

My brand new parabond and partner?

Or was he referencing our entrance in the High Council coven?

I took my eyes off the magnificent two-story doors to glance his way.

The rest of my life... Either way, it was a bold thing to say.

The rest of *our* lives.

But he was right. We were entering our futures. A future I'd chosen to spend with him.

"I'm ready," I told him, trying to match his confident tone. We both smiled. I started to blush. I felt warm and alive under his gaze. My skin tingled in his proximity. I wanted to play it cool, but I couldn't help my nervous hands. I twisted my brown hair over my shoulder, excited to hear what he'd say next, but our reverie was interrupted.

"Holy crap," Greg exclaimed, pulling our attention

back to the castle doors. He'd yanked one open and caught his first glimpse inside the entrance.

"Eeee!" Marcy squealed, coming up behind him. "You guys!"

The rest of us hurried to see what they'd seen. We poured in through the grand entrance.

"Whoa," Hilde said and let out a small gasp.

Even Rick and Vince seemed impressed. Their heads tilted back in wonder.

As I entered the space, I couldn't help but float my eyes heavenward too. It was an involuntary reaction. The room felt so large and so grand. It was an atrium built out of beautiful slab marble floors, exposed brick, and industrial railings. The ceiling soared high above us in the air. Little pods of furniture broke up the space to let you know that it wasn't meant to be too precious, although none of us dared to sit down on a perfectly curated couch. The wall of windows through which we had entered now gave the impression from inside out that we were living inside the forest. There was also a spectacular view of the fountain back down at the base of the drive. Above our heads shone a thousand twinkling lights in an extravagant chandelier. At first, I thought they'd painted the ceiling navy and dark, but then I realized what I could see was the true night sky. It was a skylight. The whole ceiling was white support beams, windows, and sky. More impressive than the light fixture, the ceiling was cut into a thousand little pieces that highlighted the stars in the sky. It was spectacular.

Having given us time to ogle enough, the ladies started their official tour.

"Over here, we have your dining hall." Lady Gray pulled our focus and collected us back together. As we had entered the lobby, our group had naturally widened and spread out in the hall, but now we gathered tightly. She opened the dining room doors, and we stared inside. There were rows of tables and benches on either side of a great aisle. The whitewashed wood ceilings were punctuated with dark, impressive beams and gave the room a chalet-like vibe. It was pretty but felt a bit empty. Without a wonderful spread of food, there wasn't much to see in the space. It was big enough for the whole coven to convene together.

"What time is breakfast?" Nicolette asked.

"Seven to eight thirty. We'll provide you a schedule," Lady Gray assured her.

"Yes, where is she? Blue Moon is late." Lady Mauve frowned.

"We're a touch early," Lady Gray disagreed.

Lady Mauve didn't care. "Good help is hard to find."

"Right this way," Lady Gray said, continuing the tour. We ducked out a different door from the cafeteria. She pointed down the hall. "Professor offices, hours are listed."

"If a door is shut, take the hint," Lady Mauve added.

We could see all the offices were currently locked. But that was no surprise late at night.

"That leads us to the library," Lady Gray continued.

The ladies pushed open another heavy wooden door, this one rounded into a wooden archway. It led into the third majestic room of the day.

"That's a lot of books," Hilde murmured.

We all paused behind her, eager to take it in. There were rows and rows of books of all sizes.

"This is so great," Marcy said.

"Do people read anymore?" Greg sounded skeptical.

"No, this is great," his girlfriend countered.

"That's what the internet is for." He shrugged.

"But think of all the fun in the stacks." Marcy giggled.

"I'll take a search engine."

She whispered something more in his ear.

"Ohhh... Best room in the house!" Greg announced.

And he was right. But not for the reasons he thought.

It was sublime.

Here, in one place, was all the coven's information. A vast sea of knowledge to take in and learn. With each title or essay, I could glean a bit more about my mother. I couldn't help myself. I grabbed a book off the shelf and cracked open the tome. The old book smelled amazing. There wasn't really time to read on the tour. But it was clear, if I was to discover anything about my mom, my dad, or my whole family's history in the coven, this was a great place to start.

"There's a lot to take in," Sloane noted as we made our way deeper inside.

The ladies snaked us through the library, past study carrels and large oak tables for quiet conference, rows of books, architecture light tables, card catalogs, and old newspaper microfiche machines. Next, we marched up a single file spiral staircase that climbed to the second floor. As we ascended one by one to the second level, the layout of the library became clear. A zigzag path appeared. The stacks weren't nearly as private as Greg and Marcy had first assumed. Not that they cared.

"Second floor holds the archives, the maps, and the territories of the nearby covens." Lady Gray fell back into tour guide mode.

"There are other covens?" Hilde wondered.

"Of course. All over the world." Lady Gray nodded.

A woman in a white tracksuit and midnight blue tank top ran up, huffing and puffing. "We'll cover all that in the Treaty of Universal Law in tutorials. Hi guys, welcome! I'm Lady Blue Moon."

Lady Mauve pointedly looked down at her watch, then back at the younger guide.

"This is the archives," Lady Blue Moon added.

"Lady Gray already said that," Marcy said.

"Blue Moon wouldn't know that because at the time, she wasn't here," Lady Mauve pointed out.

Lady Blue Moon nodded, but Mauve's sharp tone didn't seem to sting.

"What are they archiving?" Greg wondered.

"The history of the coven," Nicolette told him.

The ladies approved.

"It's weird to think that someone, sometime will be recording our actions," Sloane realized.

"But it's the history of the coven," Nicolette repeated again, as if she was stating an obvious fact that we should all clearly understand. "You have to tell the coven's story."

"But will the tale be good or bad?" Sloane wondered.

"Depends on who you ask," Vince muttered.

"History belongs to the victors, so I'll come out smelling like a rose," Greg agreed.

"So will the rich." Tej nodded.

"We'll all be accurately represented," Rick said. It was the first thing I'd heard from him since the ladies had declared that we were in, that limbo was over, and the castle had appeared. Hilde nodded to her partner. The rest of us glanced at each other.

Accurately represented.

Why didn't that sound good?

"Everyone, right this way." Lady Blue Moon tried to gather us.

"We haven't got all day," Lady Mauve added.

The second floor held classrooms and spaces they called practice rooms and a giant greenhouse full of exotic plants. In the nursery, the air was warm and damp. Rick, the only chemist among us, touched a thousand leaves. I kept my hands to myself. You never knew what leafy wonder might be poisonous to the touch.

"Check it out." Beck pointed. I glanced over as Rick held out a small twig over a flowy, dark green vine. The plant species tried to snap the branch right out of his hand.

"Snap ribbons... fascinating," he murmured to himself.

Beck and I looked at each other and grinned.

As a group, we continued to march through the castle's twisty halls. We climbed higher in the manor and straight up the main staircase, which was wide enough for a crowd. It wrapped around an ancient service elevator built to hold large equipment or a flux of people, eight or ten passengers across.

"Floors three and above are all residences. Bedrooms are by private invitation only. Since you're in first year, you're located on the fifth floor. You'll find common sitting areas at the end of each hall. And that's pretty much it. The end of the tour." Lady Blue Moon brought the journey to a close.

Lady Mauve pressed the elevator call button. We all looked up. The light above the elevator lit up, but the arrow signifying the box was traveling from floor to floor barely moved.

"Fifth floor?" Hilde raised an eyebrow.

"Lucky you," Lady Gray agreed. She tried to put a smile on this new information.

"What about a gym? Weights? Calisthenics?" Greg flexed an arm.

"You're gonna climb five stories every day, here and back. What more do you need?" Marcy asked.

"Gotta do curls for the girls." He flexed again, his image reflecting off a shiny surface he'd spotted out of the corner of his eye. Fully turned now, he took in his countenance. He flashed himself a wink and a grin.

"More like grunts for the runt," Vince scoffed.

"That's not for me, babe." Marcy also teased his clear love for himself.

"Gotta get big," he said with a shrug, not ashamed. "Tej gets it." Greg rapped his hand on Tej's stomach.

The shorter boy laughed and flexed as well.

"Little big man," Greg said approvingly, but Tej was far less enthused at that. "Lookin' good."

"There's a gym and a pool and a boxing ring behind the main house." Lady Blue Moon decided to cut off the display.

The creaky service elevator finally arrived.

The oversized doors slid open.

"We'll see you below," Lady Mauve said. She and Lady Gray climbed aboard. There was plenty of room for us all to join them, but in a power play, they claimed the car for themselves. None of us, not even Lady Blue Moon, dared to climb on. We watched the doors close.

"Right this way." She led us down the winding staircase. It was so wide here that we traveled in a clump.

"I thought you said our rooms are up. Why are we headed down?" Nicolette wondered.

"In the lobby, we'll get you situated. You'll need books, room numbers, your whole starter witch pack," she told us, but gave no further details. Obediently, we followed her path. As we twisted around it, the lift lurched its arrow downward, carrying the ladies back to the ground.

"You should know, breakfast runs from seven a.m. to eight thirty sharp," the younger lady added over her shoulder.

"Gray already told us." Nicolette nodded.

"What if I want to sleep in?" Marcy pouted.

"Then you'll go hungry," Vince snapped.

"Still worth it." Marcy shrugged.

"I can get you something," Nicolette offered.

Out of the corner of my eye, I caught sight of Vince's eyes rolling back in his head. I glanced at Beck.

"I'll make sure you're up," he offered.

"What, no breakfast in bed?" I teased.

"It's great to have servants." Tej nodded.

Beck and I raised an eyebrow each.

"Or maybe talk to Nicolette," Tej said, covering his mouth with a laugh.

"Maybe I will." I nodded, letting the joke land.

We hit the ground floor almost in tandem with the elevator. The doors swung open, and the ladies unloaded.

"Alright." Lady Blue Moon's tone transformed into that of a door-to-door huckster salesman. "Grab your books. Room keys, paperwork selection. Take one of each of the texts." She yanked a collection of papers and textbooks out of cardboard boxes on a rolling cart and thumped the tomes into piles on the table as she prepared.

We swarmed over the selections.

"Hilde, yours is here," I called the youngest girl. "Tej," I read the next one aloud.

He quickened his pace to grab the envelope from my hand.

"Mae, this is yours," Marcy noted.

"Thanks." We swapped spots.

I glanced at Beck, who was already busy reading his own introductory letter. How were the rooms divided? In limbo, we each had our own bedroom. At the High Council would we still be so lucky? I opened my letter.

"Room 5112," I read.

"Right beside me." Hilde smiled.

"Me too," Nicolette added.

"And I'm across the hall," Marcy added.

"So am I." Greg grinned, looping an arm around his girl.

"Where's your actual room number?" Marcy asked him.

"5134," he read off.

Lady Blue Moon started unloading a second shelf of items when Lady Mauve held up her hand. She checked her watch and didn't bother to disguise a sigh. "Let's save the rest of the paperwork 'til morning."

Lady Blue Moon was mid-pulling stacks of textbooks off her movable shelves.

At the other lady's declaration, she looked up, surprised, three more textbooks in her arms.

"You were late." Lady Mauve frowned. "I'm tired."

"Sure, okay. No problem." The younger lady stopped in her tracks and hit rewind, a forced smile on her face.

We were all disappointed. They were cutting short the welcome? There were still so many things to learn!

But between our group and Lady Mauve, it was clear who won this battle.

"That's it for tonight." Lady Gray fell in step with her partner. She held up both hands, cutting the tense feeling in the group. "We'll see you in the morning."

"Don't be late," Lady Mauve added.

Each of us grabbed the stack of whatever paperwork and texts we had managed to gather.

Lady Blue Moon looked at the rest of the boxes of books and other goods she had clearly come ready to distribute. There was a lot to take back to her office. Her shoulders slumped as she assessed the weight. Even on a rolling cart, it was going to be a struggle.

"I can help," I offered.

"Would you? That would be great, thanks." She pushed an especially large box in my direction. Luckily, it wasn't as heavy as it looked.

"Mae," I offered my name.

"I knew that," Lady Blue Moon agreed. "Lady Blue Moon," she reintroduced herself.

"And I knew that." I grinned.

"I can take some too," Beck offered.

"Don't be silly. Mae and Moon can take care of themselves," Lady Mauve piped in. She eyed us, daring us to disagree. "Can't you, girls?"

Lady Blue Moon nodded.

"We're good," I agreed. I slid my personal books and paperwork back on the table. "I'll see you up there," I offered.

Beck seemed uncertain, but he didn't push.

I had a bit of a secret motive for helping, hoping maybe after helping her move all the boxes, I could get Lady Blue Moon to show me how all the archives in the library worked. The others were already starting to pile into the elevator on their way to the fifth floor. I shrugged Beck off with a smile so he wouldn't miss his ride. Then I followed Lady Blue Moon with the box full of textbooks.

"Down this way. My office is the third one on the right," she instructed.

I followed, obedient.

"Right, here we go..." She fussed with her keys, then opened the door.

"Whoa." I hadn't meant to comment, but I was taken aback as I took in the sight.

Her four little walls were filled to the brim with paperwork piles, old newspapers, and stacks of books. I could barely see her desk. There was only one clean spot. In the midst of the chaos was a small, untouched space and a solitary laptop.

"Mind the mess, it's not exactly organized." She shrugged, as if she weren't the total architect of this chaotic design.

"How do you get anything done?" I wondered.

"Oh, here? I don't. That's why I work in the archives." She chuckled to herself. "Anywhere will be fine." She motioned to the box of books and the room. For once, I believed it.

"Thanks for lightening my load." She shoved the rolling cart into the midst of the chaos.

"You're welcome," I said, trying hard not to stare. I hesitated in the doorway. I couldn't find the right words.

"Something else?"

"The archives…" I started. I wasn't sure what I was asking. "Can anyone work there?"

"Oh, sure, and read them if you've got free time to burn. It's one of my favorite spots in the whole place actually." Lady Blue Moon grew wistful. "Interested in history?

I shrugged. "Family genealogy."

"Well, then you've come to the right place. Or you will. When you go there. Big day ahead." All the books rammed inside, Lady Blue Moon turned off the light and closed tightly the office door. The hallway was dark and dim. Lady Mauve had been right. It was time to turn in. "See you in the morning."

I nodded.

There would be other times better suited for exploring, I realized. Better to get my books and scurry off to bed. This was, after all, only day one of my time at the High Council. As Beck had told me, we had the rest of our lives to figure it out.

"Night."

I was tempted to stay up all night and dig in and read everything I could about my mom and this place and everything the record books might have to offer, but I held the desire in check. I had no idea what was in store for my second day, and if it was anything like this first, I wanted to be rested and prepared.

I crossed the atrium looking for my books, trying to decide between taking the stairs and risking the creaky service elevator by myself, when I realized they were no longer there.

Strange.

This was where I'd left them.

I hurried to look around, but quickly realized the lobby wasn't empty. Sloane sat in an armchair, looking out towards the forest.

"You're still here," I noted, checking out her pack of goodies.

"Oh yeah, just taking a moment for myself," she agreed.

"Well, I'll leave you to it." I stepped back.

"Nah, I'm done." She offered a smile. "A little self-reflection never hurt anyone."

"This is a lot to take in," I agreed.

"Just wait 'til the training begins."

I hadn't even thought of the training.

Together, we exited the lobby, her stack of books in

her arms. My tomes were nowhere to be found. But there was also no one left to ask. I guessed I'd worry about it in the morning. Lady Blue Moon could probably hook me up with another set of books.

"Stairs or elevator?" she asked.

"Elevator," we both said at once, then laughed.

Sloane swung her fingers round under her books and pressed the call button. We could see the descending arrow located above the elevator box travel down its path.

"That gives the thing a real old-timey feel," I noted.

"The whole place," Sloane said, nodding, "is both wildly new and terribly old."

We watched the elevator come down.

I wasn't exactly sure what Sloane meant. It sounded like a compliment and an insult all at once. But neither of us were doing a great job of putting words to how we felt. To say the whole experience had been overwhelming was not enough. It was like touching our toe to the sand. Before us loomed an ocean, calm and peaceful on the surface, but dark and dangerous in deeper waters. A person could float safe and happy on the top or be dragged violently below without warning. There were monsters hiding in these waters. Unspoken as it was, I knew she felt it too.

When the arrow hit our floor, the elevator doors slid open, but we paused before climbing inside. The car wasn't empty. Two girls stepped out. They were only a year or two older than Sloane or me, but they walked with the confidence of knowing. Their tenure in the Council was at least a few years old. We shuffled to the side to let them depart, but the prettier of the two, the one with the long black hair that fell in waves around her shoulders and the piercing violet eyes, stopped between me and the lift.

"You're new," she noted. "Mae Kingsley."

"And Sloane Lolant," I introduced my friend. "We've just arrived."

But she wasn't interested in introductions.

"This is the one who got in by default," the pretty girl told her friend.

"Oh." Her companion looked me up and down.

My cheeks flushed bright red.

"Mae didn't default," Sloane jumped in.

"No? That's right. She beat the girl with the bum leg." The girl's face twisted into a cruel smile. She didn't look so pretty then.

"I heard that the limpy one didn't have any powers," her friend added. "Total loser."

"Well, Mae wouldn't know anything about that." The black-haired girl winked at me with a nasty grin.

I was too shocked to reply.

"Good luck with first year, ladies," she said.

The two girls laughed over their shoulders as they left.

"Come on." Sloane led me onboard. She pressed the button for the fifth floor. We ascended in silence. "Ignore her. She's the worst. They both are."

I forced a smile. "No, I know." I rolled my eyes. "Real mature."

We both nodded.

But the damage was done. I felt a new feeling, and it found a home deep inside my heart. I had hoped that once I was accepted into the High Council, things would get a little easier.

Fat chance.

TWO
A LATE NIGHT VISIT

"ARE YOU SURE YOU'RE ALRIGHT?" Sloane broke the silence that started building between floor two and three.

"I'm fine. Really. Golden." I flashed a phony smile. I didn't need her to believe me. I just wanted Sloane to drop it, but she wasn't picking up on my signals.

"What does she know anyway? You shouldn't listen."

"I'm not. I didn't."

My cheeks hurt from the phony grin. Why was this elevator so slow? I felt like we'd been passing the fourth floor forever.

"There's more than one way to be admitted to the High Council. We all play to our own strengths," Sloane assured me again.

Easy for you to say.

You didn't live in the limbo's rock bottom, I thought to myself, but my plastered grin never faltered.

"Can we please talk about something else? Seriously. I'm good," I told her. "Totally, totally good."

"Sure." Sloane nodded and looked into her stack of books.

I did too.

Suddenly, her paperwork was wildly interesting.

One more floor to go.

When the elevator doors finally opened, we both breathed a sigh of relief. Assuring each other that nothing was weird in a moving box of hurt feelings was a full-time job. Remind me to take the stairs, I told myself, ready to disappear into the hallway's crown molding.

The fifth floor looked more like a mid-range hotel chain than a beautiful castle, with a large elevator lobby and a new cookie-cutter dorm room every twenty or thirty feet. I guessed by the time they'd reached the upper levels, the designing architects had run out of steam. I didn't mind the straightforward layout. Without bells or whistles, it was easy to locate my room. I tried to pretend I wasn't curious which one would house Beck. I had no way of knowing tonight. Before I'd left with Lady Blue Moon, I'd forgotten to ask.

"See you in the morning," I told Sloane.

"I'm just glad you're okay." Her room was two doorways away.

Without another word, I slipped into my dorm. Behind my back, the lock gave off a satisfying click as it snapped into place. It was safe behind these four walls.

Someone had transported my bags from the old motel room, and they were waiting for me in a pile by the single bed.

I leaned up against the door, closed my eyes, and breathed in and out.

The one who got in by default.

"Hey."

"Jesus!" I jumped out of my skin. I opened my eyes, and Nicolette was peering out at me from a doorway inside the room.

"Sorry. It's a Jack and Jill bathroom," she explained, worried she'd given me a heart attack. "I'm next door. We're sharing the space."

I followed her to the tunnel between rooms. She was right: between the two dorms was a small ensuite bathroom with a door on each end. Two sinks, one tub, one toilet. The first thing to cross my mind was how glad I was not to be sharing with Marcy... and by proxy, with Greg.

"I didn't mean to disturb you," she added.

"No, you didn't." I shook her off, but she frowned anyway. "You surprised me, is all." I poked my head in and looked around. "I'll just have to remember to lock this. I'm neat, I promise. We'll get along just fine. Night."

I got the sense Nicolette probably wanted to talk a little more, but it wasn't something I could manage. I didn't have another second of social grace in me. I was totally drained. I maintained my forced smile for the three steps it took to travel back into my own private sector, but when I shut and locked the communal bath-room door, I released that very last ounce of poise.

Confirming for myself much more thoroughly this time that I really was alone, I flopped down on the bed.

The black-haired girl's words just kept rattling in my brain.

The one who got in by default.

Is that what everybody thought? To me, it hadn't felt that way. For this spot in the High Council, I had fought within an inch of my life. But the pretty girl was correct, Josie did quit before the final battle, letting me become the final parabonding girl uncontested. I assumed that was designed by the hands of fate, but I guess you could hear the same facts and look at me like a consolation prize the boys were stuck with at the end. I hadn't considered that interpretation before she chimed in with her opinion. Now it was all I could see.

Pretty girls were the worst.

Suddenly, at my door came a gentle rapping.

"What now?" I frowned but dragged myself to check it out. "Who is it?"

"Beck."

My hand fluttered to my hair, and self-consciously I patted my strands. I peeked out the peephole. There he stood. Handsome and tall as ever, slightly skewed by the curve of the looking glass. He was looking up and down the hallway, nervously raking his brown hair back from his forehead with one hand. My textbooks were propped on his hip.

Of course.

He'd brought up my books and my welcome package. That was the kind of sweet, considerate thing Beck might have done for Josie in the past. Now he was doing it for me. I straightened my T-shirt and did a check for flyaways.

And he remembered my room number.

The tiny morsels of proof that he had been thinking about me caused my arms to goose bump. I couldn't help but grin. Beck made everything better. Once I felt sure I looked prim and proper, I turned the knob.

"Hey."

"Hey." Beck smiled.

My heart fluttered.

"Got your stuff," he offered.

"Yeah, thanks." I reached out to take the books from his hands. He loaded them into my arms. He'd made them look light as air, but I struggled to carry the weight. I tried to hide it.

"Just wanted to double check you got back okay." He nodded. He couldn't help but look over my shoulder to the unpacked suitcases in my room. "I guess you just arrived."

He'd probably already made himself at home.

"Yeah, thanks." I nodded. I thought about inviting him in, but I wasn't sure what the rules were about letting the opposite sex into your dorm. The last thing I wanted was a social ding for inappropriate fraternization, but I had to put the books down. It couldn't hurt to hang out for a second. He was, after all, my parabond.

Whatever that meant.

"Do you wanna come in?"

"Sure." He nodded.

I moved back from the entrance and let him step through. I couldn't help but glance in the hall, but there was no one to watch who'd come in or out. I shut the door and walked us back into the space. Happily, I managed to put all the books down without drawing too much attention to myself.

"I love what you've done with the place," Beck teased.

I grinned. "Does yours look the same?"

He nodded. Awkwardly, he looked around. Now that we were both in the area together, I realized there was only one piece of furniture to sit on in the whole place. The bed. My bed. Beck was doing his best not to look at it.

"It's a pretty big improvement from the motel rooms in limbo," I offered.

"Yeah." He chuckled. "You should have seen it, Josie's bed had a spring standing straight up—" He seemed to catch himself and realize the awkwardness of telling me about the bed of another girl mid-phrase. "In... the air," he trailed off.

"That's crazy." I nodded, trying to chuckle. "Hopefully this bed is nothing like that."

There she was. His ex-girlfriend.

Me, Beck, and Josie.

What a weird little trio.

I tried to think of something else to say. Something non-bed-related. Non-Josie-related. Beck did too. The silence between us grew larger. Neither of us sat down.

"Have you been to—"

"What'd you think of—"

Both Beck and I started at once.

"Sorry," he backed off.

"No, you go."

"I was just wondering, have you been to the sitting room at the end of the hall?" he asked.

"I haven't."

"Me neither," he agreed. "We could check it out?" He raked his hair again.

"Uh, yeah. Sure. Okay. Let's." I grabbed my room key, and we headed out of the space together. Even though we were only going down the hall, I locked the door behind me.

Anything to get out of the room with the bed.

"All good?" Beck checked, though he had just seen me go through the motions.

"Good," I agreed.

It was weird.

We both offered a quick smile to the other and started to make our way down the hall. Being back in a public space felt more normal, but we were walking at a strange pace. Almost meanderingly slow. We both easily fit in the hallway width, but it didn't feel that way. For some reason, I had no idea what to do with my hands.

"Which one is yours?" I asked.

Was that odd?

Was it strange if I wanted to know which one was his room? I hoped he wouldn't think I'd come knocking in the middle of the night.

"5127." He pointed in the opposite direction.

"Ah. Good. An odd number. Better than even," I mumbled. "You're an odd guy," I joked. "Not that I'm saying you're *odd*. But your room is."

I could kill myself.

"No, for sure," he agreed.

I clamped my mouth shut for fear something even weirder might trickle out.

"This is it." Beck nodded at the door right in front of us, also stating the obvious. He pushed open one of the two double doors.

"Nice," I added.

No one could accuse either of us of being sparkling conversationalists.

The French doors had ornate wood details and brass handles. They looked a bit out of place on such a sterile, personality-less floor, but the inside of the common room looked a bit cozier than the dorm rooms. I flicked on the light to get a better look.

The room flashed into view, and there was a bit of a flurry as Greg and Marcy quickly disappeared behind the couch. I was pretty sure I'd seen a bare shoulder and a wild and robust flash of unkempt hair. Slender fingers reached out and snatched a woman's button-down shirt from where it had been tossed on the ground.

"Oh, hey guys," Marcy greeted us as she threaded herself into her clothing. Greg's face also popped up from where he was lying on the couch. Marcy gave a quick swipe to her boyfriend's face to remove any smudges of lipstick from his face. "We were just—"

"You know..." Greg wiggled his eyebrows.

"Watching a movie," Marcy corrected, giving her boyfriend a little frown.

Beck and I eyed the black television screen hanging on the wall at the front of the room.

"What was the movie?" I asked.

"*The Princess Reunion.*"

"*Monster Robots Battle-a-thon.*"

They both answered at once.

"Like I'd watch *The Princess Reunion,*" Greg complained.

"You would if you knew what was good for you," Marcy shot back.

We all burst out laughing.

Marcy tamped down the last stray strands of her hair.

"Sorry, guys, we didn't know the room was taken." Beck did his best not to gape at the pair.

"That's alright. Greg and I were just headed to bed." She gave a little teasing tug on her boyfriend's shirt and stood. He followed her hungrily, holding a throw pillow over his crotch.

"Yeah, see you later," he agreed, only one step behind his girl. "I'll bring this back," he added.

"Enjoy the 'movies.'" She emphasized the fake word, then passed us into the halls.

"Great minds think alike." Greg winked and patted Beck's chest as he passed, being sure with his other hand to keep a firm grip on the pillow.

Marcy looked over her shoulder and grinned. She flashed her man just a bit of cleavage. She giggled and ran.

"Come here, girl." He raced after her, forgetting his pillow.

Beck and I watched the hurricane of energy that was Greg and Marcy as it disappeared down the hall. When they were gone, we peeked at each other, wide-eyed.

"I didn't mean—" Beck started.

"No, I get it." I nodded. "We were just exploring..." I corrected.

Greg and Marcy had explored the floor. And the couches. And every other surface, if I had to guess.

"Glad we're on the same page," Beck agreed.

And that page had a painfully awkward new parabond couple on it, I thought to myself. For a moment, we both paused.

I spotted Marcy's discarded bra underneath the sofa.

"Maybe we should—"

"You know, I'm kind of—"

Our words smashed together once more.

"I'm kind of tired," I finished.

"Yeah. It's getting late." Beck nodded.

"Got a big day ahead of us," I added. "But here it is. Now we know. The common room looks great. Super comfortable."

"Now we know," he agreed.

We flicked off the lights and retraced our steps. I didn't pick up her bra. There was no way I'd go tonight and knock on that door. She could get the undergarment for herself in the morning. Beck and I walked the return route in silence. We both slowed as we got to my door.

"Well, this is me," I told him.

"I'm just down there." He pointed.

"5127." I nodded. "I remember."

"If you need anything, just knock on my door."

"Will do. You too. Like the reverse. If there's a thing that you need. I'll be here. Not right by my door... that would be weird. But, you know, generally here in the room. You know what I mean."

I wished the floor would open and swallow me whole.

Beck watched me squirm. But he didn't go anywhere.

Together, we hung out in the doorway.

I felt like the world's biggest dummy, but he wouldn't still be standing there, still waiting for something, if he didn't want to. He wanted to be here. For a second, I thought he might try to hug me or kiss me, but instead he just flashed a delicious smile.

"I'll see you in the morning, parabond."

It was perfect.

Just the tiniest hint of teasing. A little joke we could both enjoy.

I smiled back. "Goodnight, parabond."

He smiled.

I wanted to kiss that smile right off his face.

He started to stroll away, and I felt relieved our interaction was over, ecstatic I'd made it out in one piece, my dignity still intact. But still, I couldn't help it. My mouth opened. I called him back.

"Beck."

He looked up.

I'm so glad that I chose you. And you chose me. I can't wait to get to know you. To really see all the exciting places this partnership could lead. It's super weird without Josie. She's this dark shadow looming over everything we say and do. But that's the thing about shadows: at the right time of day, they just totally disappear.

"See you tomorrow," was all I managed to say.

THREE
DREAMING OF KATE

I BUMPED into Nicolette over toothbrushes and face cream twice more as I readied for bed, but we merely nodded and spit in our sinks. The day was so long and the ups and downs so exhausting that I had no trouble falling asleep.

In dreamland, I heard a familiar voice.

"Mae." It grew more insistent. "Please help."

I looked around. Hay stuck into the small of my back. The room smelled of wet straw and distant cow dung. But then, it wasn't a room at all. I regained my senses in the loft of Kate's barn.

Kate Hucklebee hung from an old wooden beam two stories up from the ground. Holding on for dear life.

My high school friend, Kate.

The girl who died in her barn.

Kate, who slipped and fell to her death when Josie and I went to confront her about hijacking our parabonding process. Stealing our offerings. Forcing our hands. Here she was, alive and well in my dream.

For now.

"Oh my god." I took in the situation.

In real life, this wasn't how it went down, but this version of Kate didn't know that. She gripped the beam with both arms. Her legs kicked below her as I struggled to understand what was happening.

"Kate?" I sat up in the rooster perch. "What the hell? Oh god. Kate, hold on."

As I shuffled positions, little strands of hay slipped over the edge of the small wooden platform I was clinging to. The fibers sprinkled down to the floor two stories below.

"Oh my god," I murmured again.

I looked all around for a way to help her.

"I don't want to die, Mae," she said, weeping.

Her arms started to slip.

She flailed around the beam to fasten her grip, but I could see it was a losing battle. Her legs hung down precariously over nothingness at first, then over some rusty old farm equipment we both knew would do a terrible job of breaking her fall.

"Kate, please hold on... Josie?" I cried out for my partner. "Josie!"

Somehow I knew she should be there, even though I couldn't see her in my mind.

But Josie didn't answer.

And Kate was too far gone.

The beam she was holding was only a few inches in diameter, and we were on opposite sides of the barn.

"Kate, I'm coming."

"What are you going to do without her?" Kate wailed. "You can't do this on your own."

"Yes, I can. Kate, I'm coming," I repeated.

I slid on my stomach out on the wooden beam, wriggling towards her. Kate struggled. Her weight was growing too much to handle for her arms.

"Kate, I'm coming," I repeated, inching forward.

Bit by bit, I closed the gap.

"Please help me. Please save me." Her arms were slipping. "Save us all."

I was almost to her. "I've got you."

"No, you don't."

I made it to her trembling body. I put a hand on her arm for comfort, trying to figure out how to hold her. How to pull her up. She was far too heavy and too far gone for me to lift her to safety myself. I wasn't that strong.

"I can do this," I lied. I tried to pull her up.

"Mae, I'm slipping."

One arm gave out.

I reached out and caught her. I gripped her remaining arm. She was too heavy to hold. She was slipping through my palm.

"Just hold on. Where's Josie? Josie!"

But no one answered.

"You didn't call her," Kate whimpered.

"Yes, I did. I'll call her. Josie! No... no... Josie!"

My fingers couldn't hold.

"Mae—"

Kate let go. Her body fell through the air, her eyes looking up at me in terror, her hands grabbing for support that wasn't there.

I looked away in disgust as her bones and the farm equipment met.

The crunch was sickeningly alive, then deadening and final.

"Oh god." I closed my eyes, refusing to look, willing myself to wake up from this replay of the tragedy, but my unconscious mind wouldn't release me from the show. Finally, I looked back towards the farm equipment. Scared out of my mind and grossly entranced all at once.

Maybe she was okay.

I hoped she hadn't suffered.

Down on the floor, I saw Kate's limp, lifeless body, broken and bloodied. A murky red pool expanded beneath her chest. It coagulated in her hair. She swam in her own lifeless puddle.

Beside the dead girl stood someone else I didn't want to see. The pretty black-haired girl with the purple eyes. She looked up from Kate's shattered body.

"Why didn't you get help?" she asked. Her frown cut me in two.

I sat up in my bed with a start.

Moments later, my alarm clock rang out.

Day two in the castle had arrived.

FOUR
NO TALK 'TIL COFFEE

"MORNING." I dragged myself out the door and ran into Sloane and Tej as they were leaving their dorm rooms. They had clearly agreed last night to meet to go to breakfast, but now that the early time slot had arrived, all Tej could muster was a grunt. Sloane, on the other hand, looked like she'd had the best sleep of her life.

"How'd you sleep?" she asked.

"I've had better," I admitted.

"Tej feels the same."

"No talk before coffee," he murmured.

I glanced in the direction of Beck's door but didn't bother to wake him. Instead, I fell into step with the pair. Beck and I made no plan for a morning meetup. If he was still happily dozing, let him. At least one of us would have a good night's sleep.

The horror of last night's nightmare was only starting to fade.

Just a dream, I reminded myself. It didn't mean anything.

At the elevator and staircase lobby, we found Hilde waiting for the lift. The down button in front of her was lit.

She shrugged. "I'm not sure that it's working," she admitted, glancing up at the floor indicator. "It's been stuck on three for a while."

"Well, come on. It's all downhill from here." Sloane waved her into our little group.

"Morning, Mae. Morning, Tej." Hilde smiled at the older boy.

"No talk," he complained. "Coffee."

"Is this your first time away from home?" Sloane asked the girl as we descended the stairs.

She nodded.

"Well, I think you're pretty brave."

"It's my first time away from home too," Tej noted. "Am I brave?"

"What happened to not talking 'til coffee?" I laughed.

Tej shrugged. "I had to put Sloane in her place. Someone should open a coffee shop on our floor. They'd rake in the cash."

"I don't think they charge for breakfast," Hilde said, concerned. "Do they?"

"I hope not," I agreed. "I didn't bring any cash."

Other sleepy teens stumbled onto the staircase from their floors as well. We all made a zombie-like approach to the cafeteria. Everyone looked as tired as I felt, although I felt pretty sure I held the record for worst nighttime experience. We trudged down in slow progression.

"I bet Lady Mauve has her own espresso machine," Tej added, still in a caffeinated dreamland. We giggled at the idea of barista Lady Mauve turning her own tumblers and dials with the squirt and hiss of hot foam.

"Maybe she just imagines her morning joe." Sloane pretended to lie-guard a mug of coffee into creation.

"Can she do that?" Hilde wondered.

"I don't know," Sloane admitted.

They looked to me. I shrugged.

"I bet she can," Hilde decided, admiration squeaking into her voice.

As we got closer to the lower floor, new waves of students joined the procession, including two I did not want to see: that pretty girl and her snarky friend.

She'd made such a horrible first impression on me she'd even interrupted my dreams. Now she was flanked by two new compatriots: a handsome guy and a new homely friend.

Great, I thought. Her obnoxious crew was multiplying.

I slowed on the stairs. Then stopped.

I just couldn't face her.

Not after the way she'd looked at Kate. Even if it was in dreamland.

"What's wrong?" Sloane asked. The others paused as well.

The river of students threaded around us; we were

just a couple stones in the flow of progress. All around, the others continued their march down the stairs.

"Nothing," I stammered, left without a reason to give to them. "I just realized that I left something upstairs."

"Well, you're not gonna get it now." Tej looked up at the waves of students descending around us.

"No," I realized. "I guess not." I nodded.

I couldn't run or hide.

"Alright, forget it." I waved our little group on.

At least I'd bought a little time and distance. The others tromped onwards ahead, completely unaware, but Sloane fell a step behind to my side.

"Why'd you really stop?" she asked.

"It's nothing." I shook her off.

"No?" She purposefully looked down the stairwell at the black-haired girl from the elevator. "You should face it head-on."

Sloane was right.

The school was small.

It wasn't practical to run and hide every time the pretty girl appeared in the hall. Besides, dreams were just dreams, and mean girls only said out loud what everybody else was thinking in their thoughts. The nice ones held the exact same beliefs. The only difference was they gladly kept their opinions to themselves. Still, being called a default was a tough pill to take.

I'd thought I really earned it, this place in the High Council.

For a few moments, almost a whole day, I'd thought

that this was my spot, and I'd held my head high. I fought hard through all of limbo. I'd scratched and clawed for my position on the roster. It wasn't my fault that Josie decided to quit the High Council. Just like it wasn't my fault she and Beck had broken things off. Her choice to leave in the final round, mid-contest, wasn't easy. It had actually put me in an awkward and awful position. I'd had to pick my parabond from the two guys still competing. And it was not an easy choice. I was guaranteed to hurt someone and destroy their paranormal advances. It was an agonizing decision to choose between Beck and my sort of ex, Spade.

But I did it.

I did what was right. Even at the expense of the other boy's feelings. I stood up and did the right thing for me and the High Council.

That didn't make me weak. It made me strong.

I was meant to be here in the coven, with Beck as my partner. We were destined to parabond forever. The fact that she quit didn't change that. I would have tried my hardest to fight head-to-head with Josie and earn my spot at the High Council, but I didn't have to. Fate intervened on my behalf.

In that random girl's eyes, that made me the default choice.

Who cares what she says, I reminded myself.

She was just one snarky nobody.

Things were going great so far with Beck. We were on the right track.

Last night was sweet. Him showing up at my door.

I really liked him. And I felt he liked me too.

We'd just have to figure out how to give ourselves permission to be more than friends. We were partners now. Real partners, partners forever. Whether that meant romance or anything else was up to us. Being friends first had put comfortable barriers on our relationship and rules to live by, simple things to guide our way. They served us well while we were in high school and in limbo, but now we'd picked each other, and those other walls had given way. We were creating a new set of boundaries. It was weird, and a little awkward, but I had faith that we'd be okay.

That was why I picked him over Spade.

Spade Polari was a risk.

An unfriendly face.

A snake in the grass.

He was such an unknown commodity; I never knew what he was going to do or say. There was only one guarantee of where his alliances lay: he did what was right for himself.

Beck was an unknown too, I knew, but in a different way. I wanted to learn more about him.

"Check it."

As we hit the ground floor, Tej tapped our arms and pointed across the lobby to Nicolette. She had loaded up a tray with coffee and breakfast goodies and was waiting for an elevator car to take her back up to the fifth floor. "I want that," he complained. "A breakfast delivery service. Do you think she made it special for Vince?"

"Keep dreaming." Sloane grinned.

"Probably Marcy." I laughed.

"And Greg," Sloane added sagely. Nicolette wouldn't get one without the other.

Tej pouted, wishing there was also a servant for him.

A guy could dream.

Instead, we rounded the corner into the cafeteria.

"Wow," Hilde murmured.

She was right. The room looked a thousand times more impressive this morning than it had on the tour. There were people streaming in and out in every direction, groups of friendly discussions being held over tables, and all around we smelled delicious wafts of fresh breakfast foods. The space felt alive and kind of intellectual. It was teeming with conversations. I clocked the mean girl and her crew. They had journeyed towards the baked goodies.

"I'm gonna get some coffee," I told Sloane, purposefully heading the opposite direction.

Tej and Hilde had broken away at the first sight of food, but I didn't worry. We'd all reconvene and sit together soon. We didn't know anyone else. Comfort bred familiarity.

Sloane seemed to put two and two together about the girls I was likely avoiding and tilted her head in a frown.

"What?" I defended. "I'm thirsty. It's breakfast. I'll get you one too."

"Fine. Two milks, no sugar. What do you want

from the spread?"

"Buttered toast, double toasted. Thanks so much, you're the best!" I spun away before she could change her mind.

The hot drink line moved quicker than the food counters, and soon I found myself camped out at an empty table, waiting for the others to return. I drank it all in, sipping my coffee, purposefully posed facing away from the buffet table and watching the doorway as other students and ladies and fellows streamed in.

If I didn't see any mean girls in my peripherals, maybe I could pretend they didn't exist. Plus, I was looking forward to Beck's arrival. I wanted him to know I had saved him a seat.

"Don't say I never did anything for you," Sloane teased as she slid the food in front of me.

"You're the best," I agreed, digging into a brown, crispy piece. "So this is it. The real deal. The High Council. Is it what you thought it would be?" I asked her. I recalled a similar conversation we'd had during limbo, by the old motel and pool.

"Time will tell," she said. Sloane was clearly comfortable not knowing. It was like a superpower with her. Calm civility. I wasn't sure I'd ever seen her hair out of place. "Are you happy you chose Beck?" She turned the question back on me.

I glanced at her face. Her blue, inquisitive eyes cut right through me. She cared to know the answer, but not in a nosy way.

"So far, it's going okay. Yeah. It's great. I'm happy."

That was the first time I'd admitted it out loud. "Spade tried to trick me. He always felt the need to manipulate. But with Beck..." I let the conversation trail off as he and Vince rounded the corner and entered the cafeteria. They were steeped in conversation, a smile on the tips of their lips. Was it possible he looked cuter before breakfast? I couldn't stop my face from lighting up.

"There's hope," Sloane finished for me.

"Maybe," I agreed. I raised my hand to give him a wave or call him over, but before I could gain his attention, someone else caught his eye.

He nodded goodbye to Vince, broke into a huge grin, and slapped a guy I didn't know on the back after a bro-style high five. I slightly frowned. He looked familiar, but I couldn't place him. We certainly hadn't been introduced. Where had I noticed him before?

Then, suddenly, I remembered.

He was a new part of the entourage on the staircase.

The mean girl's entourage.

Beck raked his hand through his hair and grinned with the new guy and some of the others I recognized from that group. Then the black-haired girl slid through the crowd. Her head tilted, watching him. At first, he didn't see her, but when he did, she cut her way straight to him.

Beck's eyes lit up.

Without hesitation, he wrapped her up into his arms.

FIVE
HIGH COUNCIL IS NOT FOR YOU

"YOU MIGHT BE WONDERING why the High Council exists." Lady Mauve barely waited until our butts were in our chairs before she began our first lesson.

No, what I want to know is how Beck and Ms. Purple Eyes are such huggy-buddies.

I snuck a peek over at him sitting beside me in the lesson. He'd chatted with her friend group for so long he didn't even have time to sit down to eat with us before the first lesson of the day, but things weren't a total loss. He'd fallen into the seat next to mine in the classroom.

"Hey," I greeted him as he collapsed his butt down at our table for two.

"Morning." He grinned right back.

I liked that it was just assumed that we'd sit together. But we'd barely had time for a second word before the lesson had begun. I hadn't figured out a polite way of asking what he was doing with his arms around some other woman. It struck the wrong note to in any way admit I was watching or policing his behavior, but I was dying for a clarifying hint.

Center stage, a group of ladies and fellows marched in, all lining up behind Lady Mauve. They stood at attention and stared us all down. I shrunk back a bit in my chair.

"What is this all about? You might have asked yourself that. Or maybe you were so concerned with your own crap—making it into the coven, making new friends, confirming your social status—you forgot to care." She stared us all down. "I don't know what you thought this world would be, and I don't care. Because it's not about you. Let that sink in. The number one truth you should know is this: the High Council isn't for you." She let those words hang in the air. Her sharp eyeline picked us off one at a time until we couldn't help but look away.

Lady Mauve was the ultimate alpha dog in the room.

"I don't care about your powers or your fate-kissed parabond partners. I don't care about your lessons or your development. None of us do."

The men and women lined up behind her nodded in solidarity. They were all dressed in the same white sweatsuits with single color piping and tank tops that no doubt matched the color of their coven names. Our teachers and trainers stared us down.

"The High Council is not for you. It's for *me*." She let her words sink in. "For *Gray*."

In the lineup, we recognized our other teacher from limbo. She nodded.

"For *Burgundy*," Mauve said.

A handsome man in his fifties waved.

"For *Moss*."

Another woman nodded her head.

There were thirteen instructors before us, each with a different color name.

"What happened to Red and Yellow?" Greg whispered.

Some of the others giggled.

"Red and Yellow are dead," Lady Mauve snapped. "So shut up."

This silenced the group. Lady Mauve had a knack for doing that.

"Being a witch is dangerous business," she continued. "We are other. And the human race barely likes its own kind. Throughout history, there have been mistakes and some flare-ups and slaughters. Witches have been hunted down, publicly drowned, skinned alive, and burned at the stake. Your powers put you at risk. But more importantly, they put *me* at risk. Me and all the other witches that you meet." Like an evangelical preacher, she let her words sink into the air. "So you must do exactly what we say. We've put the Judicial Studies together, three years of training, so you and your foolish mistakes as baby witches will not get me murdered." Again she let the words hang in the air. "You will take the rules and regulations of the coven seriously." She eyed Greg. "Or we will make you. No one will spell it out again. There are serious consequences to face. Break the rules, and we aren't kidding. Banishment, imprisonment, or elimination."

She dragged her index finger across her own neck, a universal sign for the threat of death.

Not a single face on the panel flinched.

She definitely had our attention.

"Through the first three years, you are required to live here on the campus, learning our history, obeying our rules, and honing your skills. After that, you may decide where life will lead, if you want to become a full member of the coven or if you leave our walls for good. You will become smarter, better, stronger. And when we're sure you pose no danger to any fellow council member, you'll be free to decide what comes next. You may continue to practice or abstain from the skill set. You can stay local or move on and travel at will."

Beside me, Beck nodded.

"But mark these words. You will not put a fellow witch in jeopardy. The outer rules, the society, the family you've known—those norms no longer exist. Justice comes alone from the High Council. Our decisions herein will be swift, and they will be final. Any mistake will be met with the harshest possible punishment. Don't make it rain down on your head."

The silence fell over the whole group. Lady Mauve's sharp eyes pierced into our brains. I thought she might hold us hostage there, on pins and needles forever.

Finally, Lady Gray stepped in.

"Thank you, Lady Mauve." She nodded to her friend. They traded places. Now the good cop to her bad. "Over the next two weeks, we'll hold introductions and classes with each of your instructors, but for now... let's give your faculty a hand." Lady Gray led us in a polite round of applause.

The other men and women in the line waved. Then, their duty complete for this morning's show of force, they turned to exit. As they filed out, some went out of their way to smile and put us at ease, while others frowned or scowled, more in line with Lady Mauve's methods. I couldn't even imagine all the lessons they'd have to give, let alone what curriculum could go on for three years, but I was ready.

I hoped the coven history lessons would help me learn more about my mom.

Once all the other instructors had filed out, I recognized Lady Blue Moon from our first day. She waited out in the hallway with her rolling cart of paperwork. At the departure of the last staff member, she promptly rolled in.

"This morning, we leave you in the capable hands of Lady Blue Moon." Lady Gray invited her in. "Take it away."

She gave her younger peer a warm smile, waved to us, then disappeared.

"Right, okay." Lady Blue Moon stepped forward.

"Hello everyone, I'm Lady Blue Moon, but of course, she just said that. I am the Paper Master here. I collect all the permission slips and expense reports and keep the High Council members apprised of important data. In your case, like your grades."

"Aw, man. It's like school?" Greg was disappointed.

"It sure is!" Lady Blue Moon was enthusiastic, until she clocked her audience's frowning faces. The wind dropped out of her sails. "So, yep. That's me."

She nodded and waited. Whatever reaction she was hoping for, we couldn't provide it.

"Right. Well, okay. Let's get you started." She dragged a heavy box off her cart and onto the table and started passing the contents out to each member of the class. It was a whole set of documents tucked together in a manilla folder. This wasn't going to be fun at all.

"Time to sign your life away," she joked.

But we could see the joke was pretty thin.

There were bushels of paperwork before us.

"Everyone, please direct your attention to the first packet labeled Estate Planning, Last Will, and Testament."

"Who knew High Council would be so fun," Beck whispered, leaning over.

I grinned.

We weren't the only ones she'd lost almost immediately.

"What is all this?" Nicolette wondered, flipping randomly through the papers.

The others dug into their folders as well.

"Standard boilerplate non-disclosure, estate planning, liability releases, and the parabond contractual agreement," Lady Blue Moon rattled them all off. "Did I say non-disclosure? Yeah, it's all standard stuff. The signature spots are clearly marked," she added, as if that was what was stumping the group.

Greg and Marcy immediately started signing every signature slot. Vince stopped on the first page and started to read.

"You're gonna read every word, there, Mod Squad?" Greg joked, using Lady Mauve's nickname for the sourpuss. Greg had already signed off half the dotted lines in package number one.

"You're not?" Vince shot right back. "Hope there isn't a clause about testicles."

"I said testament," Lady Blue Moon helpfully said.

I snuck a peek at Beck. He was keenly reading, his forehead stitched into a confused little frown. It was cute.

"Why a last will and testament?" Sloane asked.

"And bank and credit statements?" Tej had noticed.

"I don't have a credit statement," Nicolette said.

"We're kids," Hilde added.

"Sure... now. But at some point, your pockets will run deep. Your family's inheritance, for example..." Lady Blue Moon tried not to draw too much attention to the eventual death of each teenager's family. "It's just a matter of fact." She shrugged. "But you can take solace in the idea that the Council isn't free. We all pay at some time. All the stuff you see around you? This infrastructure? The High Council is propped up by the gifts of our patrons."

"The *mandatory* gifts," Vince commented, clearly reading new things in the fine print.

"The return is more than fair." Lady Blue Moon shrugged.

"I don't wanna sign my life away," Greg complained, although the ink on his papers was already set. "Why don't you just steal all the stuff the Council needs with an illusion?"

"Good old smash 'n grab," Marcy agreed.

"I think you misunderstand." Lady Blue Moon shook her head. "The coven is free while you're here. All your room, your board, the lessons, you name it. The Council only gets paid when you're gone," she said. "Long gone." She emphasized again.

"You expect us to sign over the entirety of our estate?" Vince pushed the contract away.

"What, like your skateboard?" Tej teased. He added his signature to the line. "If I'm dead, they can have it."

"He rides a scooter," Nicolette defended Vince, but the surly boy didn't want her help.

"What I want is freedom of choice," he snapped back. He slumped back in his chair.

"Well, this is it. Your choice has come. It's time to pick. Nobody said this was a free ride," Lady Blue

Moon said. "If you wanna stay..." She gently slid the papers back under his nose.

"Can we change our documents later?" Sloane asked. "You know, make an addendum, something of that sort?"

Lady Blue Moon nodded. "Any time you want."

"Come on, Vince." She signed the documents. "It's a fair trade-off."

Beck and I glanced at each other.

The Council didn't have much to glean from my pockets. Aunt Abeline and I barely kept the family budget in the black. From me, it wasn't much of a commitment. I signed the paperwork.

Beck must have had similar thoughts of his dad's barbershop. He added his signatures as well.

One by one, the others went through the documents and added their own sign-offs.

Even Vince.

"There, that wasn't so hard." Lady Blue Moon swooped the completed paperwork away and tucked it out of sight in her cardboard box. "Next up, liability releases."

From there, no one put up much of a fight.

Lady Blue Moon would instruct us to pull out a certain titled paperwork, and once we did, she would vaguely explain the intricacies of what the document entailed. She used common language instead of the in-depth legal jargon, which of course helped, but we could all see plainly that throughout each contract, there were miles and miles of bullet point official language that actually required very delicate reading. It didn't matter. Our collective will to worry over protecting our individual rights had simply disappeared.

Joining the High Council was a given.

If this was what we needed to do to be here, Lady Blue Moon could walk us right through. In her skittish way, she pointed to the correct dotted lines and initial spots. Then, when it was all complete, she diligently swept the signed documents out of view. And so it went all morning.

Again and again, we signed the dotted lines.

My hand started to hurt from the thousand autographs I was signing, but still, I bumped the crooked pen across the page. I had completely zoned out of the meeting when she got to a topic that made me sit back up in my chair.

"Next up, the parabond partnership agreement."

She pulled a large packet from the paperwork pile. Our folders were getting smaller and smaller. Thankfully, we could all see the finish was coming, but now I realized one of the biggest mysteries of the supernatural organization of the High Council was about to be spelled out in challenging language and pages of legal subheadings. I couldn't wait. She held it up. When we all had it at the ready, she flipped it open, ready to begin.

"As you know, fate has selected your special parabond partnerships." She nodded at each duo, and we dutifully nodded back. "No one really knows exactly how the supernatural energy does this. Some bonds are much more magical than others, kind of like that mythological first kiss. Will it be fireworks on prom night or a lip lock behind a dumpster? You get what you get, and no one knows why it shakes out how it does."

There were a few twittering giggles from the already-kissed in the group. They knew exactly what she meant.

"What was your first kiss?" Marcy asked, leaning forward on both hands.

Some of the other girls nodded.

"Mine? Uh, locked in the archery shed, last day of summer camp at Lake Happy Cod." Lady Blue Moon blushed.

"How romantic." Marcy let out a moony sigh. Nicolette and Hilde nodded.

"See, Tej, there's hope for you yet." Greg laughed, swatting the boy, who smacked him right back.

"I hate to camp," Tej disagreed. "All the bugs. Yuck."

"There's s'mores," Hilde offered.

The idea of Hilde and Tej camping together struck me as hilarious.

"You ever been in an archery shed?" Beck leaned over, asking in a whisper.

"I am a good sport," I agreed.

I wiggled my eyebrows. We both grinned. I could have sworn that his blue eyes checked out my lips just for an instant. But before we could flirt any further, Lady Blue Moon cleared her throat.

"Anyhow." She could see she'd led the room off track. It was time to right the ship. "As I was saying, I had to revise some of the regular boilerplate this and that due to the fact that... well... your unusual induction into the coven. This year was a bit out of the ordinary, what with Katherine Hucklebee stealing the potential offerings, followed by her sudden passing, and the ripples and impacts on the reaping that posthumously caused. The Council created limbo and they put you all through thorough testing, so here we are. We're back in the running after a few tweaks and minor rearrangements, and lucky for us, the essential talking points are the same." She pointed back to specific text blocks on the document and rattled on. "Your parabond is a metaphysical partnership between you and one solicited other, and you will act in concordance with regards to the High Council procedures and the conduct therein. You will be fully accountable to your parabond partner, as they are to you in a herein mutual, benefacto relationship. Any performance taken by you or your fated other, signified hereto-ever-after as your quote-unquote parabond, will be directly attributed to you as a member of the Council, and/or to your other, which may result in prosecutable action against one or both party members," Lady Blue Moon read out.

"You're getting a little lawyer-y on us," Greg complained.

Others nodded.

"Oh, right. Sorry." She looked up. "Basically, through accepting this bond, from now on you are responsible for any action taken by you or your partner. And if the Council deems their or your behavior to be an infringement to the High Council social rules and regulations or even our societal norms, both you and your parabond will be held equally accountable."

Beck looked at me. He looked as confused as I was. I squinted.

Did that mean what I thought?

"No way," Vince said.

"Absolutely not," Sloane agreed.

"Wait. What?" Greg didn't get the point.

"I'm not taking on Nicolette's problems." Vince shook his head.

"You're not some picnic," she shot back.

"Take her on what, where?" Greg asked.

"They're saying if *she*"—Vince pointed to Marcy—"screws up, as her parabond, *you're* at fault."

"You're toast." Tej nodded.

But Lady Blue Moon was undeterred. "It's an accountability metric built into the Council population." She nodded.

"You and your partner both carry equal loads," Rick said.

We all looked towards him. He spoke so infrequently that his words, when they sounded, held heavy weight.

"So if Greg screws the pooch," Marcy said, catching on, "I'm at fault?"

Out of all of us, she was right to be worried. Her man was a definite loose cannon, history had shown.

"Well, yes. You are responsible."

The general din of disapproval grew louder.

"But not to worry," Lady Blue Moon spoke over the volume. "There's an escape valve. The Council has thought of everything. Has anyone told you about that?"

We all shook our heads.

"If you report your partner's malfeasance for judgment and evaluation, you will be siloed from their bad acts and inspection. The vocal partner will not suffer their parabond's final fate." Lady Blue Moon nodded.

"So we're supposed to rat each other out?" Vince summarized this supposed good news. "To avoid punishment."

"Well, no. The real solution is for you and your parabond not to break any of the coven's rules." Lady Blue Moon shook her head. "Then you won't ever have to worry about it. But if they *do*... then, yes, rat away."

"So... it *isn't* romantic?" little Hilde wondered.

All eyes shifted her way, and she blushed. Rick shifted in his chair. He crossed his arms and frowned. No, his body language seemed to say, it *isn't* romantic. She didn't look at the older boy.

"It's not," Lady Blue Moon gently agreed. "Although lots of bonds do go on to date... and some marry."

I snuck a glimpse at Beck. He was sneaking a look at me as well.

"Well, I still think it's romantic." Greg nuzzled Marcy.

"Thank you, baby." She snuck him a kiss on the lips.

"I think it's crap." Vince frowned.

"Just sign the thing so we can go on and do cool stuff like learn how to turn over a table using only our minds," Greg complained. "Or fling some stuff across the room with our brains."

"He does know it's a witches coven and not super-hero camp?" Beck muttered to me.

I just grinned.

"Fine." Vince, the last of us to give in, signed the final forms. "Now what?"

Lady Blue Moon collected the files and busied herself repacking the box they were in.

"Right. Well, in a minute or two"—she glanced at the doorway; it was still empty—"someone will return, and we'll continue your introductions and orientations."

She went back to her filing.

The rest of us relaxed in our seats.

"It's awful to think we have to rat on each other," Nicolette murmured.

"Why, are you planning to do something bad?" Marcy teased.

Somehow, Greg had leaned himself all the way out

of his seat and snaked himself around her slim shoulders.

"No, but..." She looked around.

I thought I understood. "It's weird to think your closest friend might turn you in for something you did," I agreed.

"That's why we need to do everything together," Beck told me.

I couldn't help but smile.

"Not every parabond will be your closest friend," Rick said.

"Amen to that," Vince agreed.

Nicolette frowned.

"Respecting each other, respecting the coven, these are the things that matter," Sloane reminded everyone.

"Respect and trust," Tej agreed.

Rick and Hilde also nodded.

I looked at Beck. His eyes had already found me. We both grinned. Our boundaries had yet to be built, but if respect and trust was all it took, we were good.

"And sex." Greg added in. "If you're lucky."

The whole room burst out laughing.

"You wish." Marcy swatted her man.

"What can I say? I'm a lucky guy," Greg agreed.

"Shhh." She winked. "A lady never tells."

"Um, the High Council does not recommend the casual fraternization of its members," Lady Moon said, cutting into the playful atmosphere.

"But it's not a rule," Marcy said worriedly.

We glanced at the giant rule book we'd been given.

Lady Blue Moon hadn't even touched it. Now Hilde began to leaf through.

"No..." Lady Blue Moon agreed. "But think of it like an instruction of best practices," she corrected. She glanced towards the door again. She checked her watch on her phone. "Flirtations can get messy. It's best if you can avoid it." Distracted, she checked the door again. "In the long run, you'll be better off."

I didn't dare glance at Beck now.

"But what about love?" Little Hilde's voice was so sweet and tentative, we all turned.

"Ah, well... I suppose love is okay," Lady Blue Moon agreed. "And long-term relationships."

"Love you." Greg nuzzled Marcy's neck.

"Love you too, babe," she agreed.

"Give me a break... Are we done?" Vince wanted out.

"I think... another fellow should have relieved me by now," Lady Blue Moon admitted, glancing towards the door for what might've been the hundredth time. "I'm sure they're on their way. This is good; ask more questions. Keep 'em coming. What else have you got? I'll answer as best I can."

This was such a new attitude I almost choked on my tongue.

I guess now that we'd officially signed our lives away with all these contracts, the secrets of the High Council were officially ours as well. My eyes shone wide with possibilities.

"When do we start using our powers?" Nicolette asked.

Lady Blue Moon checked a schedule. "You'll have training seminars four days a week, both to develop your primary skill sets and to see if you can develop another."

"A twofer." Tej nodded.

I glanced at Hilde. In limbo, she had already proven to be both a dream-cast and a harness. Maybe some of the rest of us would be too.

"I might develop all of 'em," Greg supposed, shooting his palms out in all directions as if he might secretly be Spiderman.

Hilde nodded, but Rick slid a hand out to silence her. He shook his head.

"How do you develop a dream-cast?" Sloane asked Lady Blue Moon.

"Oh... well, guided meditation, visualization; there are dream image catalogs, but they're not very good." Lady Blue Moon shuffled towards the door.

Whoever was meant to replace her must have really been pushing the envelope.

"What about the archives and family histories?" I called her back. "Will we learn about them?"

"What, like genealogies?" Lady Blue Moon put her hand on the doorknob.

"Don't look too close; Greg and Marcy might turn out to be related." Tej chuckled.

"Ew." Marcy turned up her nose.

"Wouldn't stop me, babe." Greg kissed her cheek.

"No? You're the best." She kissed him back. Their lip-lock grew more amorous.

"Alright." Vince stood up, pushing back his chair. The scrape across the floor called the lovers up for air. "Time for a break."

The rest of us also fidgeted. At the very least, we could stretch our legs.

Lady Blue Moon nodded and opened the door to poke her head out in the hall. Almost immediately, we could feel the temperature changing. Outside our class room, something was wrong.

Very wrong.

Other members of the coven were racing back and forth down the hallway.

"What's going on?" Hilde asked.

A shiver went down my spine.

Lady Blue Moon, who had the best vantage, didn't know what to make of it.

"What is it?" Vince asked, coming around the desk. The rest of us stood. Others tried to look out the door.

We could all tell something was off.

"Sapphire, what's happening?" Lady Blue Moon asked someone she recognized as they hurried by.

"There's a fire at the Orson Bell," the witch recounted, then disappeared onwards.

"A forest fire," added someone else running by.

They were both gone before Blue Moon could offer a follow-up question.

"A forest fire..." Lady Blue Moon turned back to

us. Her face was worried. Her eyebrows twisted into knots.

"Is it nearby?" Hilde feared.

Rick shook his head.

"Closer to Prince Martin," Beck agreed.

"No, it's not that far," Nicolette countered. "More like Alderton."

I still wasn't great with directions, but I knew they were both a township away. A fire that far away didn't seem cause for so much chaos and fear at the castle. The property wasn't in any real danger.

Lady Blue Moon seemed to forget all about us. She raced back to her paperwork and tossed the last of the papers into a box that she shoved onto her cart.

"Aren't there firefighters to take care of the damage?" I wondered.

"It's not that type of fire." She shook her head.

"Well, should we help contain it? I can move water," Vince suggested.

"I can call on rain," Beck added.

"You'd just add to the flames!" Lady Blue Moon almost shouted. She grabbed ahold of herself and tried to put on a calm face while she packed the final bits in her bags.

We fell quiet.

"It's not *that* kind of fire," she told us. "It's a *forest fire*." She rolled the cart towards the door.

"I don't understand the difference," Nicolette admitted.

"Forest fires are *magic*," she explained, exasperated. "*Magic* fires. Made by extirpated energy fields." We looked amongst each other. It was clear from our facial expressions that none of us had heard of such a thing.

"Ex-ter what?" Greg frowned.

"Just... sit tight. Stay here," she instructed. "*Stay here.*"

She rolled her cart out into the hall.

"Don't move," she told us. "Everything's fine. Nothing to worry about."

With that, the door slammed, and she and her cart disappeared.

SIX

I, FOR ONE, WANT TO LEARN ALL WE CAN

"COME ON," Greg instructed.

Everyone started gathering their things. I looked to Beck; he shrugged and packed up as well.

"What are you doing? She said to stay here," Nicolette countered.

Hilde nodded.

"Uh, she said there was a magical forest fire. I'm not missing that," Greg said. "That's why we're here."

"But we've only been here for one morning." Nicolette wasn't moved. "She said not to leave."

"I don't think it was an order." Beck looked to me for confirmation.

I checked with some of the others.

It wasn't... was it?

No one seemed sure.

"At the very least, we don't have to stay here in this class," I suggested. "We could go out to the lobby. Suss it out. See what we learn?"

"You're not curious at all?" Marcy asked Nicolette.

"I am, but Lady Blue Moon said—"

"She said a lot of things," Greg interrupted. "I would argue she gave mixed messages. That's what I heard. Who really knows what she meant?"

He looked around for support. Tej nodded. Nicolette wasn't convinced.

"Come on, Lettie. Come with us. It'll be fun," Marcy enticed her.

At the personal nickname, Nicolette's eyes lit up.

"What do you think?" I asked Sloane, not entirely willing to let Greg lead the group.

"Well—"

"We won't learn much in a locked room," Vince complained.

"Already done that," Tej agreed. He rolled his eyes, maybe thinking back to our challenges in limbo. I could see Beck was also in agreement with the boys.

"Alright," Sloane agreed. "We won't leave, but we'll go to the first floor. See what we see."

I looked around. Everyone nodded in consensus.

Beck peeked out the door. "Where's everyone going?" he asked a random fellow caught mid-scamper.

"Fire at the Orson Bell!" The guy didn't bother to slow down.

"What *kind* of fire?" I shouted after him, but he had already disappeared. Without him, the hall was empty.

"The second floor's a ghost town," Beck noted.

If the building was now basically drained of

witches, or if the others were hunkered down in small rooms like ours, it was impossible to tell, but an eerie silence fell over the halls.

"Well, I for one want to learn all that I can." Tej pushed past our logjam in the doorway and out into the hall. Others flowed through behind.

"Guys, it's gonna be awesome," Greg added.

"It better be," Vince agreed.

"Maybe we can help," Sloane added, trying to refocus the plan.

The others weren't suitably chaste.

"That too." Greg nodded, not even hiding his grin.

"Come on, L." Marcy held out her hand to Nicolette. She and her ever-shortening nickname eagerly stood side by side with the more confident girl.

"L?" Tej looked over.

"Short for Lettie. Short for Nicolette," Sloane said, filling in the gaps.

"It's cute, right?" Marcy grinned.

"Wouldn't it be N, short for Nicolette?" Vince muttered.

"You don't know how nicknames work." Nicolette scowled.

The rest of us grinned.

"You guys coming?" Greg turned to check in.

Beck and I stepped into the hall with Sloane and Hilde.

"We are," Beck agreed.

Then all eyes floated to Rick. For the entire discussion, he had remained silent. What would he think?

For a moment, he didn't flinch; then he gave a small, accepting nod.

"Yes!" Greg pumped his arm.

"That settles it," Marcy cheered, hugging Nicolette to her side.

As we left the classroom and headed for the exit, our little group gathered excitement and steam.

"I've never seen a real forest fire," Hilde admitted.

"What about your s'mores?" I joked.

"I think this one will be a little bigger," Tej told me.

"Do you think it'll be dangerous?" the younger girl worried.

"I don't know," Sloane admitted.

"It'll be fine," Marcy assured them both.

"We'll keep you safe," Greg added.

"Don't make promises you can't keep," Vince snapped, but then seeing Hilde's face, he couldn't help but add, "But yeah, it's probably no biggie."

"You can stick by us," Beck added.

I nodded.

Suddenly, the hallway lights flickered and dimmed, cut to half-mast for emergency procedures.

"Whoa," Nicolette murmured.

"Come on!" Greg led the charge.

By the time we reached the end of the hallway, our group was jogging, excited to see what the fuss was about, ready to get our hands into the fray. Lady Blue Moon's instruction to stay put was totally out of our minds.

Greg, Marcy, and Nicolette turned the corner to the stairway, but abruptly stopped in their tracks. The route was blocked. By Lady Mauve. She stood, arms crossed.

"No," she said in her simple monotone.

For once, I was glad I wasn't near the front of the group.

"Go back."

"We wanna see it," Marcy said.

"The magical fire," Nicolette added.

"And maybe some witches in action," Tej added.

Others also nodded.

"Or maybe we can help?" Hilde's little voice topped us off.

I stayed silent. I'd seen such dark and stormy eyes from Lady Mauve before.

"Blue Moon said to stay where you were," she said.

"She said a lot of things," Greg tried to counter.

"Well, let me make it abundantly clear. You are not to go to the fire. You are not to help."

"But couldn't we—" Marcy started.

"No."

"Just give us a—" Greg tried again.

"I don't have time for discussion. Turn yourselves round and wait it out," she ordered.

Obediently, we slowly turned and trudged.

If Lady Mauve was refusing to let us join the sidelines, the magical fire at the Orson Bell must really be something, I realized.

It could be dangerous or scary.

Maybe it was better that we stayed safe on the grounds.

"How about this." Greg turned back to negotiate once more.

But Lady Mauve was already gone.

"What the hell?" At his surprise, the rest of us peeked back over our shoulders.

"What happened to the stairway?" Hilde wondered.

"It's an illusion," Sloane realized.

"A lie-guard." I nodded. "Lady Mauve must have created it."

"What is it?" Beck murmured.

The ten of us spread out to have a better look. The hallway was now covered in plant life. Walls of foliage had sprung up where the staircase should have been. In every direction was a large, rustic hedge with sharp, trimmed sides. The greenery grew ten or twelve feet. We moved forward to touch the branches.

"It's a maze," Tej realized, finding the entrance. "A hedge maze. They have them on my grandfather's property."

"It feels so real." Hilde fondled a branch.

"Do not touch," Rick critiqued.

She immediately pulled back her hand.

"Hilde's right," Marcy said, ignoring Rick's command. "It feels exactly like a real tree."

"Hilde, come," he instructed, pulling her from us.

"Where are you going?" I asked.

"Upstairs to wait. As Mauve said."

Hilde looked like she wanted to disagree with her partner but didn't dare.

"You heard her. We wait." Rick turned and marched away.

Hilde gave us one last, longing look, then followed her parabond.

I checked in with Beck with a raised eyebrow. What should we do? Were Rick and Hilde right to follow instructions?

"But it's so real. It's awesome. Don't you want to check it out?" Marcy brushed a pine branch needle on her skin.

"She said don't go out to the fire, not don't go through my lie-guard maze," Greg tried to reason, but Rick and Hilde's minds were made up. They just walked away.

"She *did* put this here to stop us," I countered Greg's argument.

Beck nodded.

"True... unless this is a test," Tej said. "I mean, the whole thing. It could be an elaborate ruse. You know they do that."

"What do you mean?" Nicolette wasn't following.

She touched the same branch that Marcy had just felt.

"Think about it. Everything we know of this world has been one test after another. Nothing is what it seems: the motel, the seven trials, the competition to get into the High Council." He recounted some of the things we'd just been through.

"But those were all in limbo." Vince wasn't convinced. "This is the High Council."

"What's the difference?" Greg asked.

We all looked at each other. No one had a good answer.

"Well, she didn't say we had to sit in our rooms, just that we couldn't go to the fire," Beck kind of agreed.

If classes were indeed postponed for an hour or two, maybe I could use this time just for me... to start to search for information about my mom in the library. But to get there, I'd need to make my way to the other side of this maze.

I looked from one face to another. "I say we do it!"

"Alright, Mae!" Marcy and Nicolette cheered.

"Yes!" Greg and Tej were also in.

Vince shrugged and nodded.

"We figure out an exit. But we don't go to the fire," I said. Sloane and Beck nodded.

Everyone was on board.

"Let's do this! Where do we start?" Greg's enthusiasm immediately waned.

"This way," I said.

We hurried to a cut passage in the plant wall that Tej had already discovered. Two turns into the shrub maze and we eclipsed any sign of the school hallways. The ground was soft underfoot, with a layer of needles that had been picking up new dead donations for years. It smelled like a pine forest, a real-life version of the pine wax Aunt Abeline and I sometimes used to protect new wood floors. Fresh and slightly minty. Only these wafts weren't fake or synthetic; the scents in this garden were the real, delicious deal. The lie-guard had thought of every detail.

We jogged forward through the hedges, keeping our eight members tightly grouped together so as not to lose a runner as we threaded our way through the field. Greg and Tej led at the front. They just turned right every time we were presented with a fork in the bushes. But soon, even with that simple guideline, we were very, very lost. We stopped at a new division with three separate paths instead of the usual two and weighed our options. There was no way to accurately judge which route to take. They all looked identical.

"What are these?" Vince asked, bending down to get a closer look at some wild pink mushrooms.

"Don't touch," Nicolette warned.

But Vince was smart enough to keep his hands to himself.

"Those are poison."

"Well, that's not fun," Marcy complained.

"Guy," Greg added and giggled. "Fun-guy?"

"Oh boy." Tej rolled his eyes.

"You're just jealous you didn't think of it." Greg puffed up his chest.

"Which way?" Beck wondered.

"No clue," I murmured.

Sloane pushed her way forward to the front of the pack.

"Should we flip a coin?" Nicolette wondered.

"Who carries money?" Vince rolled his eyes.

"I have plenty of money," Tej countered, "but none of it's coin."

"Well, that isn't helpful," Nicolette told him.

"Enough of Daddy's wallet." Greg rolled his eyes.

"I wasn't—" Tej objected.

"Why don't we split up into teams?" I suggested.

"Sounds good to us," Greg said and immediately partnered with Marcy. "We'll go together."

The rest of us groaned. Who wanted to pair off with the love birds?

"That shouldn't be necessary," Sloane said.

She'd finished her examination.

"I've been here before."

SEVEN
I'VE BEEN HERE BEFORE

"YOU'VE BEEN HERE? In the lie-guard hedge maze?" Marcy frowned.

"Guess your family's not the only one with cash," Greg muttered to Tej. "No wonder you partnered together."

Sloane pulled off a small twig and crumpled the pine stems together. She watched them trickle down to the mossy ground, taking their time to float to a landing, only slightly heavier than the air.

"When were you here?" I asked.

"In last night's dream." She shrugged. "You didn't cast?"

Kate's dying breath gurgled in my memory. I shook my head no. Sloane's eyes narrowed, surprised.

"Well, which way?" Vince prompted, getting impatient.

Greg and Marcy looked left, Nicolette quickly followed their lead, Beck and Tej and I looked right, and Vince wondered about going back the way we came, but Sloane shook her head.

"We climb."

We all looked up.

The hedge was tall. At least ten feet. Maybe more. Twice as tall as me.

"It'll never hold," Greg said. "I mean, the little ones, sure."

Our eyes avoided Tej.

"But me or Beck?" He shook his head.

"It'll hold," Sloane said.

Vince grabbed a vine and started climbing.

"What are you doing? Vince, you're gonna fall," Nicolette complained.

"I'm fine. Don't worry, Nick." He called her his own nickname, accenting the final consonant with a sharp letter *K*. It didn't sound friendly. "Sloane just said the branches will hold you. They'll definitely hold me."

"I prefer L, or Lettie," she told him.

Marcy nodded, proud as punch of her junior girl.

"I get it. But sorry. That's not how nicknames work." He stared her down, daring her to stand up to him again.

Nicolette broke first.

"How'd you do that?" Tej complained. "Climb so effortlessly?"

The rest of us tried to follow his lead.

"Tuck your butt," Vince criticized as we elevated.

Sloane easily scaled the wall of plants as well. Nicolette wasn't as graceful.

"Unfortunately, some of us have more butts to tuck," Tej noted in regards to his own boney behind, but Nicolette wasn't aware. She seemed to think the comment was about her. She flushed bright red.

"Amen to that," Greg agreed. He cupped his girl's cheeks.

"Watch it." Marcy giggled. "Whatcha doing?"

"Just givin' my baby a boost."

"Sure you weren't getting fresh?" She giggled.

"I can multitask." He grinned.

"Wanna lift?" Beck asked me.

We watched Greg fondle Marcy's hindquarters as she scooted up the plant life. He squeezed and caressed all the curves he could grasp.

"Not like *that*." I laughed.

"How about this?" Beck threaded his hands together to cradle my foot.

I stepped in with a hand on his shoulder.

"Perfect, thanks."

"Up!"

I pushed off the ground and he raised his hands with me, helping me get pretty high, easily on par with Marcy and Tej, but as I climbed aboard, the trees started to fall. With the weight of all three of us so concentrated in one spot, the walls of the hedge started to fold. Nicolette was right. Several boughs bent.

"Whoa." Vince rode the wave on the top.

Sloane also held tight.

"I was wrong, you're too big." He frowned.

"That's what I said," Nicolette snapped.

"Just spread farther out," Sloane suggested.

We stepped farther from each other to try again. Tej, who hadn't fallen with the rest, managed to pull himself up over the top. Sloane and Vince also spread out. That seemed to work.

"I'm not going back up to fall to my death," Nicolette complained.

That seemed a touch dramatic, but she held her ground.

"Can you see the route from there?" I asked. "Maybe you can guide us?"

Vince shook his head. "The maze isn't real. All the routes seem to loop. I think it's purposefully designed to fail. You can't get out walking. I can see the far side. That's our out, straight left across the rows." He pointed over the shrubs.

We couldn't see what he was seeing, but I trusted it was right.

"So we climb, but we space." Beck nodded.

"Move in tandem, not together," Sloane agreed.

"We could go back…" I trailed off. I was starting to have doubts.

"It'll be okay," Beck assured me.

"Lady Mauve said—"

"She said a lot," Greg snapped. "What's she gonna do, punish us all?"

We glanced at each other, unsure.

That was, in fact, entirely possible. Wasn't that the

key message behind a lot of the complicated contracts we'd just signed?

"Remember, this could all be a fraud to test our skills," Tej added. "No real maze, no real fire. Only one way to find out."

Even Sloane had come around to the plan. Probably because she could see the exit.

"My partnership's solid," Greg added pointedly. Marcy giggled.

"So is mine." Beck smiled at me.

I blushed and nodded.

"So we're good. We can travel in tandem," his logic said.

All the others stared me down, waiting.

"Okay," I agreed. "Let's get across."

EIGHT

WHICH WAY TO ORSON BELL?

BECK'S EX-GIRLFRIEND would have climbed the shrubs, I felt confident.

So would the mean girl from the elevator.

It seemed like a dumb reason to risk my status in the coven, but when Beck smiled at me, I couldn't keep up the fight. It's not that I wasn't curious about the fire; of course I was. I had never seen a *real* forest fire, let alone a magic-related one. But I felt pretty certain it was important to keep the ladies and fellows on my side. There was so much about the history of the High Council that I wanted to learn; I didn't want to alienate the adults in charge. But... I also didn't want to let down my friends. One particular friend.

It was a fine tightrope to tread.

Of course, once we'd actually climbed on the top of the hedge, the maze was much easier to progress. Vince was right, the pathways just looped around and around in circles, designed to never end. I don't even think we could have found our way back to the castle now that we were inside of the maze. But climbing hedge to hedge wasn't hard. The lie-guard was really only designed to hinder one specific action—walking the path—and climbing above that vantage point made the whole thing a pretty easy task. The fact that the illusion didn't simply disappear as soon as we got to higher ground also meant that Lady Mauve expected us to consider and use this new vantage. She had known, once we went in, climbing up top was the only way to escape.

At the end of the maze, we hopped down off the shrubbery to discover we were outside, back at the edge of the High Council grounds.

When I tried to look back at the maze, it drifted away.

The illusion was over.

"Freedom!" Greg bellowed.

"Which way to the Old Mill?" Marcy dusted the smell of pine off her hands.

"Orson Bell," Nicolette corrected.

"Whatever. Who knows where that is?" Marcy grinned.

"I do." Vince nodded.

"Well, what are we waiting for?" Greg rubbed his hands in glee.

The others started to head for his car, but Sloane and I stopped.

"We hypothesized this was a test. But it wasn't," she said. "It was a block."

"Lady Mauve doesn't want us to go," I agreed.

"We're just gonna take a peek." Marcy shrugged.

"No one will know that we're there," Tej added.

Sloane was unmoved.

"They said don't go to the bell, so we'll just go near," Marcy offered.

I glanced at Beck and gave a small head shake. "I'm gonna stay."

It was clear to me that the ladies and the fellows expected us to follow their rules. If they said no fire, that meant no fire.

"Fine." Greg shrugged. "Just don't spill the beans."

"She's not your parabond, baby. I am. You don't have to worry about Mae. Let's go." Marcy tugged his arm.

That wasn't how the laws at the High Council worked, but it didn't matter. I had no intention of turning anyone in.

"Let's go, Lettie." Marcy said. Greg, Tej, and Nicolette followed her route.

I looked to Beck. He gave a small frown.

"I think... I'm gonna check it out," he told me.

"Oh? Okay. Sure." I nodded, forcing a smile. It hadn't crossed my mind that he and I would part ways, but of course that would be fine. Just because we were parabonds didn't mean we had to do everything together.

"I just wanna see what's up," he added. "A magic fire."

"No, it's cool. I get it," I agreed.

He took a step or two to follow the group, then jogged to catch up.

"Don't wait up." Vince gave Sloane and I a wink.

"You don't have to stay," I told her.

"I know."

We watched the small group head out to the parking lot where they'd all squish into Greg's car. For a moment, Sloane and I stood still.

"I thought I might hit up the library," I offered.

"How about we go into town?" Sloane flashed a grin. "I could go for an iced mocha."

I checked over my shoulder. I wanted to get started on my research as quickly as possible, but the allure of a cold, bitter drink and Sloane's sparkling grin enticed me. We had been isolated and landlocked at the school under so much pressure; blowing things off for an afternoon had some serious appeal.

She raised an eyebrow.

"Alright. What the hell!" I agreed.

Lucky for us, Sloane also had her own vehicle.

"Plumpkin, Alderton, or Prince Martin?" Sloane listed all the closest towns.

"Whichever is farthest from the Orson Bell," I suggested.

"I actually don't know where that is." Sloane laughed.

"Me neither." I giggled. "I think someone said Prince Martin."

"Okay, Prince Martin's out," she agreed.

Suddenly, Spade's face popped into my head.

My ex-boyfriend... Well, my ex-*something*.

"And not Plumpkin," I blurted. "I mean, I wouldn't want to see anyone who was just rejected from the Council."

Sloane raised an eyebrow, but nodded. "Smart."

When I first arrived, there were times when I thought I'd be matched forever with Spade and his long list of manipulative problems. There were even brief moments that I was happy about that option, but like most ex-relationships, it had ended in a messy, ugly manner.

Plumpkin was his home. Better to avoid it like the plague.

"Alderton it is!" Sloane agreed.

A carefree skip in our step, we headed to the car. It felt strange to be leaving the High Council. I'd fought so hard to arrive, and now we were driving away. But it was good to have a temporary reprieve. These castle walls carried a lot of weight. I was already pretty exhausted, and it was only our second day.

"I'm surprised you didn't cast last night," Sloane said in the car. She watched me closely. I thought about blowing her off, but I kind of wanted to talk about my dream.

"Actually, I kinda had a nightmare," I admitted.

"Oh?"

I could tell she wanted to dig in, that she might love to hear the details, but I just shrugged in my seat. "I mean, it was nothing. You know... just kinda awful."

What was worse? I wondered. Not casting at all, or

having a powerful vision arrive but failing to recognize what it meant?

Sloane just nodded, keeping her opinions to herself.

"Maybe my powers aren't that strong. After all, I'm here by default." I tried to slide that in, put it casually on the table, but my voice caught in my throat as I did.

"Maybe," Sloane agreed.

I was surprised to hear her accede, but when I looked over, she was smiling, looking at me out of the corner of her eye.

"You plan to doubt yourself through your entire tenure at the High Council?" she asked. "It's not a great look."

"Point taken." I sighed.

Better to keep those opinions to myself.

I watched the farmlands passing, the fields dotted with goats and cows. "But you dreamcast every night?"

"Like clockwork," she agreed.

"For me, that's not happening. Casting is the weakest of the witch powers, and I can't even get *that* right. No offense."

"None taken." Sloane pulled into a parking spot at the start of the little town's main street. "You speak for yourself." Her breezy look told me she couldn't be ruffled by my complaints. They were my issue.

We climbed out onto the sidewalk.

"I don't think dream-casting is weak. I got us out of the maze, didn't I? My skills are pretty good."

"It's just me who sucks," I muttered to myself.

"Watch your step," she warned me.

I looked down in time to avoid a large puddle with brown, murky water. If Sloane hadn't warned me, I was so distracted I might have fallen right in.

"Did you dream about that?" I complained, goose-stepping around the puddle, mostly kidding.

"No... this."

She nodded forward just as Josie Jiu left the bookstore in front of us. When she saw us coming, Josie turned and stared.

NINE

NOT ONE TO MAKE SMALL TALK

"UH, HI," Josie said.

Beck's ex-girlfriend had a book on herbalism tucked under her arm. Her expression told me she was just as surprised to see me as I was to see her. She looked good, I thought. Her slick black hair was pulled back with a barrette behind her ear. She probably assumed, like I did, that once we'd been admitted to the High Council, we wouldn't be permitted to leave campus again. Maybe she had also come to Alderton instead of Plumpkin to avoid a run-in, just in case.

Clearly it was not an effective choice.

Sloane nodded hello on our behalf, but I couldn't find the words.

Josie looked... calm.

Happy, I told myself.

Like she was pleased with her decision to break up with Beck and to leave the High Council coven forever.

Okay, that was too simple a retelling, but she definitely looked calm, happy, and good.

"Hey, Mae." She offered me my own greeting.

I knew I should say something back, but the words were still stuck in my throat. I coughed.

Josie...

I remembered in my dream how I called out for her. She never answered.

But that was a vision. This was real life.

"Hey." I managed to greet the girl in the flesh.

"How's Beck?" she asked. The question hung in the air. Straight to the point. Josie had always been able to use her words and tone as her strongest weapon of choice, cutting clear to the bone. She wasn't one to make small talk. It wasn't mean, it was decisive.

"I'll let you two chat." Sloane gave a gracious nod and excused herself. "See you back at the car in a bit." She extricated herself and when the traffic was clear, Sloane jogged across the street, her blonde hair swinging as she stepped.

For a moment, I wondered how her dream had played out. With Josie here now. How would it all end? Not like my dream, I hoped. But it couldn't. After all, Kate was already dead.

Why hadn't Sloane said something about who we might meet as we left the High Council, especially when I specifically expressed who I wanted to avoid? Instead, she let me pick the town. Fate led me right to this meeting.

Do I tell Josie about my dream, I wondered? How

she didn't come to the fresh tragedy in my mind? That ugly night in the barn was something we'd always share.

No.

Why freak her out with unconscious rumblings?

I'd already taken way too long to answer the question she'd posed to me, but Josie wasn't interested in letting me off the hook. She simply waited.

"Beck's good," I offered. "Great."

Was that too much? I didn't want to rub it in. I tried not to squirm.

But she just nodded. "I wasn't sure you would choose him."

"I wasn't either," I admitted. "He's still pretty hung up on you. Who wants to be a parabond rebound?"

Josie shifted. She pressed her lips into a thin line.

Was she stopping a smile or a frown at that news? I couldn't tell.

She was impossible to read.

"But Spade couldn't be trusted." I shrugged.

"I heard he was pretty mad. Livid." She picked the word carefully.

I nodded.

That sounded about right.

We were both very aware of how bright his anger could burn. I had actively betrayed him and denied what he thought was his birthright. There were bound to be some feelings hurt.

"You made the right choice," she told me.

I nodded. "Did you?" I stepped towards her. "Are you happy you quit?"

She took a defensive step back.

"I don't know if I'd say *happy*." She considered the idea. "It is what it is. I'm working here now." She waved towards the bookstore from which she'd exited. "I'm doing my own studies. That's *jatropha podagrica*, better known as Buddha Belly," she explained, pointing to a vibrant red succulent sprouting in the grout on the curb. "You use it in burn salve. My folks agreed to let me complete my non-witch education via homeschool. I'll be working on independent study from now 'til the end of the year. They were pretty disappointed when I failed."

"You didn't fail," I said quickly.

The elevator girl's smirk played in my head.

Default.

Josie raised an eyebrow. "I quit. That's a fail."

"You remain untested." I polished the facts.

We both do, I added to myself.

Josie just shrugged. "So where is he?" She glanced over my shoulder, and I realized she was looking for Beck. "Now that you've parabonded, I thought the two of you would be glued at the hip."

"It's a work in progress," I admitted, not about to go into the ins and outs of our flirtations with the girl who dumped him last.

I thought she seemed a little disappointed at this news, but with Josie, you never could tell. She played her cards too close to her vest. Instead, she nodded.

"Well, I only get fifteen minutes." She started to pull away. "Say hello to Beck," she added. "Or don't." Her brow furrowed. "Whatever suits him best."

I nodded.

Josie held my gaze a moment longer.

I wasn't sure what else to say.

Thanks for your man? I'll take good care of him?

That wasn't fair. She didn't donate Beck to the cause of Mae. They weren't a good match, and she ended their relationship. What he and I were, or weren't, or what we would become, at this point, was none of her concern.

She nodded once more and headed back to her store, whatever errand she'd intended to run left for a later break in the day.

I watched her go.

Her news wasn't that surprising.

She had left the High Council, but she hadn't gone home. Not really. The weight of her parent's expectations hung heavy on her shoulders, and she didn't want to trudge back in the doors of the same old, same old. Not when she'd already come so far, seen so much. I totally understood. I wouldn't want that for her either. I hoped for good things to come.

For her.

And for me.

And for Beck.

I shook myself back to my senses. I had been so focused on Josie, I hadn't even noticed the little town. Now that our conversation was over and I'd survived, I started to see the look and feel of the stores. This was my first time in Alderton. Sloane had disappeared into one of these cute little shops. Townspeople popped in and out all around me, their errands being run with local flair. It was cute and quiet but also had a hum and a hustle. Even in small communities, the bits and bobs of capitalism turned their gears.

I began to explore.

Alderton was geographically larger and therefore more populated than Plumpkin, one town over. Both consumer centers offered darling little Main Streets with a mix of similar stores and tone. There were butchers and cheese shops and several other single-minded specialty buildings that could never survive the arrival of a come-one-come-all mega department store. You could call the available items dated, or spin them into classics, the kind of things that were never on trend to begin with and would therefor never go out of style.

I walked along the street, staring in the windows and admiring the displays, waiting for Sloane to reappear. She'd clearly overestimated how much time I would need to reconnect with Josie. That, or she really was shopping. I wondered which of the little cafes held the iced coffee drink that had drawn us here. My pleasant stroll continued all the way to the end of the strip. Store after store after store, until finally, at the end of the lane, the urban sprawl disappeared.

At the end of the sidewalk, a farmer's field of corn, already harvested and gone, brought an abrupt halt to the consumer flow. A double, rounded handrail signi-fied the end of public land and suggested pedestrians turn back around the way they'd come. I had walked right to the end of the line, and there were no more little stores to be found.

I looked out over the cornfield. It was a beautiful sight to see a never-ending crop, even now, missing the majority of its ears. I climbed the bottom rung of the handrail and elevated my viewpoint.

The sky was vast and unhindered above the field, the clouds untouched by construction or high-rise buildings. You could see a long way. On a nice day, the expanse would be stunning and bright. Today, it was murky and overcast. There were gloomy clouds coming in.

Actually, the darkness was kind of billowing.

It wasn't a storm, I realized. The clouds were building from the ground up.

The forest fire.

I could see its results from here.

Orson Bell.

The landmark must be over in that direction.

I couldn't see the actual structure so it's base was still quite a ways off, but the sky didn't lie. Something ugly was coming. I hoped the fire wouldn't reach the town.

The *magical* fire. The fire we were told not to attend.

Well, that was there. I was safe in town.

Sloane still hadn't appeared on the street, but I

hopped down off the rail and headed back the way I'd come. It was time to go. We could grab our drinks and head back to the castle.

She hadn't made her way over there, to the fire, had she?

I shook the worry away. Sloane and I were on the same page. No magical fires. No disobeying Lady Mauve's specific commandments. We would stay safe within the village. No drama. No worries. The best place to wait for her was probably beside her car.

The last store on the strip beside the field was a hardware shop. I'd passed it by on the way out of town without much notice, instead focused on the allure of the wide, golden field. But now, on return to Sloane's car, I peered in the window. The store hosted a menagerie of home improvement products. In the outbound display, they offered a selection of mouse deterrent buzzers to help homeowners keep out the tiny forest creatures. It was a problem with the coming winter. Furry friends would come running, looking for any household cracks and crannies as soon as the temperatures officially dropped.

The little white boxes with electrical prongs fit for outlets made me smile. They reminded me of my aunt. Aunt Abeline plugged those unpleasant little humming boxes in every outlet in the cabin. I couldn't blame her. The creaky old lake house built by Grandma Mim and Grandpa Charles was structurally sound but not exactly mouse proof. Who'd want to live with the pitter-patter of furry neighborhood feet?

I missed her, I realized. A lot.

In the residence, it was easy, in the flow of the Judicial Studies, in the buzz of the new coven and the High Council, to forget the places I'd been. The world outside, the things back home, all the people I loved. When you were busy, they disappeared. But here, off the grounds, was a good reminder of all the normalcy we'd left behind. Aunt Abeline was a normal person, and I loved her dearly.

She had raised me well.

When my mom passed, she brought me up, took me out, and introduced me to the world. Although my family history had been riddled with secrets while I was growing up, I was now in on the tale. And in fact, the tables had turned. I was now learning new secrets every day that I couldn't share with my aunt. It was kind of ironic. But it didn't matter. Whoever would be the keeper of the secrets, the love would freely flow. She would always want what was best for me, just as I wanted the best for her.

I frowned at my reflection.

It was a tough fact of life. I was in the coven, and she wasn't.

At my age, Aunt Abeline was rejected from the High Council world.

The world in which I was now living.

A world of secrets.

In fact, this morning, I'd signed a thousand agreements that said I would take those mysteries to my grave. But after all the non-disclosures and secret codes and whispers, it all felt kind of arbitrary, who stays and who goes. Who gets in to the High Council. After all, my skills as a witch were pretty weak.

Default.

No better than hers, I should think. I wondered what Aunt Abeline's powers were?

I didn't realize how long I had been staring into the store window until something on the other side of the pane caught my eye.

Something moving.

Not something.

Some*one*.

The silhouette of a person.

A guy, coming right towards me.

He was moving slowly. Picking his way. His face twisted into an angry scowl.

Although the boy was just a shadow, I recognized the frame immediately. The sinew of his muscles. That angry, hunched-over frown. I knew it all too well.

Spade.

TEN

NOTHING BUT CORN IN THE FIELD

FOR A MOMENT, we just stared at each other.

A world of hammers and socket wrenches and garden hoses stood between us. The glass and the door. They all held their ground. I was grateful for the in-betweeners. I had come to Alderton specifically to avoid running into any High Council rejects, but it turned out Josie and Spade had decided the very same thing.

I felt like a deer in headlights.

When he'd first seen me, Spade's movements in the building were slow, deliberate, like he didn't want to cause too many ripples. Like a cat stalking his prey. I hadn't even noticed his initial approach. But once I caught sight, I couldn't take my eyes off him. He stared into my soul, his frown trapping me in his gaze. Those dark eyes had always seemed so attractive. Now the sparkle was gone. The pupils burned like black coal.

I heard he was mad. Josie's words pinged around the back of my mind. *Livid*, she'd said.

He looked livid.

My eyes couldn't pull away, but my feet knew to be afraid. Every step he traveled towards the door, I backed up in the other direction. He weaved through the shelves and customers, coming for me. I had to get out of there. But quickly, I surmised, there was nowhere to go. His exit from the store stood between me and the rest of the street. I would only get past it as he pushed out the door. If I wanted to avoid a confrontation, that wasn't the direction to head.

There was no time to make a decision. He was coming. Quicker now, his moves intensified. His black eyes smoldered. Those sweet, teasing grins were gone. His handsome face twisted into a frown. He wasn't coming to chat.

Every step of his progression warned me he was planning his attack.

He wanted to punish me.

A punishment I deserved. Kind of.

Didn't I?

For the most part, until now, I had skated through life fairly untouched. I kept other kids at arm's length and they held me there as well. Aunt Abeline and I traveled so much through the years that I fell into the habit of making acquaintances, not friendships. I didn't connect deeply with other students, and if we did interact, it was nothing more than day-to-day little chats. But Spade had been different.

Plumpkin was my family's town, our home for generations. And he'd taken me under his wing. He'd been so sweet, so insistent, so sexy. He put on a great swagger and charm. I'd been intrigued by him from the first time I laid eyes on him, and before I even knew it, I'd let him into my life. At first, things were good, great even. An attraction crackled between us. He was a sweet talker and an even better kisser.

Such a good kisser.

And those hands. Oh my.

But he had this ugly habit of trying to manipulate me.

Big or small, he would push or pull our situation to try and make the cards land the best they could just for him. He could never let our relationship develop on equal terms. Always tricky. Always manipulating. He was scared I would leave or pick someone else as my parabond. He tried to remove all my options. In the end, that compulsion to control was the biggest thing that drove me away.

And worse for Spade, it drove me to Beck.

The guy he'd always feared I'd pick. It turned out he was right to be scared.

Unlike with Josie, who accepted the hands of fate, Spade had a pattern of lashing out at his enemies, making them suffer, making them pay. I had betrayed him at the highest levels he could think of, casting him out of the High Council and brutally rebuffing him. Beck and I had been accepted into the coven. Spade was refused entry. So here he was. Moving towards me. Coming for his revenge.

I couldn't budge.

"Mae, over here," Sloane called in a singsong. She had returned to the street, nibbling on a bag of home-made caramel corn.

Her friendly wave was enough to shake me out of the trance. I turned my eyes away from Spade for only a second, my face wild in fear. Sloane caught my expression and could tell instantly something was wrong. She immediately jumped to high alert. My stress radiated all the way across the street.

I turned back.

My glimpse at Sloane had been for only a split second, but when I looked back to find Spade, he was tearing through the store. He shoved aside displays and bewildered pedestrians, coming at me now with full speed and force.

"Run!" I screamed to her.

I turned on my heels and fled.

I heard Sloane's snack hit the ground. I prayed she escaped back into the constraints of consumerism before Spade hit the street, but I couldn't stay to find out. I bolted in the only safe direction I could.

The cornfield.

I leapt over the handrail and jumped down into the field. I hit the earth running. The terrain was spongy with fallen stalks and branches, but I couldn't stop to get my bearings. I needed to disappear before Spade exited the store. I scampered forward through the corn stalks, desperate to put four or five rows of the crops between me and the sidewalk. I ran and ran, then I dropped.

I crouched low in the field and waited.

My heartbeat pounded in my chest.

I tried not to huff and puff.

My pulse thumped so loudly it drowned out all my other senses. I struggled to stare back at the road.

I hoped Sloane had escaped. I hadn't given her much warning. I hoped at the very least, she had blended into the crowd. Spade wouldn't hurt her, I felt. That darkness in his heart he reserved for me alone.

I crouched lower, not daring to spread out. I didn't want the stalks around me to quiver or bend. I held as still as possible, completely motionless, and watched for any movement from the stores.

For a moment, there was nothing.

Silence.

A chill in the air.

Maybe he'd given up. Thought better of it. Cooled off his temper and gone home.

Then I saw it.

His dark frown.

It appeared above the corn.

He had climbed atop the metal railing I had not long ago used like a lookout myself, getting his best vantage of the stalks. We were close enough for me to see his jaw twitch. His eyes narrowed as he tried to look deep into the field. The corn convoluted the image. I wasn't visible, I hoped. I held my body still.

Deliberately and slowly, I breathed out of my mouth in a quiet hiss as if even the rise and fall of my chest might give my position away.

He watched and waited.

He could wait all day, I feared.

I was hidden and covered, but only so long as I didn't move. I stayed crouched, frozen. Offering my jangled nerves only small wisps of oxygen in shuddered gasps.

He surveyed the land, just watching. His eyes narrowed as he stared into the field.

Under my foot, I heard a tiny stalk snap as I accidentally shifted my weight.

No.

I looked up. But that tiny crack was enough.

His mouth, which had been locked in a frown, flirted with smiling. He turned his back, hopped off the rail, and suddenly he was gone.

I released the breath I didn't know I'd been holding, then closed my eyes to relax. Instead, they fluttered open.

Where was he? I wondered. Had he truly given up? Or just changed his attack? Could I return to find Sloane? Or was he waiting to ambush me out on the road?

This, I realized, was what his smile was about.

With him on the perch, staring me down, at least I knew where he was. I could gauge how he felt. Now those points of information were gone.

Was he setting a trap? I couldn't be sure.

I didn't dare reveal myself. I waited.

Alone.

The gray, ashy clouds that had been floating in the distance when I'd first arrived at this lookout were now closing in on the stores. The cornfield was growing darker. The prevailing winds blew the fire's murky clouds into town.

Still, I waited.

My muscles grew cold. I wasn't dressed to be out in the elements. I sure wasn't dressed to hide in a muddy field.

When ten, maybe twenty minutes had passed, I decided Spade must have had his fill. He hadn't shown his face again. It was likely he'd gone home. Slowly, I stood. I kept my eyes on the direction of the stores as I rose, ready to bolt or freeze at the first glimpse of his expression, but he never appeared.

I took a deep cleansing breath and huffed all the air out, physically trying to blow out my fear.

It was okay.

I was safe.

Spade was gone.

But... so was the town. I looked around, surprised.

There was nothing but the corn in the fields.

ELEVEN
WATCHING, LISTENING, GLOATING

"NO," I murmured at first. "No!"

I ran forward through the stalks towards where I knew the metal handrail at the end of the field should have been, and I searched for the sidewalk, the stores, the town. But all I found was more corn.

My heart beat loudly in my chest. Becoming lost was far scarier than being found.

Spade had created a lie-guard illusion to twist me into confusion. But I knew it wasn't real.

"Spade, come out," I called. "This isn't real. I know what you've done."

It sure felt real. But giant fields of corn didn't spring up the second you closed your eyes. Illusions did. And Spade was a lie-guard.

"Let me out," I told him, snapping a corn stalk with my hands. "Let me out!"

But if Spade was close by, watching, listening, gloating, he didn't feel the need to reply. Why would he? The silent unknown was far scarier than any ugly words he could say.

I needed help.

I pulled out my phone to text Sloane or to call Beck. I wasn't sure what my next move would be, but it didn't matter. The signal was dead.

Another part of the illusion, I guessed.

I moved forward, snaking through the field, headed to the spot I knew should be home to the stores. There were only more crops.

The smell of smoke and char filled my nostrils. The dark clouds from the Orson Bell were getting closer as well. Bits of ash fluttered in the air, landing like snowflakes on my shoulders, and the stalks around my head had started to exhibit an ashy dusting. The smoke was growing nearer.

"This isn't real," I said to refocus. "I know it's fake, Spade!" I shouted. I took all the crops in view.

That was actually a lie.

It was impossible to differentiate between what was fake and what was real in the farmer's field; the illusion was too detailed. The dark smoke was too thick. Maybe I should never have moved from where I started. I was starting to lose my bearings. I should have just stayed in one place.

Or stuck with Beck.

Or gone to the library like I wanted.

Why did I come into town?

Getting out of this on my own was impossible. I shouldn't have run. I shouldn't have hid. I should have faced off with Spade. Let the confrontation unfold. Let him have his say. He was right to be mad. I had hurt his heart, his ego, his future. Hearing him out would help him move away from the pain.

"Do your worst," I finally said, giving in. "Spade, just do it. Give your best shot. Then move on with your life."

Josie had moved on.

Beck and I were finding our new path.

Even Aunt Abeline at home was adjusting to life in a new way.

Spade could adjust too. If he wanted to.

"Come out!" I called. "Let's talk."

It was an ironic request since it was my cowardice that had driven me into the field. I listened for a response, but he didn't give in. All I could hear was the sweet, gentle crackle, sizzle, and pop of the fire. The licks and snaps grew louder as it engulfed stalk after stalk. The smell of fresh popcorn wafted. I felt warm.

Too warm...

I turned, recognizing the peaceful sounds as they grew far more dangerous.

The ash all around wasn't just wafts from the far-off Orson Bell blaze.

The cornfield was on fire.

TWELVE
POPPING AND SMACKING

WHAT THE HELL? The hanging ash in the air hadn't just floated in from some distant clouds. The danger was building here, in this field. How had I become so complacent? My mind was so twisted up dealing with Spade Polari, I didn't see the danger right in front of me. Now that I had, it was unmistakable. The air was thick and gray. It was becoming difficult to see. The plumes of black were getting bolder, and the fire was close on my left. The terrible heat wave moved quickly; the dried out crops were easy food for the flames.

I took a few steps backward, watching for signs that the fire was coming.

The sounds were growing louder.

Then I saw them: the first flickers of orange flame.

The fire licked its way up the dry stalks ten or twelve rows away. The whole field was a tinderbox. In seconds, the fire could surround where I stood.

I turned and fled.

"Spade!" I screamed. "Spade!"

There was no way to know if he was still holding me in the bounds of a false illusion, which way was out, or what direction to head. The crackling foliage burned all around me. Sputtering and spitting. Popping and smacking. The sweet scent of fresh popcorn turned sour.

I raced blindly into the charred vegetation. There was no sky or landmark to guide me, only the crackling sounds at my back to drive me forward and let me know where I didn't want to go. The heat and fire folded in behind me. Dead, yellow stalks smacked into my face and shoulders as I ran by. Their brittle, dried leaves were just waiting to be consumed. Soon the whole field would be ablaze.

This couldn't be Spade.

Could it?

Had he intended to burn me alive?

I had seen his capabilities before, and this chaos and destruction was too dark. It was beyond his abilities. It couldn't be his. I refused to believe it.

The fire wasn't an illusion.

It was real. But that did nothing to calm my nerves.

Magic illusions could be stopped. How did you end a real fire?

At this point, I knew I had been running far too deep in one direction. Clearly, I'd made a wrong turn, and my path had raced deeper into the field, not out of it. But it was too late to correct the course again. I had no choice. Staying ahead of the fire was the only option.

I ran as quickly as my feet could take me.

My legs ached.

Little scrapes from a thousand stalks of corn carved ugly scratches into my skin. I covered my face with my hands.

Soon, my pace was slowing.

I was exhausted, and the fire seemed only to be quickening. In moments, it would overtake me where I stood. I moved forward, like through quicksand, struggling to keep going. A stitch in my side sucked out my breath. My vigor had escaped me.

Some fields, I knew, were acres wide.

What if I'd found my way into the middle of one of those fields?

I tried to regulate my breathing.

You can't stop, I told myself. You have to keep going. My muscles kept crying out. I trudged ever forward. All I could see was more corn. Yellow and brown in every direction... Yellow and black as the fires licked the fields. Yellow and... What was that?

I turned back.

I stumbled towards it.

Yellow and *black*.

There was definitely a change in my depth of field.

The world around me was yellow and brown, still yellow and something, but the darker color told me something was there. Was it a mirage?

I marched towards it.

A tiny color discrepancy.

The hue called out towards me. It wasn't much. Anything to escape the endless repetition of the field.

As I dragged myself towards this new color, the blackness actually grew larger. Darker. I gasped, so relieved. The darkness was actually something. My instincts were right. It was a burned out, grassy field!

Through the stalks I saw it.

What was once a meadow lay charred and crumbling now, but it was wide open. An open field already burned. If I managed to get there, there'd be nothing to scorch. The fires couldn't follow me there.

The gray skies opened up.

If I could just get to the meadow, I'd be free.

It was the other side of the field. A meadow on a farmer's property, far away from town. I'd gotten so turned around in Spade's illusion, I'd walked my way right through the acres of corn.

But here waited salvation. There had to be a house... or a barn... or a something. Maybe I'd find a road out. An exit of some kind was waiting. Once I was free of the stalks, I'd figure it out.

I picked up speed.

A blooming smile hurt my cheeks. Relief bloomed in my chest.

I could see it—freedom—getting closer.

Safety.

My feet closed the gap.

Thirty, then twenty feet.

Tears started to stream down my face. I wiped them away, sliding the black ash around on my cheeks. My skin had grown thick with the stuff.

My heart leapt in my ribs.

Ten... only five feet more. I was going to make it.

With dramatic flair, I burst through the final corn stalks and busted free!

The change in terrain caused me to stumble, disoriented, ungraceful. I threw my hands out to halt my momentum, my fingers digging into the black, ashy ground. I hit hard, but in the rubble, I felt safety.

I cried openly.

Exhausted.

Catching my breath and myself.

I was free of the fire.

Free of the terror.

Free of the maze.

"She is one of yours, yes?"

Shocked, I looked up.

The voice was distinctly other. An accent from another land. The woman who'd said the words stood in front of a pack of other people, adults who all stared down at me. It was clear they were from the same clan. The group was almost all blonde with piercing blue eyes. They were different heights and different ages, but they all wore wardrobes in shades of red.

Most of the women had tight, dramatic curls framing angry stares.

The men, with hair cut short, tossed their wavy

locks sky high and to the right. They glared in my direction.

But their animosity wasn't aimed at me alone.

On my other side, I recognized my people. The familiar white tracksuits of all the ladies and the fellows.

Led by a rotund man with fiery orange hair and a wicked scowl, there was the collection of ladies and fellows that had come from my home. Our leader leaned over to listen intently to the whisperings of someone I knew well.

Lady Gray. She was there, in the heart of the crowd.

The whole coven was present.

Arms crossed. Death stares.

Lady Gray seemed to be filling him in on who I was.

I didn't dare budge. On hands and knees in the center of this confrontation, I froze, an ashy ball of nerves.

"Yes," he agreed, claiming me as one of his tribe. "Just a student."

Lady Gray seemed to have more to tell, but he waved her away.

I had no clue what I'd stumbled into.

There were far more ladies and fellows than people in red, yet still they faced off as equals, a great divide between them. No one in either crowd moved towards the others; the two people in the forefront seemed to work as voices for all.

Everyone stood on edge. Both factions looked ready to pounce.

This, I realized, was where the fire had started. I was lucky the wind had blown it off before I'd come.

I had landed at the origin of the magic forest fire.

My eyes raked over the groups, then traveled to the outbuildings in the distance as well. There were crumbling barn buildings with some fire damage and an untouched stone tower. Constructed of ancient techniques built to last, it still towered above everything. At its top sat an old gray bell.

Orson Bell.

This was the very place we were told not to go.

First by Lady Blue Moon, then more firmly by Lady Mauve.

And I was in the middle of the grounds.

My eyes floated down from the structures to a nearby tractor. Something flashed behind it. A quick little motion. It caught my eye.

My friends were hiding there. Far up on the hill. Hidden from everything. How I longed to be by their sides. I could feel their wide eyes. I quickly looked away, fearful my stare would draw attention to their hiding spot. Instead, I looked further around.

There was Lady Blue Moon. She looked worried.

And... Lady Mauve. Her disapproval slit a hole into my soul.

To her left and behind her, I found another scowl. The pretty, black-haired girl and her judgy friends were watching. In fact everyone stared. Every face in the crowd was a frown.

Why hadn't I stayed home?

"But she is yours?" the blonde woman confirmed. "A coven member?"

Grudgingly, the orange-haired man nodded.

"We pick this girl. Final selection," the foreigner said.

Lady Gray whispered something to the man.

"Very well." He grimly nodded. "Mae Kingsley: our final competitor. When the fires no longer rage, the Battle of Four will begin."

WHAT? I looked left and right, bewildered.

With the woman's final proclamation, the meeting was over. Both the ladies, the fellows, the older students, and the strange group of others began milling and chatting with their own friends.

There was no interaction between factions.

I climbed to my feet and dusted the soot off my hands and knees, but cleaning off was a losing battle. I was covered in grime. I could shake off the large, crumbly flakes, but a gray, ashy powder remained. I glanced in the direction of the tractor and barn ruins with the vague hope of reconnecting with Beck and the others, but the first year students had already disappeared.

Lady Gray and Lady Mauve were marching towards me. The look of animosity in their eyes burned metaphorical holes in my heart.

Thankfully, as they approached, Lady Blue Moon swooped in by my side.

"What are you doing here?" She forcefully tried to help brush off the char from my skin but only succeeded in adding the gray powder to her own hands. "I told you to stay put at the castle." Her eyes were worried and sad, not angry like the other two.

"I didn't come on purpose," I squeaked out. "I got lost in the corn. Then the field turned to fire."

"Did you use magic?" Lady Mauve snapped.

"No, I—"

"Fires don't start themselves, Mae."

Fires don't... I didn't know what to make of this phrase, but suddenly I was starting to put it together.

The magic had *started* the fire?

All these fires?

"It wasn't me," I admitted. I looked up, a guilty feeling settling in. "It was Spade."

The women bristled at his name.

"We're in a state of extirpation," Lady Blue Moon explained to me, as if that would mean something.

At my blank look, Lady Gray sputtered out the definition. "Extirpation: extinction, annihilation."

"The energy field is at the brink," Lady Blue Moon clarified. "He can't use magic." She shook her head, like I should tell him. But to be fair, she didn't know who he was. "No one should. The energy here is too thick. Even a small spell will cause a new blaze."

I looked back at the black, smoldering clouds still

billowing out of the field. I was safe now, but the danger wasn't over. The plants and wildlife would never be the same. And destruction could spread further.

"Will it reach town?" I feared.

"No," Lady Mauve said. "We caught it in time. Although your little stunt didn't help."

It wasn't a stunt, I wanted to say. But there wasn't room to share my thoughts.

"We've reached an agreement. Diminutive magic from either side until the energy field clears." Lady Gray eyed the remaining people in red clothes.

"Without a full reset, the extirpation will continue to build," Lady Blue Moon said.

"Enough. Blue Moon, introduce our champion to her new teammates; we've got more important things to do." Lady Mauve gave me an especially cruel once-over, then she and Lady Gray turned on their heels.

Instinctively, I wanted to follow. Beg for more forgiveness. But I knew our conversation was over for today.

"What's she talking about? Teammates?" I asked. "What the heck is going on?"

"Ah. Right. Well, your dramatic entrance had particularly bad timing," Lady Blue Moon admitted. "The two factions can't continue warring, or the kinetic energy will destroy everything in its path."

"Causing magic forest fires. I get it."

"Yes. Great. And Cornelius ordered the Damocles coven to leave, but they refused. Of course, they've come for Valdeez leaves." She nodded, expecting me to understand their value. "Or so people say."

"Do we have them?"

"That's above my rank." She shrugged. "But yes. Now they've arrived, and we're already here, happily existing. The geographical area can't handle the qi. That's like energy."

"I know, it's a big Scrabble word. A *Q* word, without the *U* vowel. It's commonly used."

"I didn't know you played Scrabble.."

"My aunt and I compete." I nodded, hoping Lady Blue Moon would get back to the people we were now on a crash course to meet with.

"Right... Well, when there's a huge new influx of paranormal power with nowhere to go, so something's got to give. Hence, the Battle of Four. You're our fourth," she quickly added, slipping that last detail in before we stopped abruptly, arriving at the new group.

"I'm the what?"

"These are your co-competitors," Lady Blue Moon offered. "Fellow Silverfox..."

An older fellow nodded. He had auburn shaggy hair longer than his ears, a chin strap beard, and a mustache of ruddy red hair. His stance and his style pegged him around forty years old, although he might have been aggressively dressing younger, as his age was starting to show. There were a lot of crow's feet around his eyes. But his face looked kind. He whipped his hair over his shoulder and offered a grin.

"Nice ta meet ya."

"Third year Ferris Bean..." Lady Blue Moon continued.

Ferris was young like me, but hardened. She looked tough.

"She's already completed the first two years of training," Blue Moon told me. In that time, she must have seen some rough moments. Her arms were crossed in front of her chest. As she nodded to me, a cute boy with black hair whispered something in her ear. She cracked a smile that was for him alone, then tightened her expression again. I could tell she wasn't pleased to meet my acquaintance, but I didn't blame her. In her shoes, I'd probably feel the same thing.

"And Lady Rain." Lady Gray completed the introductions.

The last competitor was a well put together middle-aged woman with short, slick blonde hair. If she weren't a witch, I might have assumed she was a socialite or influencer. She had stood straight and tall, her lipsticked lips flatlined into a frown.

"Nice to meet you," she offered with proper manners, but it was clearly not how she felt. Somehow, her tracksuit looked more expensive than the rest.

"Everyone, meet first year—"

"First *day*—" Lady Rain interrupted.

"Mae Kingsley," Lady Blue Moon finished.

There was a flash of recognition in Fellow Silverfox's face at my name.

Did he know the name Kingsley? He was about the

right age. Maybe a year before or behind my mom. Had he known her? Or my dad?

I filed away these questions.

Now was not the time to ask.

The others stared at me.

"Hi." I awkwardly waved, having no clue what the proper etiquette was in an introduction like this. I wished I wasn't such a gray, ashy mess.

"She's just a baby," Lady Rain moaned. "We're doomed."

"Nice to meet you." Ferris offered me a sturdy handshake.

"Welcome to the club! The place you don't wanna be," Silverfox announced with a grin. He shoved his hand in mine and pumped enthusiastically. "You got some powers, girl?"

"She's a dream-cast." Lady Blue Moon put a protective hand on my shoulder.

"Well, alright. You'll, like, tell us the future and where to go to win the battle and things. Nice." He grinned again under his spikey facial hair. With his whole head, he tossed his hair out of the way. His hair-line showed no sign of aging, and he swooped the mass of wavy auburn hair often as a dramatic exclamation point as he spoke.

He reminded me of Greg.

A bigger, hopefully smarter, middle-aged Greg with a great head of hair and a grin on his face. Silverfox clearly loved that flip-flopping mop of hair, and it showed.

"We'll see." Ferris tapered his expectations. "A first year has a ways to go."

It wasn't meant to be mean, just true.

She probably remembered her own first year experiences all too well.

"We might as well quit," Lady Rain moaned. "Pack your bags. All of the High Council is riding on a girl with one day."

"Ah, it's alright. The Red Queen sniffed out a weak link, but it's fine. She made a mistake picking this one and me." Silverfox hugged Ferris from the side, squeezing the shoulders of the young girl. The redhead accepted his gesture but didn't reciprocate, just frowned.

If Lady Rain noticed he'd left her off his list, she didn't show it.

"And Cornelius chose wisely too," Lady Blue Moon added.

"It's a battle of the weakest links," Lady Rain snapped in case I wasn't following. "Both Cornelius and their leader tried to find them."

"Great." I nodded, frowning.

"I told you not to come." Lady Blue Moon sadly shrugged.

"Come on. Don't write this one off yet. Maybe they picked wrong with you as well. You look a fine mess, but there's fire inside, yeah? Like yer mom. Prove 'em wrong." Silverfox pointed his stumpy finger in my direction.

My cheeks burned.

A fire inside like Sierra. He *did* know my parents. Or at least, he'd met Mom.

"Enough chit chat. Time for lunch. This tum is starving. You'll make our schedule soon?" He looked to Lady Blue Moon. She nodded. He tossed his auburn mop once more. "Well, what are we waiting for? Let's fill our bellies." He shook his stomach and wandered off in search of food, not interested in trying to lead the charge.

"Welcome to the team." Ferris nodded to me. She peeled off in the direction of her black-haired boyfriend.

Lady Rain looked me up and down. "This is the worst," she muttered and left.

"Nice to meet you too." I rolled my eyes. But I didn't leave. I turned to Lady Blue Moon instead. "Give it to me straight. How bad is this?" I asked.

She considered things before she answered, probably trying to decide how honest she should be. Finally, she nodded and sighed.

"I wouldn't want to be you," she said.

FOURTEEN

THE BATTLE OF THE WEAKEST

PSSST.

The shrubs hissed as I walked past.

I had begun the long walk across the farmer's field to the road back to town. I'd been gone for so long I had no idea if Sloane would still be waiting around or not. But on the off chance she was, that was where to return.

Pssst.

The bush called again. No, not the bush. It was Marcy, still in hiding.

Other ladies and fellows still milled nearby, also exiting the field. I checked no one was watching, then disappeared around the shrubbery. I was surprised it wasn't touched, but the fires hadn't reached this part of the vegetation. The magical fire seemed to be a concentrated burn. Behind the foliage, the whole group was waiting.

"You look terrible," Greg blurted out. "What were

you thinking?"

"Nice to see you too." I wiped my hands again, but cleanliness was impossible without the aid of a hot shower.

"I thought you weren't coming," Beck said. He looked a little hurt.

"I wasn't. Sloane and I went shopping."

"And then you accidentally strolled into a burning cornfield?" Vince wasn't buying.

"Where's Sloane?" Tej looked around.

"We got separated," I admitted. "When I ran into Spade," I added.

Beck's eyes flashed.

The others registered surprise as well.

And Josie, I didn't say out loud. But that was wrong. What Beck and I had started wasn't some secret. We weren't doing anything improper. He deserved to know the truth.

"Josie too," I added. "They were both in Alderton." I nodded in the town's general direction. "She's working at the bookstore."

Beck's face twisted in a frown.

"And they did this?" Nicolette worried.

"They didn't team up to fight her, dummy," Vince snapped.

"They weren't together." I shook my head and glared at Vince. No need to be rude on my account. He rolled his eyes.

"How is she?" Beck asked quietly.

I looked over to him. He'd come back into control

of his expression.

"Good, I think. She seemed good."

He nodded.

"Spade, on the other hand, chased me into the field," I added.

"The burning cornfield." Marcy nodded sagely. "Which is why you're covered like that."

I looked down at my ashy mess.

Tej let out a low whistle. "That bridge is torched," he agreed.

"He's basically a murderer. You could have died." Nicolette folded her arms across her chest.

"To be fair, he didn't know his illusion would make the field start burning."

"Extirpation." Nicolette nodded.

"We all heard the new vocab, Nick," Vince shut her down again.

"He just wanted me to freak out. Get lost among the stalks," I said.

I don't know why I felt the need to defend a guy who I had run blindly from to escape, but I did. I couldn't blame him for all of today's actions, and I didn't want the others to blame him either.

Beck had fallen away from the conversation. He just kept nodding. No longer following what was said. His mind on other things. Other people.

"Bet you wish you'd come with us." Marcy grinned.

"Yeah. You should have seen it! The Council members were, like, burning with anger. They were, like, flinging these boulders, and then they'd be shooting these rockets and the sky would rain down with hail." Greg, Vince, and Tej playfully reenacted some of the drama. "There were cracks of lightning and Cornelius Child could do this, like, boss teleportation."

"It wasn't teleportation." Vince fell out of character.

"Then what would you call it?" Tej wondered.

"Dude, he jumped from one spot to another without moving a muscle," Greg said.

"It was some sort of lie-guard." Vince shrugged.

"Well, whatever it was, I want to bottle it," Tej agreed. "You could make a fortune!"

"It was fast," Beck agreed, finally coming back to the group.

"So fast," Marcy agreed.

"Which one's Child?" I wondered.

She nodded. "Orangey-red hair. Big stomach, but he could really move," Marcy described.

"It wasn't that big." Nicolette frowned.

Of course.

The man with the booming voice. With Lady Gray in his ear.

As the head of Judicial Studies, he also appeared to be head of the coven. The leader of the High Council. Cornelius Child was someone I knew immediately I did not want to interact with. Vince agreed.

"I don't think you made a good first impression," he sneered.

I did my best to ignore him. "What about the Battle? Did you learn any more about it?" I asked the others.

"The Battle of Four," Nicolette corrected, as if what was most important about the upcoming competition was to say its proper name.

"When the Red Lady picked Lady Rain, she burst into tears." Greg sniggered.

"Shut up, man. She's part of our team." Tej smacked him.

"I can't help it if she's a crybaby." He shrugged.

"She might be a powerful sorceress. You don't know," Marcy chided.

"I don't think so." I shook my head. "Blue Moon told me it's basically a battle of the weakest," I admitted.

The others stared at me in disbelief.

"The weakest... to represent the coven?" Nicolette asked.

I nodded. "That's why the other coven got to pick our battalion."

Finally, Vince vocalized what they all must have been thinking.

"And lucky us," he said. "They chose you."

FIFTEEN
IT'S A LONG STORY

AFTER I REJOINED MY FRIENDS, I noticed some of them were able to use their phones, so I stepped to the side and checked my cell again. Whatever issue it'd had in the midst of Spade's lie-guard had worn off. I sent a quick message to Sloane, and Greg offered me a lift back to town as her message pinged back. She was still waiting by the store, wondering where I'd gone. I happily accepted his lift but reconsidered when I saw the backseat was a serious squish. His car was so full I had to sit on Beck's lap just to fit in.

Luckily, I didn't really mind. Plus, it was a short trip.

I sat sidesaddle on Beck, with Vince on the far side of the bench and Tej in the middle of things. As a short guy, he was used to being stuck in the worst carpool location, but that didn't mean he was happy about the move.

The front seat wasn't much better. Marcy perched on Nicolette's lap too.

Beck wrapped his arm around my waist to find room for his broad shoulders, and our heads tucked dangerously close together. Our scents intermingled.

"Hi," he said as I climbed aboard.

"Hi," I returned, tucking in.

"Hi," Tej added his two cents as well.

"Hi." Vince finished the row.

We all laughed.

Sitting so near, Beck's skin and clothes gave off the tiniest hint of sandpaper and pine needles intermixed with just a touch of store-bought musk. It was intoxicating. I must have smelled like sweat, burnt popcorn and charred vegetables. I hoped Beck and the others wouldn't breathe too deeply.

"Bet you wish you'd decided to come with us," Beck teased.

"That's what Marcy said." I frowned.

So I was right. He had totally zoned out in the field.

"Well, I missed you," he added. When I didn't give an immediate reply, he got a little worried. "You okay?"

The boys readjusted the best they could.

He wiggled a little underneath me, trying to find a comfortable place, as if the lack of legroom was what was bothering me.

"We're all hunky-dory." Tej laughed, using my knee as an armrest.

"Get a move on, Greg," Vince added.

"I'm fine," I said.

What else could I say?

He was all cute and cuddly now, but he didn't seem too focused on us when I happened to mention his ex-girlfriend.

That wasn't the kind of complaint you brought up in a car full of your peers. To your not-quite-sure-what-the-heck-we-are-but-I-thought-we-were-starting-to-be-something guy, it's not the kind of thing you brought up at all.

"I'm not too heavy, Lettie?" Marcy giggled in the front chair.

"Nope, you're good." Nicolette's clipped tone gave away the truth that her friend was maybe a bit heavier than she'd hoped, but she wouldn't tell Marcy that.

"The girl's all skin and bones." Greg tickled Marcy.

She squirmed and giggled. "Greg!"

"Ahh! No wiggling," Nicolette complained.

"I really appreciate the lift," I told the whole crew.

"If Sloane's not there by the stores, you're finding your own way home," Vince replied.

"We're fine. And if we weren't, Greg would make two trips, wouldn't you babe?" Marcy turned back and smiled.

"Ahh, no turning," Nicolette groaned.

Greg grabbed Marcy's hand and kissed it. "Whatever baby wants," he mused.

Marcy giggled and leaned off Nicolette's legs to kiss Greg's cheek. She peppered his face with kisses.

"Watch the road!" came the other five voices at once.

"Okay, geez." Marcy plopped back on Nicolette's lap.

"I'm watching," Greg complained.

"I got you," Beck assured me. "I'm your human seatbelt."

"Thanks." I tried to warm to him. I could see he was trying. "Sorry, I'm getting ash on your shirt... and your pants..."

"It's like a new pattern. That hopefully comes out in the wash." He grinned and cleared a smudge off my cheek.

"If Mae dies in a car crash, can they choose a new competitor?" Tej wondered.

"One can only hope," Vince muttered.

"No one's dying," Nicolette complained.

"If Greg crashes..."

"No one's crashing."

"First of all, she wouldn't die. You'd be thrown clear," Greg informed me.

"Like me." Marcy nodded.

"The ones thrown clear are definitely dead," Tej countered. "That's why we have seatbelts."

"Didn't you hear? He's my human seatbelt," I told Tej. "Beck's got me."

"I got you," Beck assured me again. This time, his hand around my waist pulled me farther in. This physical tug broke through the final piece of disgruntled wall I had started to build. My worries about competing for the coven, my run-in with Spade, Beck's reaction to Josie, and even his random hug earlier with the elevator girl all fizzled away with the grip of his hands. Here he was, rebuilding our connection, and he was literally pulling me in.

I blushed. "And I got you," I told him playfully.

It didn't mean anything, but it was the kind of mushy, gushy thing Marcy might have said to Greg. Beck ate it up.

I leaned farther into his chest, putting my head on his shoulder. He shifted more in my direction as well. Using the excuse of the crowded car seat, we cuddled closer together. For a moment, the rest of the world slipped away. It felt so warm and safe on his lap. His hands were strong. They tugged around me, radiating with energy, pulling me closer. His broad shoulder was a soft place to land. I put my cheek against his shirt.

This afternoon with Josie and Spade, then the fire and selections... It had all been so rattling, but now, I fit perfectly against the curve of his neck.

The others in the car kept on chattering, but Beck and I tuned them out. Our focus turned in. I could feel his heartbeat and the rhythm of lifeblood in his body as his breath rose and fell next to mine. We were completely in sync. His thighs were warm beneath my butt. Sitting on his lap was intimate and exciting. Beck took a deep breath, his diaphragm gently rocking me, then released a small sigh.

I hoped the car ride might go on forever. It was exciting to be in his arms.

We had hugged a few times in the past, an embrace here or there to help celebrate a moment or in some sort of friendly hello or goodbye. Quick and dirty those squeezes had been, a bump of chests, a pat, a handshake, always dropped within seconds, mindful of who might be watching and careful to avoid any lingering pause. None of those previous interactions had prepared me for what I felt in this car.

He was meant to hold me.

One hand around my waist, the other cupping my bottom.

I fit every nook, every cranny, every fold.

Our body language was perfect. Positively delicious. And then, it got even better.

He curved his face in towards mine. Looked down at me on his shoulder. I looked up at him. Into his eyes.

Until that moment, we had been separately enjoying each other's company, taking pleasure in silent companionship, but now that I could see him, face to face, I knew it wasn't just in my heart. He felt it as well.

Our desire was growing.

"Hi, parabond," he said, so quietly that only I could hear him.

"Hi, parabond," I whispered back as well.

His eyes stared deep into mine, drinking my soul in. Then his gaze flickered down to my lips.

I couldn't help myself. In desire, I bit my bottom lip. My teeth pinched the pink orifice, then released it.

He watched with appreciation.

My fingers, which had been resting on top of his T-shirt, gently tugged at his fabric and skin.

His upper hand squeezed me towards him. His lower palm grazed down on my thigh.

His lips looked so plump and inviting.

"Is that Josie's bookstore?" From the front seat, Nicolette pointed to a shop.

"Where?" Beck sat up so fast I had to catch myself on the passenger seat headrest.

"Where?" Tej asked too.

The others turned as well.

Beck craned his neck, so intent to see the girl.

"Yeah," I admitted, frowning. "That's what she said. She works there."

The carload peered around, anxious to catch a glimpse. Beck rubbernecked as we passed. The shoulder that moments ago I'd been safely tucked on now turned and aimed towards the other girl.

There she was, set up at the counter. There wasn't a customer in front of her, so she leaned on her arm and casually read a book.

"Gave up the coven for that." Vince shook his head.

The others turned around again and lost interest, but Beck never did.

Suddenly, the lap I sat on felt strained and boney.

He'd completely twisted in his chair. There was

nowhere left for me to comfortably balance above him. I frowned and turned my energies forward, holding on to the backrest to hold me, but I didn't say a word.

Let Beck strain his neck for Josie.

My cheeks flushed in anger. I felt so dumb.

Moments before, I was swimming in the deep end of Beck's pheromones, picturing our lives together. Romanticizing our hearts.

Our lips.

Our love lives playing out.

It was so clear he was still hung up on her. And of course! Why wouldn't he be? They were together forever. It wasn't even a week since they'd been broken apart.

The car ride couldn't end quickly enough.

Thankfully, Sloane was still patiently waiting, leaning up against her car with a half-drunk iced coffee in her hand. A second drink waited for me on her hood. The sweet girl had bought one for me. When she saw Greg's car loaded down with coven members, she smiled. He pulled up beside her but didn't bother to park. Greg just stopped halfway off the road and waited for the rest of us to hop out.

"Thanks, sir." I patted his shoulder and popped open the door. From my awkward vantage, it was actually easier for me to stand and let Beck climb out first, then unload myself.

"I got you," Beck tried to tell me, but I was done playing around.

"I'm good," I said, and I climbed out myself.

In the back seat, Tej also slipped out as Nicolette unpeeled herself from the front row.

"I can't wait to hear all about this." Sloane raised an eyebrow, looking me up and down. I'd forgotten, on top of everything else, I looked like I'd gotten lost in a chimney.

"Sorry," I muttered. "I'm such a mess."

She shrugged, handing me my drink. "I'll see if I have an old blanket," she offered.

"Tej, if you wanna stay with these guys, I'll ride back with Mae and Sloane," Beck offered, his eyes still lingering on the bookstore.

We couldn't even see Josie from the street, but still he continued to stare.

"Nah, we're good." I gave Beck a little push. "You go with Greg. Tej'll come with us. I'll see you in a bit." I nodded.

I tried to play it cool but there was an edge in my voice. I cleared my esophagus to play it off, coughing once, twice to sell it, but nobody was fooled.

Especially not Beck.

"Are you sure?"

"Yeah, of course." I nodded. "See ya." I offered a big smile to prove my point.

"In or out?" Vince complained, leaning out the window.

"I'm in," Beck agreed, getting back in Greg's car.

I felt almost bad about casting him away, still covered in my ashy gray remains. Then I saw him sneak another peek at the bookstore. The boy couldn't keep his eyes in his head.

I turned to my other friends. "This iced coffee is amazing," I told Sloane as she returned.

"Yeah, where's mine?" Tej complained.

"At the time, I didn't know you'd be joining." Sloane smoothly rebuffed him. "Here." She handed me an old blanket. "I was starting to think you were dead… I guess I wasn't far off." She raised an eyebrow.

"It's a long story."

"You didn't answer your phone," she noted.

"Apparently, cell phones don't work when you're trapped in an illusion," I told them, laying the blanket out as a base to sit on. This technical news was surprising to the other teens.

"Like, not at all?" Nicolette wondered.

"Good to know." Tej nodded, impressed.

I just shrugged, sinking low in the passenger car seat. The others loaded into the back.

"Long story?" Sloane prompted again.

Exhausted, I nodded.

She smiled. "I look forward to every detail."

SIXTEEN

MAYBE THE ELEVATOR CHICK WAS RIGHT

SLEEP, I told myself.

Sleep.

I stared at the drywall. *Close your eyes and count backwards.* I willed the slumber upon me.

Come on, dream. Give me a vision.

If you don't sleep, you can't access your one and only power, I worried to myself.

The sheets itched my bare legs.

The whole coven is counting on you. You have to prove you're not a default. Close your damn eyes and help. I frowned, no closer to unconsciousness. Beating myself up wasn't helping. I sighed and rolled onto my shoulder. If only I were a chemist and could contribute some real, concrete magic, or maybe if I were a harness, I'd be bold with magic realms. Best case, I should have been a lie-guard. I could have conjured like nobody's business. Being any one of those types of witches was a real skill. Not like what I was. A lowly dream-cast.

Maybe the elevator chick was right.

It should have been Josie here at the High Council. Not me. Not my parabond.

During the trials set out in limbo, I had thought about walking away from the coven so many times, but I had always stuck around. It was Josie who bailed. Now, bailing wasn't an option.

The fate of the whole coven rested with me.

Plus the other three battalion members as well.

I couldn't quit, and I couldn't bail.

These thoughts were not helping. What I needed to do was sleep.

Sleeeeeeeeeep.

If Josie were here, she'd be sleeping, I complained to myself.

Beck was clearly not over her.

In the car, he was practically spinning in his seat. He didn't even realize he was doing it, swiveling around like a pinata. I had been kidding myself to think we might have a future. At the chance to see his previous girl, he had practically thrown me from his lap.

At least I had my friends.

Sloane had listened to every detail of what had happened since we parted, and she didn't judge me for any of it. She didn't say a negative word. Plus, she knew what I was going through. She was also a dream-cast. Of course, that skill set seemed to work much better for her.

Time for beddy-bye. I tried again.

Sloane was a much more powerful witch than me, I knew. Every night she immersed herself in visions for the coming day. That was why she always seemed so calm and happy. She knew exactly what was going to happen. She always knew how to interpret the day. Her visions were clear. She didn't spend her nights staring up at the plaster on the walls. And if she did, when the time was right, she'd drift away, and then her visions would appear.

I took a deep breath and rolled on my back again.

I'd already tried on my side. It was hopeless.

I clicked on my table lamp and dragged the High Council rule book off the shelf. Maybe reading would help. I thumbed through the pages, not sure where to begin.

What was that word Lady Blue Moon and the others had used? Exitation? No. That wasn't it. I flipped to the index at the back. My finger scanned the *E* words until there it was.

Extirpation.

That was what she'd said.

I'd never heard it before, and that said a lot about a word. Aunt Abeline used fancy language peppered throughout her common conversation. But she had never used that term.

I felt confident I would have remembered it.

I flipped the book open to find the reference.

Extirpation, the passage explained, was the destruction of energy fields through the repeated overuse of magic in a geographic range. There was a layer of unseen energy all around us, mixed in with nature, free to be manipulated for gain. When a witch harnessed an element through an otherworldly skill, he or she used that unseen power. But every spell thinned out the vitality and intensity of the invisible world. Instead of running out or using it all up, overuse sparked a reaction. Tiny bursts of heat and flame. Stretched thin enough, the universe itself would sputter and spark. At the point of extirpation, the energy in the space flashed into fires. Once past the point of no return, any spell could cause instant combustion.

And it would keep blazing, the flames sparking over and over, until the build-up in the atmosphere had time to release or could die out again.

Time and space was the only way to solve it.

Luckily, if left alone, the tension in an environment would eventually equalize again. The energy would calm. When it did, regular magic could exist once more.

I read on.

Over the history of the coven, there had been several huge fires, some changing history forever, until all the covens learned how to recognize the stages of extirpation as it began to build. Once they recognized the pattern, they could accordingly act and back off the location and let the energy imbalance redistribute.

I sat back taking it all in. There was a whole new world of knowledge out there that would need to be discovered. The witch world where regular science and physics didn't apply but there were new, very specific rules. No wonder the council required each coven member to undergo years of training. I read on through two more chapters of rulings and terminology lessons until I finally drifted off into sleep.

"Mae... please help..." Kate's maudlin voice returned to my dream.

Eyes blazing in fear, I sat straight up.

Wide awake in my bed once again.

SEVENTEEN
SHUT UP AND TAKE IT

THE KNOCK CAME EARLY the next morning.

I roused from the ugly, reoccurring nightmare and rubbed my eyes. All night, every time I drifted off, I was greeted with Kate's same strained voice and my complete inability to help her, followed by her eventual fall to her death.

The knocking grew louder.

"Coming," I murmured to Sloane through the door.

I pulled myself out of bed, dressed, and took the time to make myself presentable. Staring at my blood-shot eyes in the mirror, I brushed a wide tooth comb through my hair. With nimble fingers, I swooped the long brown mop into a top knot bun and dragged a few wisps down to frame my face. I dragged lip gloss on my bottom lip, black mascara on my top lid, and headed for the door. We had only a few days, five at most, until the energy field would calm.

Did someone tell me that? Or was it in last night's reading?

I was too tired to remember.

Either way, once that happened, the Battle of Four would be thrown into action and I'd have no choice but to protect the whole coven from the Red Faction. That was what I'd taken to calling them. The other coven.

"Ready." I flung open the doorway, but it wasn't Sloane waiting behind it. "Oh, good morning."

Lady Blue Moon stood ready, impatient. "Morning. Muffin?" she offered. Without waiting for an answer, she forced the baked good into my hand. "No time for the usual schedule." She swooped behind my back and pulled my door closed. "I was sent to grab you so your training can begin. Off we go to the library." She pushed me forward.

"What's happening?" I tried to shake out the cobwebs.

"I'm your escort." She tried to chuckle. But then the truth trickled out. "Lady Mauve was a bit worried you might..."

Run off? Bail out? Leave the others to fight by themselves?

"Need an escort," was all she said.

"Right." I sighed. I guess with Mauve that reputation was well earned. She knew during the limbo trials I had tried to leave. But I didn't. The follow-up choice should also count for something. And I was definitely committed now.

I stifled a yawn as we took to the staircase. We were

the only ones in the hallway. It must have been super early.

"Eat. Breakfast. Yummy." Lady Blue Moon pushed the muffin towards me. "The most important meal of the day... and who knows when you'll get the next one," she admitted, then forced another grin. "Training can be difficult."

Dutifully, I took a bite.

The carbohydrates dragged through my throat and sat like a lump in my stomach. But I managed to force the whole thing down.

"Over this way." On the second landing, she caught me before I could go farther down the stairs and steered us into the upper floor halls. She swung open a large, rounded wooden door.

"This is the library." I remembered it from the first day's orientation tour.

"My favorite place in the whole building," Lady Blue Moon agreed. "The archives," she announced with flair.

The sun took its cue and like magic, a cloud cleared, and beautiful morning light streamed down through the windows above. It washed the room in a soft orange glow. The sunrise filtered through the architecture, creating pockets of apricot and tangerine light on the floor.

"Wow," I murmured.

"I know. Take a whiff of all that paper," Blue Moon gushed. She took a deep breath. "All that history and lore."

"This is where we're training?"

"Reading trains the mind," she informed me. "But no. Your actual trainer will be here soon. While you wait, it couldn't hurt to gain a little knowledge." She spun around like she was the heroine from an animated movie. "Or a lot of knowledge." She waved dramatically at the world of books.

"I used a High Council rule book to help me get to sleep last night," I confessed.

"Oh." Lady Blue Moon was pleased. "I bet you read about so many fascinating things."

Not exactly, I thought to myself. I fingered the closest books with interest. "As paper master, I guess you know a lot of rules."

"So many." She grinned. "And when you slept, did you dream?"

"I've kind of been having the same nightmare since I arrived," I confessed.

"Well, that's not good." She seemed disappointed.

"I thought maybe... if I bored myself out..." I shrugged.

"With books? How could you be bored? A set of norms and rules creates the expectations for a whole world! There's literally nothing more exciting."

Literally? Nothing?

But I didn't speak my doubts out loud.

"Genealogy's this way." She steered me with a delicate side-eye, clearly not having forgotten my specific question in class yesterday before the chaos began. "You can look around, but your trainer will be here, like, any second, so don't get too wrapped up in anything."

"Who is it?"

"Beats me. I just do what I'm told. But life is good. Don't worry. Your trainer will be awesome. Do you hear that?" She cupped her hand to her ear.

I didn't hear anything.

"An Excel sheet is calling my name. Knock 'em dead, Mae." She gave my shoulder a little pat, then slipped down the stairs. I watched her cross the library floor. She looked like a mouse in a maze, dodging between the stacks, scurrying as fast as her little legs would take her. Then she was gone. I glanced around at the rest of the place.

Where was that trainer?

Time was ticking away.

The others in my class had probably realized by now that I wouldn't be spending my morning with them. It was too bad; we were really starting to get to know each other. I didn't love the idea of now being ostracized from the group. But I was used to the general feeling of dread.

I didn't like anything about this Battle of Four or its demands, and training hadn't started yet.

I wondered if Beck would care that I was gone.

We hadn't reconnected since the carpool. I'd said "see you later," but in truth, I was kind of avoiding him. His thoughts were probably so wrapped up with his Josie sighting he hadn't even noticed I wasn't there.

Well, that was fine. I wouldn't waste my thoughts on him either.

While I waited, I picked my way through the coven's historical records. Most of the documents had been duplicated into computer files, I was sure, but there was something romantic about looking through the original records and books. It reminded me of my family's secret basement and the old photo albums I'd found on those shelves. The papers were full of history, but they were also historical artifacts. This was the closest I'd been to learning more about my mom since I'd arrived on the grounds. Seeing the depth and breadth of the coven's historical documents gave me hope. I felt confident I could learn more about my family's history here. There were literally hundreds of books to go through. The ones that really called my name were ancient, crumbly tomes that were filled with aged wisdom and delicate pages, but I left those to the side. For now, I focused my search on books from twenty-odd years ago. Luckily, by dates on the spines was how most of the texts were shelved.

Back then, I could see there was a hand-mailed coven newsletter. I also found newspaper clippings of notable interactions. Prolific photographers had captured all the High Council's key events. I flipped through some pages.

A few times in the records I saw an S.K. noted down in the listings.

Sierra Kingsley?

It was possible, but there was no way to be sure.

And then I saw her.

Mom.

In a yellowed newspaper photo.

There she stood, in a two-photo story spread. The headline shouted across the top of the coven newsletter: "Which Witch is Best?" *Winner and village victor*, the caption read. Sierra stood atop the Orson Bell tower, her hand thrust up in a victorious punch. Her other hand held a camera to her own eye, as if she was celebrating and taking a picture as well. A huge smile danced on her lips. The second photo was the view from her camera: a cow field, then a cornfield, with the town a ways off to the left.

Back then, Alderton wasn't a whole strip, just five or six stores, but it was clearly still the same little Main Street.

A view from the top, the second caption boasted.

My mom was the winner.

She looked on top of the world.

I scanned the fine print. The story told of how she bested fourteen other witches in the Village Victor competition. I still had no clue what her powers had been. Not a dream-cast, that was for sure.

I leaned in and looked at her eyes. Even in the aged photo, her inner confidence glowed. She was a strong and fearless woman. We had the same mouth and nose. Was it possible I'd also inherited her award-winning skill?

"Your mom was a great lady." A girl's voice shocked me out of my reverie.

But it wasn't a voice I wanted to hear. I looked up into the elevator girl's face.

Great.

"Too bad the apple fell so far from the cart," she sneered, her arms crossed in front of her chest. "Almost a blessing, isn't it? That she's not around to see?"

My mom's dead and that's a blessing?

She stared me in the eyes, daring me to answer.

Please don't be my trainer.

First, I closed the book. Once my mom's photo and article was safe and secure, I ventured a reply. "Look, I don't know what I've done to you..."

"No?" The girl's stare cut me to the bone. "Poor little you. You stole a spot in the Battle of Four, the entire coven now rests on your boney shoulders, and you don't know what you've done?" her sickly sweet voice asked. "Any witch in this place would have been a better contender than you. You're untalented, ungrateful, and—"

"Thank you, Brandi. That's enough."

We both looked up, surprised. Lady Mauve had approached and stopped to watch the encounter without either of our notice.

"She's going to destroy the coven."

Lady Mauve just frowned in response.

"Yes, ma'am." The girl lowered her eyes, deferring to her elder. To me, she snuck in a final, disgusted shake of her head. Without another word, she departed.

I looked up at the older woman. "Thanks, I—"

"Save it. I agree with the girl. You were stupid, and you were selfish. Even now, on your first day of training, the whole coven is in your hands, and here you are, thinking only of yourself." She shoved the record book I'd been reading across the table. "She's right. Any other member would have made a better opponent, literally any person in the coven, but you and your friends just couldn't stay away. You defied my direct orders. And now here we are."

"That's not what happened, I—"

"Do not talk back." Her tone was so cold, it blasted into my face. "We have a day, maybe two, until the fire dies. In that time, you will train as much as your pea brain can handle. You will not waste even one of those seconds feeling sorry for yourself or making excuses. You will shut up. You will take it. You will do your god damn best." She shoved her own pointed finger in my face. "Because this is my home and this is my family, so you better pray that your work ethic can save the day. I will not let a bunch of red-dressed outsiders burn my home to the ground. And neither will you." Her point made, she backed off.

I nodded. "I'm sorry, Lady Mauve. I'll do it. I'll do whatever you say."

"Prove it. Come on."

EIGHTEEN
TRAINING BEGINS

WE STARTED WITH BOOKS.

I had wanted to dig into the library for days, but now Lady Mauve pulled so many texts off the shelves and shoved them into my arms that I may as well have taken home the entire database. I think she added a few of the heaviest choices just so I'd suffer while carrying them around. At least I hope she did, because there was no way I could read through all of that information in such a short amount of time.

"That's a good start," she murmured to herself, adding an eight hundred page botany textbook to the top of my pile.

My arms quaked under the pressure, but I refused to let it show.

"Come on." Lady Mauve pushed out of the library and led us down the castle hall.

"Does the High Council have some sort of witches training facility?" I asked, trying to keep step with the older warrior who wasn't carrying four hundred pounds of paper in her arms.

"No." She gave me a sigh. "We just create the space we need."

"I thought we couldn't do magic."

"Three hundred witches can't all perform magic in the same space at the same time or the energy won't hold, but one or two of us is fine." She rolled her eyes as if this was just another obvious loophole specification I should have known. "This way."

She pushed through the doors into a magnificent training room with high ceilings, bright lights, and blue walls with red racing stripes painted in strategic patterns. There were physical training apparatus like rock climbing walls and punching bags, kitchens and labs with chemical concoctions, and a playground of earthly materials intended to help you practice your harnessing skills. There were even cots and chaise loungers intended for beds or psychoanalysis sessions. These, I figured, were for dream-casts.

I wondered if I should tell Lady Mauve about Kate and the recurring dream in my head.

For now, it seemed best to shut up and follow.

All around the facility, there were already plenty of witches, including my other three battalion members. Each contestant was already working with their own lady or fellow trainer.

Ferris was having some sort of stick battle with a lady who I guessed was twice her age. They lunged at each other with bamboo rods that they used to attack, but they also employed their poles to deflect and repel each other away. Their hands were lightning fast. In any opportunity that arrived, one or the other would also drop their opposite hand and manifest some new illusion into existence to either help them defend their position or use in their attack. Both Ferris and her trainer created shields to protect themselves from blows, other weapons, and tools like nets or deflectors. Whatever ideas their imaginations could create, they would manifest them. It was impressive.

Fellow Silverfox was bent over a stovetop. He added ingredients, watching a big cloud of smoke erupting from his pot. He and his trainer quickly stepped back as they mixed in another chemical. The mixture flashed white hot, but they knew it was coming and stood a safe distance back from the reaction. They whistled. Silverfox mimicked the explosion with his mouth and hands, laughing, then dove back to the cauldron, madly concocting again.

Lady Rain stood in the double-doored exit to the outside world. Balling her hand into fists, she called on the weather. Outside, it began to pour. She twitched her fingers, and a crack of lightning filled the sky. It smote the pavement right where she stood. She could turn the weather on and off like a switch. She stood with her hip cocked, unimpressed with the world.

All around them, other ladies and fellows watched the threesome's abilities develop. The milling observers whispered tips to one another. Some took notes. The whole coven was cataloging how each contender could improve. Their faces brimmed with judgment. Every witch in the room seemed to assume they were far better at the tasks than the chosen four. Perhaps they were right. But I'd still give it my all.

At my arrival, a hush came over the room.

Silverfox, surprised at the change in energy, added the wrong ingredient to his pot, and whatever reaction he was trying to make fizzled into a purple, bubbly mess. Ferris looked up, distracted. Her trainer used that exact moment to smack the third-year student off her feet. She splattered on the floor with a thud. Rain relaxed her balled-up fist and looked over her shoulder. The rain immediately stopped, and the sun came out once more. Catching a glimpse of me, her eyes rolled back in her head. Every other witch turned. Mauve and I stopped in the center of the room.

"Enough." Lady Mauve didn't raise her voice. The space had already come to such a stop at our entry that her quiet word echoed through the room. My hair stood on end. "Leave me with them," she instructed.

The ladies and fellows looked at each other, uncertain. No one objected, but nobody moved. In the doorway, I noticed Lady Blue Moon had reappeared. She nervously bit her fingernails and waited, like she knew a storm was brewing.

"Now," Lady Mauve added.

She flicked the fingers in one limp hand, a dismissive action. Her tiny whisper lent her instruction more strength and authority than barking orders ever would. At this pin drop direction, the room burst into motion, ladies and fellows streaming out of the doors, the facility immediately emptying.

Silverfox, Ferris, Rain, and I silently watched them decamp.

At the doorway, Lady Blue Moon collected the coven member's notes and observations as they departed. They passed them off in a pile. All the notations quickly developed into a large stack. Lady Blue Moon carried the listings in her arms. When the last straggler had departed, she scurried forward to Lady Mauve's side.

"I'll have these classified and collated as quick as a bunny. But you should know, one of the data sets will be blank." She pointedly scooted her eyes in my direction.

"It's fine. Leave Mae's. We already know she's insufficient in every category." Lady Mauve nodded.

Lady Blue Moon snuck a peek at me to see how well I handled such an ugly evaluation, but behind my stack of books, I didn't flinch. I died a bit on the inside of course, but showed nothing to the group. I was tougher than that.

"Right. Right away." Lady Blue Moon nodded and scurried out of the room.

The other battalion members had stayed at their posts, awaiting further instruction. A flicker of Mauve's hand told them to convene in the kitchen. We collapsed into a small huddle in the enormous, sterile space.

Thankfully, I felt free to put the large pile of books on the ground.

Lady Mauve slid herself up onto the marble countertop and faced our little collective. She waited for the rest of us to find stools and settle in. "Thank you for meeting me here."

"Like we had a choice." Silverfox laughed.

No one else joined in.

"Our coven has called Plumpkin home for the last hundred and sixty-two years, and you lot are tasked with keeping us safe in our homes. We have until the end of the fires to prepare."

"Won't all this extra magic just stoke the forest flames?" Ferris asked. She looked around the room at all the fancy equipment that even yesterday hadn't been here. Our eyes flashed in her direction.

Lady Rain was about to answer, but Lady Mauve passed it off to me. "Mae?"

Rain frowned and tilted her head to listen.

"A little magic will be fine. The four of us aren't enough to harm the energy fields. As long as the rest of the coven has their powers shut down completely, the duality in nature can restore," I parroted back the information.

"Well, look at you, little Ms. Know-It-All." Lady Rain frowned. "Our own little first day genius."

I thought I detected a smile on Lady Mauve's face.

She probably intended to elicit that jab.

"This team is particularly weak," Mauve admitted.

Silverfox sputtered at this evaluation. "I don't know about that."

"No. It's true."

"I'm pretty good with my skills," Lady Rain disagreed, a proud smile pushing up her cheeks.

"Doesn't matter. A chain is only as strong as its weakest link," Lady Mauve told them. All eyes flashed in my direction. My jaw stiffened.

"Blue Moon said she's not casting, only having nightmares," Lady Rain complained.

I raised an eyebrow.

I had only mentioned that to Lady Blue Moon this morning. Word sure got around the coven quickly. I'd have to be more careful with what I said.

"I'll do what I can to train her, but each of you will need to compensate for this weakness as well," she added.

The others nodded as if I weren't sitting there, party to these insults.

Still, I kept my thoughts to myself. After all, Mauve was right. I wasn't ready for the Battle of Four. I didn't even know what the battle was for.

"Lady Rain is a harness," Lady Mauve said. "Weather, right?"

"Specializing in downpours." Lady Rain nodded. She held out a hand, and a single droplet landed in her palm.

"Very aptly named," Silverfox approved.

Lady Rain beamed.

"It's a little on the nose." He chuckled. "Silverfox

here. I'm a chemist. With a focus on the pyrotechnic. Things that go boom, yeah? Light up the night." He tossed his mass of reddish-brown hair twice. His eyes sparkled, and he shot me a tiny wink, a blink almost, like your favorite uncle might do. The nod of an inside joke. "Your mum was a great lady," he added to me.

At this, my jaw fell open.

"Thank you," I murmured.

A million questions flooded my brain, but Lady Mauve marched on from that aside. She nodded to Ferris.

"Ferris Bean." The third-year student gave an awkward wave. "I'm a lie-guard."

Both Silverfox and Rain shifted a little taller in their chairs.

"Do the others have a lie-guard?" Rain wondered.

"We're still waiting for information to come in." Lady Mauve shook her head. But I could see this was good news. Having a lie-guard on our team was a notch for our side.

"How many of these Battle of Fours have you done?" I asked. The others all glanced over. "Oh, sorry. I'm Mae." I waved. "As you know, dream-cast." The lift the group had gained from hearing of the skills of a lie-guard collapsed again at the mention of my brand.

Being a dreamer didn't come with the same social cache.

"How many battles?" Rain repeated.

"None." Silverfox shrugged. "This is a first for us all."

Ferris nodded.

"Oh, alright." So we were all on the same page.

"Have you had any visions?" Ferris wondered.

"No. She's had nightmares. I said that already. Weren't you listening? What were your nightmares about?" Lady Rain asked.

"Well, I—"

"But overall, are you any good at visions?" Silverfox jumped in.

"I wouldn't say good, I..." I thought about Sloane. She always seemed so calm and sure. Her dreams were clear. The messages were succinct. My dreams weren't like that. They were jumbled and strange, with lots of random stuff thrown in. And that didn't take into account my recent nightmares. But I wasn't sure how much I should share.

Was it best to be coy? I didn't want to discourage the group... but I also couldn't give them false hope.

In the end, Lady Mauve answered for me. "She's crap. But she'll improve."

For a moment, we all thought about the training for the coming battle.

"So what do we know about this challenge? I mean, I've heard of a Battle of Four a hundred times, obviously, but I've never, like, seen one. Not in real life," Silverfox admitted.

Ferris and I nodded. For once, it wasn't just me who was ignorant.

Lady Rain again rolled her eyes. Seeing her disdain

wasn't reserved solely for me but was more her general temperament, I felt a bit better.

"When two covens come to blows, the Battle of Four is the only answer that works within the bounds of extirpation, or at least, it's the best solution we have. The other options being to kill everyone or to burn our whole way of life to the ground," she said.

The casualness with which Lady Rain shrugged off these other two options sent a shiver through my spine.

"The Battle has been used to settle disputes over land or resources for generations. Unfortunately, our coven has really great land. I mean, we like it, we use it. But everyone wants a piece of the pie. It was bound to come up at some point. We simply cannot all live in this space. When too many witches gather..."

"It's like a frickin' tinder box." Silverfox nodded.

"It's very dangerous." Lady Rain felt the need to finish her thought in a classier manner.

"That's where you lot come in," Mauve said. "There will be eight contenders, four on each side, in a square-mile wooded area. I don't think it's yet confirmed, but usually the battle takes place where the fires were started, and the burned-out char serves as a neutral location to observe. So there, the covens will gather."

"And you should consider yourselves lucky." Lady Rain jumped in again. "Early battles were fights to the death, gladiator style, 'til only one contender remained. Over the decades things have grown more civilized, which is good because I don't want to break a nail. Or have to kill."

"Some leader's kid was probably called into the battle, so suddenly they didn't want the contenders to be stabbed in the head," Silverfox scoffed. "Which, you know, good for us."

We nodded.

"The battle is now a retrieval mission," Lady Mauve started again. "Each side will be gifted an untouchable glowing orb, too hot to hold or to physically move with one's hands. The globe will glow too brightly to easily hide. They call it the Evil Eye."

"Silly dramatic nickname." Lady Rain rolled her eyes.

"The battle is simple," Lady Mauve cut her off. "The opposing teams will split with their own glowing orb and hide it."

"Precious cargo." Lady Rain nodded.

"You must protect the orb at all costs. The contest is over when the first team returns with the other coven's Evil Eye and presents it," Lady Mauve finished. "Find. Retrieve. Return." She let those words sink in. "Whichever coven succeeds first earns the right to claim the land. The other coven must immediately move on."

"And the people do? Leave? The losers?" I wondered.

"Sometimes, no," Lady Mauve admitted. A far-off look flitted momentarily on her face. "But today, they will." She was sure.

"If they don't, we circle back to option two," Lady Rain piped in while examining a chip in her nail.

Kill everybody or burn it all down.

Silverfox made the universal signal of slicing a finger across his neck.

"It's not really fair," Lady Rain moaned. "We have so much at stake. I want my children's children's children to grow up on these lands. I mean, I'm not pregnant yet, but I could be. The Damocles coven wouldn't know."

"We all have plenty to fight for," Ferris agreed.

The contest results, I realized, were heavily skewed in the visiting team's favor. If they succeeded in this battle, that meant claiming land that was already rightfully owned. But the battle itself favored our coven's knowledge. There was a serious home turf advantage. Our assembly's knowledge of the fauna and terrain of the region should give us a sizable lead. Too bad I was so unfamiliar with the area. Just another fault line where I was the weakest link.

Lady Mauve was right in her evaluation. I was insufficient in every way.

I could barely get myself out of a cornfield.

"Our four person battalion can be divided in any manner. To win the war, you must both hide or protect our own Evil Eye and return with the other coven's orb. Don't worry about strategy. We'll decide how to divvy you up, likely two and two or three and one. But that is none of your concern. The elders will come up with our plan. Once in the field, however, it will be up to you to enact it. You must adjust and adapt as strengths and weaknesses evolve," Lady Mauve said.

I sat a little higher in my chair, choosing to focus on the evolution of strengths. I could do that.

"Until the fires cool, we train. Two days, three tops. The ladies and fellows will watch. Get used to it. Observation and hive mind thinking will help with our competitive factors. Our trainers are the best. Do everything they say. First time."

We all nodded.

Lady Mauve hopped off the counter, her insights complete. She slipped two fingers into her mouth and let out a loud wolf whistle. It echoed through the empty space and ricocheted to the halls.

Our private chat was over. The stream of ladies and fellows who'd been waiting in the wings flowed back into the training center.

"They were all chilling outside in the halls?" Ferris wondered.

Silverfox shrugged. "Guess we were the lucky ones to hear the lesson in chairs." He smirked.

It was odd to hear us referred to as lucky, I thought, seeing how every eye in the coven stared me down as they walked back in the room. We'd be under the looking glass, our every flaw dissected, from now until battle end.

"You're with me," Lady Mauve said, marching right by.

I immediately followed. I was growing more used to this brash instruction.

"We'll start with practical," she added, leading me to a climbing wall apparatus. "Climb this."

The instruction was simple.

The task was not.

The wall stood nearly twenty feet high.

"Is there some... gear?" I looked around.

"No." Lady Mauve narrowed her eyes. "Just do it. Get to the top."

I glanced at the crowd that was gathering. Of course my friends had all come, happy to watch. I gave a small, embarrassed wave.

"You've got this!" Hilde cheered, but Rick put a hand on her shoulder.

No one else said a word.

They were supposed to observe.

My eyes trailed over to Beck. I was still annoyed with him and his Josie head spin from the day before, but under this much strain and pressure, his face was a welcome sight for my soul.

He offered a warm smile.

I slipped half a grin back, uncertain, then turned to meet my fate.

"Climb," Lady Mauve said again.

I looked up at the gray wall punctuated with colorful little handholds. The grips were curved in unusual shapes, their little structures screwed into the wall. Some were round and protruding, others barely a sliver thick. How they would hold my weight, I wasn't certain. I had never in my life attempted rock climbing for amusement, but I didn't have to test it out to already know I had the upper body strength of a small child. Starting on this task was directly playing into my weakness.

But I said I'd do it. Whatever it took.

Lady Mauve waited.

I took a deep breath and approached the wall. I put my hands on two of the molded, rubber grips and put my foot on a lower rung. I dragged my body up.

That was it, I'd started.

My rock climbing career was rolling. I was officially on the wall.

I squirmed around to find a second rubber hold for my opposite foot, then reached up across the expanse of the wall. I had to stretch. My limbs immediately felt the burn. I wasn't used to trying to move in either horizontal or vertical directions. I managed to grab a second handhold, a bit farther to the right than I would have liked, but it was the only option in my wingspan. I stretched for it. Already, my body couldn't hold on. I tried to push and catch it, but instead, I dropped to the floor with a thud. Several coven members winced in sympathetic pain. I grimaced, dusted myself off, and stood back up again.

"What did you do wrong?" Lady Mauve asked.

"I chose a bad route. I should have found a better path."

"Your route was fine," she disagreed. "Climb."

I glanced over my shoulder.

There was Beck's worried but supportive smile.

There they all were.

I knew they were trying their best to bolster my efforts, but I wished they'd go find somewhere else to stand. This was humiliating enough without a personal audience.

I put my hand on the wall and tried again.

This time, I looked ahead, picking out what I hoped was a solid route for the first three or four moves. I managed to lift my body twice, raising up six or seven feet off the ground. My whole frame shook with the strain of gripping the tiny holds.

After the third reach, I forgot the route that I'd planned.

I held on to the wall, frozen, unsure where to go.

"Climb," Lady Mauve barked from below.

I reached up and moved to the right. As I stretched out, my bottom foot gave way. I fell like a sack of potatoes. I clenched my eyes closed, anticipating the impact, but—

Phoom!

Instead of cracking down onto the floor, my body imprinted on a thick blue mat.

"Who did that?" Lady Mauve spun on the group, anger flashing across her face. "No one but the four are to perform any magic. Show your hands."

My friends and the gathered ladies and fellows held up their blank palms. Lady Mauve's scowl cut into each of them. I got back to my feet, and the blue mat beneath me dissolved. From the chemistry station nearby, Ferris caught my eye. She winked.

I couldn't help but smile, grateful.

My audience hadn't broken a rule.

As a fellow battle-mate, Ferris was technically allowed to use her magic in the training facility, but that didn't wipe the frown off of Lady Mauve's face.

"First years, disperse." She decided it must have been one of my closest schoolmates who had saved me. "You will learn more by watching literally anyone else."

"You'll learn more watching paint dry," Brandi added, laughing to her friends. But Mauve wasn't having it.

"And you're such a prize?"

The older girl turned and stalked off in a huff.

I couldn't help but smile.

"She's right." Lady Mauve didn't let me off the hook either. "You're terrible. Mod Squad, come back." She waved at Vince. "Show her."

He looked at me. "What's stronger, your arms or your legs?"

"I'm not strong, Vince. Full stop."

"Strong-*er*. Which one?" His gruff demeanor reminded me a lot of Lady Mauve with hairier legs.

"Legs," I said.

"Good. Then use them as you climb. Don't pull with your arms. Push with these." He hopped up on the wall like a cat and smacked his own thighs. He demonstrated the difference between arms-forward and legs-forward methods. He made both look much, much easier than I ever could. "You've been pulling," he said, literally followed my path. I could see it was an ugly, difficult stretch from hold to hold, even for him. He peeled back down the wall to my original grip. "That's way too hard. But if you push..." This time, he brought his leg up first, secured its next spot higher on the wall, then straightened his front knee, raising himself up in the air. At the new height, he grabbed a fresh handhold for balance, then did it again.

Knee up, straighten, tall.

"Enough." Lady Mauve nodded.

Almost ten feet up, Vince simply let go of the wall and dropped back to the ground. He landed with almost no impact, his lithe body able to completely absorb the jump.

"Now you. Climb." Lady Mauve nodded thanks to Vince.

"Alright," I muttered, trying to take in the lesson.

This time, I found the foot grip first and didn't lead with my hand. Vince nodded. I bent and straightened my knee like I'd seen from him. Bent and pushed.

It was easier than pulling, he was right. But it still wasn't easy.

Proper technique aside, my whole body was weak as toilet paper.

"Keep your butt in," Vince instructed, as if I wasn't already multitasking fourteen other new techniques in my mind. "She'll never descend," he noted to Mauve. "She needs a mat."

Far above them, I knew he was correct.

My fingers started to shake.

Lady Mauve nodded at one of the fellows in the

half-moon of the watching crowd and suddenly, a thick, protective mat, wider and plusher than the illusion Ferris had designed, appeared beneath my feet. I breathed out the oxygen I didn't know I was holding in. Seeing protection beneath me was a relief, but I still didn't want to go down. I was too high on the wall. Mat or no mat, the impact would hurt. I clung to the hand and footholds.

"I'm trapped," I called down.

None of the lessons had discussed how to go back down.

I tried to find a new grip, but my fingers were starting to burn.

Soon, I'd lose all control.

"Use your feet. Bend and stand," Vince coached.

"I can't."

"Yes, you can."

"The footholds are too small."

"Grip with your toes."

I looked at my toes. There was no way the little nubs inside my shoes could hold up my whole body. I couldn't even feel them on the wall.

But there was no other option.

Every muscle cried with agony. I had to go up.

Bend and stretch...

Phoom!

My body hit the mat.

Hard.

I lay still for a moment, then slowly raised my head.

Lady Mauve flashed a signal to her fellow. The blue mat beneath me disappeared. I dropped the final two feet to the ground with a thud.

Ow.

"I can't do it," I admitted.

"Not with that attitude," she agreed. She nodded to Vince, who stepped back and disappeared. "Moving on."

Next up, we ventured into the kitchen.

Here, there wasn't a test to pass or fail, but knowledge to be learned. Lady Mauve utilized the expertise of several different chemists to explain the various properties of plants and animals. Simple ingredients made up a complex collection of spells. Results could be achieved through consistently applied practices. I did my best to take in the basics. Some plants could be used to harm, others to heal; still others provided energy or fuel. Chemical reactions could be large or small, immediate or slow reacting. Almost every item was safe on its own and only dangerous when correctly combined, although some foliage did cause skin reactions if you brushed up against the leaves.

Even the poisons, while unpleasant on their own, only became truly harmful once consumed.

The chemistry of the human body was a very specific test tube, unlike any other, that held a certain biological mix of saliva and other bodily fluids and enzymes. Introducing new products into that environment caused a lot of different reactions.

I took it all in.

The lessons were far more practical than anything I learned in a high school science class, but after the second hour of plant identification, myself and all of my observers started to grow bored.

It was pretty obvious that the real chemists would be concocting all the chemical reactions I'd be carrying into battle, and it was enough as a non-chemist contender to expect that my pockets would be full. The ladies and fellows knew that once I had a solid base of knowledge, my training could move on to other, more pertinent things.

Like practicing magic.

But Lady Mauve didn't agree. She waved in instructor after instructor.

"Mother Nature can tell you a lot, all on her own," a fellow named Stone told me. "You don't always have to manipulate her." He was scruffy like a survivalist, but his wire-rim glasses gave him an intelligent air. "Look here." He knelt and pointed at a rock that no one had bothered to lift onto the counter. "What can she tell you?"

"It's a rock. An immovable force. You can use it, maybe like a hammer?" I suggested. "Or a weight."

He nodded, pushing his glasses up his nose. "Sure. But that's still *you* using nature for your own purpose. What can this nature tell you on its own?"

"Maybe the weather?" I wondered.

A guess seemed better than an uncertain shrug.

"Look closer."

We bent together. He wrapped his hand on the

hard stone surface, then down around the edges. On the bottom corner, his hand returned with a spongy green moss. He showed me the formation.

"This isn't a rock, it's a compass," he told me. "Moss grows on the north side. Most people think it's on trees where you'll find it, and you can, but the spongy stuff loves a hard surface. And when available, it always chooses to grow to the north. It's darker and more humid on that side. Less sunny. It's nonvascular, so there's no root to pull from. In this way, it can tell you where to go."

Fellow Stone knew all kinds of details about nature. He showed me nests and the meaning of the different holes you might find in a forest. He differentiated between the tunnel systems and the burrows animals used to hide from the world. It was interesting, but I wasn't sure how it could serve me. I had no plans to go into the forest on an expedition alone.

After the third hour, even Lady Mauve was ready to move on. "That's enough. This way."

Fellow Stone simply bowed and stepped aside.

Exiting the kitchen, Lady Mauve and I renewed the coven's interest. We'd all been in the training facility for hours. Even the observational witches were starting to look like they needed a break.

I was ready to rest too, but until Lady Mauve gave the nod, no one broke ranks.

None of them had departed the training facility. They had been watching the competitors for hours. But diminishing returns had set in. As I passed them in the facility, I held each of their gazes and tried to smile. Out of all of them, Rick's gentle nod gave me the most comfort.

We do what we can, it seemed to say.

Or at least that was what I imagined.

He was always so stoic and proper. I wanted to crumble into a trembling little ball. But, like Rick, I carried on with all the strength and grace I could muster.

Lady Mauve moved us to a carpeted corner of the room with a club chair and a chaise lounge, each facing the other like the kind of setup you might see in the movies between a patient and shrink. She waved me into the chaise and sat herself down in the chair. This was supposed to be the kind of environment, I knew, where a patient felt safe and anonymous, but here, all around us, a crowd started to form.

A lady slipped forward from the group and put a writing utensil and pad of paper into Lady Mauve's hand. From nowhere, a fellow arrived with a stationary set for me as well. I took it, surprised, but before I could ask anything, he quickly disappeared.

Mauve poised her pen above the paper. "Tell me about your dream."

"Here? Now?" I looked around. There must have been thirty sets of eyes on me. Eventually, my gaze returned to Lady Mauve.

"Yes."

"They haven't been dreams. I'm seeing night-mares," I murmured.

I wished the crowd would disappear.

"Nightmares are ugly dreams. Just semantics. They're still visions."

I shrugged.

"They will tell you the future," she said.

"This wasn't that. It was the past." I squirmed.

"What happened?"

"Kate died..." It came out as no more than a whisper, but the surrounding witches all started to murmur.

Lady Mauve held up a hand. "Details, Mae." She leaned forward.

"I don't know. She was there... and I was, and there was this beam, and she was holding on, but then she couldn't, and that's not how it really happened, you know? In real life. It wasn't right. It wasn't... accurate. But it felt so real, and... I don't... know."

These weren't the kind of details I wanted to share.

"You don't know?" Lady Mauve sat back.

I shook my head, miserable.

"Perhaps if you saw it again?"

"I guess, but I can't control what I envision and—" I started to object.

But Lady Mauve wasn't listening to me. She nodded to someone in the crowd from the row of witches that had accumulated behind me. That person came forward and pinched my shoulder. The grip was surprising and quite rough, but when I turned to see who'd taken hold of me, everything went black.

NINETEEN

WHAT HAPPENS AFTER?

WHOOSH!

"What the hell?" I sputtered, struggling to sit up, the shock of water still wet on my face. Had I been asleep for several hours? Or only minutes? I had no way to tell.

But I knew how I'd awakened.

Brandi stood beside the chaise, an empty bucket on her hip. She grinned from ear to ear. All the contents from the tub had been doused over my head. My hair and clothes were soaked through. My T-shirt clung in revealing peaks and valleys. I felt exposed, wet, and attacked. I wanted to smack that smile right off the awful girl's face, but I knew all eyes were watching. I ignored her instead. Just pretended she wasn't there. I wouldn't give her the satisfaction of even a glance in her direction. I tried to shake off the excess water.

"Sit back," Lady Mauve instructed.

Begrudgingly, I did.

I wanted further instruction on how to get better at dream-casting, how to help the tribe, how to do my part, so I would do what was I was told, but I felt humiliated. How could this public degradation possibly help my casting improve?

"Tell me." Lady Mauve leaned forward.

If it was possible, there was now an even bigger crowd around us.

"I heard her," I admitted. "Kate called me."

"What did she say?"

"I don't know. It's... Her words aren't important, you know? It's just a feeling. She needs my help, and I fail."

"Just like in real life." Behind me, I heard Brandi snark to her friend.

My cheeks burned, but I didn't turn around. I wouldn't give her that satisfaction.

"What happens after?" Lady Mauve asked.

"After what?"

"You fail."

"I don't know. Nothing."

She sat back. "You don't know? Or nothing?"

"I don't know."

"Then we look again." She nodded, and the other fellow came forward. He pinched my shoulder. I wanted to object, but I immediately fell unconscious.

TWENTY

SHE SWAM IN HER OWN GORY PUDDLE

"MAE... PLEASE HELP."

In dreamland, the voice returned again.

"No..." I looked around. "Not again." Hay stuck into the small of my back. The room smelled of wet dew and distant cow dung. I had regained my senses in the loft of Kate's barn.

It was all the same. So familiar. So ugly.

Kate hung from a wooden beam two stories up from the ground. Desperately, she held on.

"Kate, oh my god."

She gripped the post with both arms. Her legs kicked below her.

"What do I do?"

"I don't want to die, Mae," she said, weeping. "You have to help." Her arms started to slip. Her legs hung down over the old farm equipment below.

"Kate, don't let go. Josie?" I cried out for my partner. "Never mind. I'm coming."

Kate's eyes went wide in her sockets. "You can't do this on your own."

"Yes, I can. Kate, I'm coming," I repeated.

I slid out on my stomach, across the wooden beam, moving towards her. Kate struggled. Her weight was growing too much to handle for her arms. I reached out and caught her. I gripped her arm. But I could see that she was right. She was too heavy for me to hold on my own. She was slipping through my palm.

"Mae..." Her first arm gave out. "You're not enough."

"No... I am. I'm here."

My fingers couldn't hold.

Kate's body fell through the air; her eyes looked up at me in terror.

"No! Not again! Oh god." I looked away in disgust as her bones and the farm equipment met.

The crunch was sickeningly alive, then deadening, then final.

At last, I looked back towards the scene.

Down on the floor, Kate's lifeless body lay limp and bloodied. A murky red pool expanded beneath her chest. It coagulated in her hair. She swam in her own gory puddle.

She was gone.

Brandi stood beside the dead girl. She took in the grisly sight, tut-tutted, then stared up to me in the rafters. A wind started to blow in my hair.

"Why didn't you get help?" she asked. Her frown cut me in two.

"I tried," I objected.

"Not hard enough."

"You should have called me." Suddenly, there was another familiar voice. My head whipped up. Josie plopped onto a seat in the barn loft near where Kate fell. I sat up to face her, surprised. Beside her, my aunt was also watching.

"She's always gonna need us." Aunt Abeline giggled to Josie.

"She's basically lost without me." Spade joined Brandi on the lower ground.

"No, I'm not. I'm good," I tried to correct.

"Not good enough." He shrugged.

"That's what I've been trying to tell her." Brandi nodded.

"This is what happens when they let losers in to the High Council." Aunt Abeline nodded.

"You didn't even enroll." Spade laughed.

"Nor did you," the older woman shot right back.

"Who would want to?" Josie rolled her eyes.

All four of them raised a hand to enroll. They cackled.

"I'm not in Sierra's dumb club." Aunt Abeline laughed like this was the funniest news. "We were barely sisters."

"Rejects should stick together," Brandi scoffed.

"That's what I said!" Josie laughed. "Mae, you need help."

"You definitely do," Aunt Abeline added.

"You're just not good enough," Brandi told me.

"I wouldn't help if she were the last girl on earth," Spade muttered. His toe tapped gently at the edge of the blood. Suddenly, Kate's hand snatched his ankle. Her head turned, soaked in blood. Her face was cracked open by the deathly impact, and her eye hung out of its socket, oozing down her cheek. She twisted around to stare at him. At me.

"Well, maybe she is," her bloody voice gurgled.

The others started to laugh.

Whoosh.

I shot straight up in my chair.

I coughed errant water out of my lungs, struggling to see beyond my smattering of wet hair.

"What the hell!"

"Sit back," Lady Mauve instructed.

"Oh my god," I sputtered. The horrible imagery in my dreams and the heart-stopping return to earth made my ears ring. It took a moment to regain my bearings.

"What happened after her death?"

"There was blood. A lot of blood." I wiped my own face.

"Good." A tiny smile flickered on Lady Mauve's lips. "What does blood mean?"

At such a rough entry, I was having trouble regrouping.

"I don't know. She was dead."

"I wasn't talking to you," Lady Mauve corrected, looking beyond my head to the crowd gathered around. "What does it mean?" she asked again.

"Danger," a lady answered.

"Fear," another replied.

"Peace."

"Silence."

"Death."

"The growing spread of nothingness."

"Rage."

"Something closing."

"Something failed."

Answers came from every direction, each witch having a different interpretation of what the seeping vital fluid could mean.

Lady Mauve held up a hand, and the suggestions abruptly ended.

"What does the blood mean?" she asked me. She leaned in. Her attention was intense. All eyes were on me.

"Do we have to do this... here? In front of all of them?" I asked, my wet T-shirt clinging to my breasts.

Lady Mauve waved a hand, and the audience around us disappeared.

Suddenly, it was just me and her. She waited expectantly.

"You can't expect me to believe..." I looked around.

There was no way she could have physically emptied the space, I knew. A harness could only influence the natural elements, and a lie-guard could only make you believe things that weren't true. I wasn't sure which type of witch Lady Mauve actually was, but there was no magic that would actually cause a crowd of people to disappear. It was only an illusion.

Everyone was still there. Still around me. They could all see what I was doing. And in fact, the disappearance illusion made things a thousand times more terrible, because now they could see me, but I couldn't see them.

"That's just a lie-guard. I want the audience to really go away."

"Break the illusion, and I'll send them out." Lady Mauve nodded.

She sat back in her seat. This wasn't the lesson she had intended when she started this discussion, but we were here now, and she was happy to see it play out.

The next step was up to me.

Breaking illusions was another skill I would need. She had likely planned to test these skills eventually, so now would work just as well. She steepled her hands and watched, curious and serious. If this was what it would take to get out from under the looking glass, then this was what we would do. She was studious, but so was I, so I stood, involuntarily wiggling around in my wet clothing. I would break the illusion in two. I'd done it before. A lie-guard was only as good as the details it was given. If you could see the illusion from an unexpected perspective, the specifics would falter, and the vision would shatter. I already knew this illusion was fake; I only had to prove it to my own senses. The easiest way to do that was to see it from an unexpected angle.

I walked forward towards the spot where only moments earlier, Brandi had stood with that smug smile on her face. I swung my fist fast and loose—with a twisted hope I might make contact with her cheek—but played it off like I was stretching.

The illusion didn't waiver.

My arms swung through, unencumbered, the lie-guard safe in place. I stalked around my chaise, looking for another edge to bend.

Lady Mauve simply watched me.

I hopped up on the chair and looked down, but there was no change to the illusion. The angle from atop the furniture piece wasn't high enough to impact my view.

Mauve looked bored.

I dropped down to the floor.

On hands and knees, still nothing happened.

Those were the easiest tests. Mauve had clearly thought of them.

I'd have to step up my game.

I rolled my body upside down into a backbend and looked out beneath my dripping wet hair. Still, nothing altered. The upside down vantage didn't cause even the slightest quiver in the room. So far, Lady Mauve had anticipated every move that I made. The only new vantage I earned, upside down at shoe level, was a glimpse of the underbelly of the chaise. It was fairly well constructed on what looked like a solid frame. I collapsed out of the back bend, careful to tug my soggy shirt back into the proper place.

I couldn't see them, but there were plenty of eyes now on me.

Maybe I could use it. The chaise. Worth a shot, anyway.

I picked up the heavy piece of furniture and dragged it up against the side of Lady Mauve's chair. The woman didn't flinch, but I could tell she was intrigued. From there, I tilted it up and rested the whole piece on its headboard, with its front legs raised high in the air.

I was right about the structure. The frame should be strong enough to hold me. At least, hold long enough to break through the illusion. That was as long as I'd need.

I gripped the upright chaise for support and climbed Lady Mauve's chair with her still in it. She leaned away from my approach but didn't offer to stand. Didn't matter. I climbed around her. From the top of her chair, I reached out and put my hands on the end of the upended chaise. I clambered onto the footrest portion, tucking my knees under me, balancing, waiting to see if the wood square would hold. The ends clearly were not meant to be used in this direction or climbed with this intention. A person was not supposed to perch on its end. But that was why the choice was effective. The chaise shook a bit but didn't buckle. The frame could hold my weight.

With the help of the upended lounger, I would be twice as high in the air when I fully stood. That would break the illusion for sure.

I released my fingertips from the fabric and started to extend my legs. The wooden frame shuddered but held firm. Moving gently, I switched one of my knees to a foot, then added the other slowly. I raised up to a standing position on the precarious end of the chaise. It wasn't pretty. My arms splayed out in all directions for balance, and my legs shook as I straightened to stand. But I accomplished what I wanted to do. The room took on a different view.

It was working.

I raised my center of gravity higher.

Any second, the real audience and the actual training room would break through the illusion. I could feel it. Lady Mauve hadn't expected me to ingeniously use the chaise. My strategy was working.

For the first time, I could feel I was about to succeed at my task.

In front of Beck and everybody.

In one motion, I took a deep breath, pressed my legs straight, and stood up to my full height on the chair.

Crack!

The wood frame snapped and pitched forward. The sudden motion catapulted my body, like a trap door that opened mid-air. There was no time to counterbalance. I braced for impact as my bones slammed into the floor.

Phoom!

I smashed into a thick blue mat. It appeared out of nowhere.

The material was tough but forgiving. It caught my fall and absorbed half the body slam. Hitting the mat face first in such a public, unexpected manner hurt, but nothing was broken.

But for my pride, I was still good.

I didn't break out of the lie-guard.

"Who did that?" Lady Mauve broke her own illusion and angrily jumped up from her chair. She spun around and glared at all the witches who were gathered in a circle surrounding us. I was correct; more people had joined us than those present when she started this task.

The mat that had held me disappeared almost immediately.

I flopped down to the floor in an ungraceful collection of elbows and ankles, but from this height, the secondary impact wasn't painful, just embarrassing. Once again, I found myself sprawled out on the ground. The rest of the coven watched from above. It was awful.

I looked up and saw Beck's face. He and all the other class members were watching. Their expressions all said the same thing.

Pity.

Embarrassment.

As fast as I could, I got back to my feet.

But Lady Mauve wasn't finished with her mission. "Who saved the girl?" She stalked the circle. "Answer me!"

No one met her awful gaze.

As she marched towards them, the sides of the circle fell back. Only one witch didn't retreat. Ferris held her ground, her arms crossed. Her eyes were as dark and stormy as Mauve's.

"I did," she said, facing her instructor. "I made the mat. Twice. And I'll do it again."

Lady Mauve stalked right towards her. Wordless and angry.

The rest of us cowered on her behalf.

You could feel Mauve's rage; it vibrated out of every inch of her. All the dark energy was focused on the girl.

But still, Ferris held firm.

"It won't do us any good if you smash her to bits," she said. "We need to protect her."

"She's not a child." Mauve shook her head.

"And she's not a toy," Ferris shot back.

Lady Mauve's outbursts had momentarily gotten the better of her, but now, she regained full control. Her cold, sharp demeanor was terrifying.

But Ferris wasn't about to falter.

"Leave us," Mauve told the rest of the room without losing eye contact with her prey. "Now."

The other students, ladies, and fellows who had been watching didn't need to be told again. They quickly departed. It had been a long day, and most were already ready for a good meal and a recharge. No one wanted to risk transferring Lady Mauve's rage to their own shoulders, so the facility drained in total silence.

The women stood in an angry standoff.

As the room drained out, Lady Rain, Fellow Silverfox, and all the other trainers slipped out into the halls. We were the only ones left. But I didn't move. As the subject of this controversy, I stood still in precarious fear.

Should I leave with the others?

Should I join Ferris?

Should I tell her not to fight my battles?

Ferris, for her part, gave as good as she could.

Still, tough as she was, she was no match for Mauve's commanding stand. Neither woman cowed to the other, until finally, Ferris flinched and looked away.

This was enough.

"She can have her mat," Lady Mauve told the girl. "Don't cross me again." The unspoken *or else* wasn't a threat. It was a promise.

Ferris nodded.

The tension broke, and the women stepped apart.

But I wasn't sure what that meant.

"Are we... Is it over?" I asked my trainer.

"No." Lady Mauve frowned. "Your day is complete when you climb that wall. Not a minute sooner." She shrugged and turned her back to me. Over her shoulder, she added, "But not to worry. Ferris will stay to catch you. We wouldn't want you to fall."

TWENTY-ONE

IT'S ALL TOUGH LOVE
AROUND HERE

LADY MAUVE LEFT Ferris and I alone in the training room. The space felt much larger and more intimidating without the influx of the crowd. Even our footsteps echoed. Together, we walked back over to the climbing wall.

"Thanks for catching me," I offered. I didn't want to meet her eye.

"Twice," Ferris agreed.

I looked up, but thankfully, she was smiling.

"You're welcome," she said.

I stared up at the wall with the tiny handholds. "I'm never gonna climb this."

"Maybe not, but that isn't the point."

"What's the point? To humiliate me?" My fingers grazed a hold on the wall.

She shrugged. "Come on, up we go." Ferris dropped her hand and to my great relief, created a thick, fluffy mat to land on. The best mat I'd seen all day. "It's just you and me." Instead of watching and judging and critiquing my performance, she also approached the wall. She kicked off her shoes. "Come on."

I could tell Ferris, unlike Vince, wasn't some crazy experienced rock climbing master. We had similar builds and similar reach. When she'd raised herself up two levels on the wall, she looked back. "Well, don't just stand there."

I kicked off my shoes as well. Vince said to grip with my toes. This little trick did help. I managed to pull myself up beside the older girl.

"How do you feel?" she asked.

"Like I suck at climbing?"

She nodded. "Maybe you do. The point is to push and realize you can always do better. Not do it *all*, but *more*. More than what you've done." Ferris reached for the next rung. I followed. "The fates, the coven... It's all a little tough love around here. Not just for you. For everybody. Did you know, when my parabonding season began, another coven member kidnapped me and my potential partner? Just threw us in an abandoned barn. Locked us in. No food. No water. Just figure it out or starve."

"That's crazy."

We reached for another foothold. I could feel the lactic acid building in every muscle in my body. My fingers started to shake, but I didn't want to admit what was coming.

"Yup. That was my entry into the High Council."

She reached hard for her next handhold and let out a little grunt.

I wasn't sure if my body could take much more. I reached my arm up.

"Oh, and I was naked."

"What?"

My fingers slipped off the wall.

Phoom!

I hit the mat. Hard.

Ferris angled herself off the wall and dropped onto the cushy mat, landing a few feet beside me. She laughed.

"What the hell?" I giggled.

"Sorry, should have led with that." She nodded.

Without the audience of judgy witches, I didn't feel the need to immediately stand. Instead, I lay where I fell, staring up at the ceiling.

"Ethan lent me his clothes. It's a long story." She brushed the details away. "Now, how was that?" She motioned to the wall.

"I didn't climb it," I complained, sitting up, resting on my hands behind my back.

Ferris waved the mat away and sat with me on the hard floor. "No, but..."

"But..." I didn't want to admit it, but I could see she was on to something. "I did better than before."

She tossed my shoes over to me.

"Now you're talking. End of lesson." She grinned.

"Mauve said we have to stay until we reach the top."

"What the lady doesn't know won't hurt her." Ferris shrugged.

Just then, a cute guy stuck his head in. The same black-haired guy I'd seen Ferris with before. She grinned and offered him a wave. He glanced around and seeing that it was just us, ambled over.

"I was just talking about you," she greeted. He crouched to our level. "Mae, this is my parabond, Ethan. Ethan, Mae."

We nodded. Ferris and I both tied on our shoes.

"All good, I hope." He nodded.

"I was recounting our introduction to the High Council," she said.

"Pretty crazy." I nodded.

"Right?" He grinned. "Frickin' bonkers is what it is."

"But it made us stronger." Ferris refocused the conversation.

"Super stronger." He flexed his arms.

Pretending to be annoyed, she gave him a little shove. The action tipped him off his feet. Ethan landed in a heap beside us with a grin.

"The worst part." He nodded. "Did you tell her the worst part?" he checked, but then steam-rolled forward. "Our kidnapper was also accepted into the same Judicial Studies class. You've met her."

"Brandi?" I already knew I was right in my heart.

The other two nodded.

"What's her problem?" I asked, but I could already tell it was a question without an answer.

Ferris and Ethan shrugged it off.

"When she started treating you like crap, Ferris said you must be a quality chick." Ethan laughed.

"I didn't use that word." She frowned.

"Fine," he agreed. "A quality girl? Woman? You know what I mean."

"Her and Lady Mauve... What pieces of work." I shook my head.

Ferris and Ethan exchanged a small glance.

"What?"

"Maybe don't put those two in the same camp." Ethan shrugged.

"Mauve's had a lot on her plate," Ferris agreed.

"I think she gets off on embarrassing me."

"She's tough." Ethan nodded.

"On us all," Ferris added. "It isn't personal."

I shrugged. It sure felt like it was.

"Do you know *why* she's in charge?" Ferris asked. "Why everyone jumps when she speaks?"

"Because she's the meanest?" I grumbled.

They exchanged furtive glances again.

"Just tell me," I complained.

Ethan played with his watch. "Well, word round the coven says she's been through this before." He didn't look at me. "The Battle of Four."

Instinctively, I knew her experience hadn't been good.

Ferris nodded. "Just rumors, really... but Lady Mauve didn't start her practice with the High Council. She didn't grow up here in Plumpkin or the neighboring towns. Years ago, she had another tribe. Another coven. Somewhere far from here, on the other coast, maybe. No one knows for sure. But people say her tribe of witches cultivated an impressive garden full of powerful botany, casting spells for even the most complex chemistry and then... word started to spread."

"White-water rice, Gloonship flowers... It's all about the resources." Ethan shook his head.

Ferris nodded.

I wasn't familiar with either of those plants.

"Other covens wanted to take their land and make use of their vegetation. At first, her coven shared. But as with all limited resources, there was never enough to satiate the demand. Over time," she said, shrugging, "things got out of hand. The use of their powers escalated. The covens encroached more and more. And when the energy grew too thin, the fires started. Mauve's coven tried to regain their sovereignty and reclaim the region, but the other tribes refused to back down. Their only choice for the hope of their coven was to engage in the battle. It came to a last-ditch effort. Mauve was chosen as one of the four."

"Did she volunteer?" I wondered.

"No one knows." Ethan shook his head.

"But we do know she didn't win." Ferris looked down. "Mauve lost, and after that, her coven ignored the requirements. They refused to leave their lands. The countryside burned in a terrible battle. All the life they'd worked so hard to grow, the plants they'd nourished and propagated and farmed, everything was destroyed. The tribe splintered into pieces, and eventually, every member disowned her. They cast her out on her own. She never rejoined society. She was living wild when Cornelius brought her home."

"That's terrible."

"Yeah. So now we *listen*," Ethan agreed.

"She's the only one among us who truly knows what's at stake," Ferris finished.

IN THE CAFETERIA, a plate of dinner had been set aside for me: a sandwich wrapped in plastic and a cold lump of potato salad. I knew it was mine because someone had scribbled my name on a label. I picked up the plate and looked around. The room had emptied for the night. Without other people mingling, the cafeteria felt big and deserted. Although I felt exhausted after a day of being out on display, weirdly, I didn't actually want to be alone. I decided to eat the paltry dinner back on my floor. Hopefully there, I could hear a few tidbits of what the others thought of the day's events. I'd been so busy getting my butt handed to me over and over that I hadn't had the opportunity to watch any of my other battalion-mates train. I was curious to hear how the others had done. They were, after all, the people I'd have to rely on in the field.

I was also curious about what, if anything, my friends had heard about the other coven, the Damocles tribe. So far, all I had was their name, no more calling them the Red Faction. But I felt confident the teens upstairs might have heard something more. If I'd gleaned anything today, it was that rumors traveled fast in the coven.

The other team seemed so foreboding.

If I focused on their red robes, their shocking blonde hair, or their piercing blue eyes for too long, a lump would start to build in my throat. Their entire aura was bewitching. One little glimpse would cast you under their spell. But worrying about them too much wouldn't do me any good. It was best to only focus on what I could control.

"You can only build words with the letters you're dealt," my aunt would say.

Scrabble wisdom.

I had enough words to last a lifetime in the texts Lady Mauve had given me to read. I carried the giant stack in my arms with my dinner perched on top. It was a precarious pile to bring back to my dorm room. I pressed the call button for the elevator. It felt risky to wait in the lobby to see who might be on board when the ancient doors opened. But the books were far too heavy, and I was too exhausted to care.

Ding.

The elevator opened. Safe, sound, and empty. Quickly, I boarded.

It was strange that with all that was going on, my thoughts had drifted to Aunt Abeline. But ever since the day's extended nightmare, she and my mom had been kicking around in my thoughts. Aunt Abeline had wondered her whole life what it would be like to be a part of the High Council, and Sierra was proud to call this place home.

I would like to know more of its story.

Since I arrived, I'd barely had any time to rest or explore my family's history, but I was moving forward. I'd found a clear record that Mom was present and even met a guy who'd known her. Once we won this stupid battle, I'd have further time to dig in.

Huh.

Once we *won*...

After today's final round with Ferris, I guess I'd started to believe for myself that winning could happen. Lady Mauve was a tough broad and a powerful sorceress; she was gruff and sharp.

Not just with me, with everybody.

And now I understood where she was coming from. In my heart, I knew she was trying her best. But one evening working with Ferris had given me more tools and information. There was something to be said for focusing more on the *love* and less on the *tough* in the tough love of these lessons.

I was improving, and that was all anyone could ask.

Including me.

I arrived on the fifth floor and marched down the hallway. I was a bit surprised to discover the space was empty. I half expected the others might ambush me with questions the second I stepped out of the moving compartment. But the elevator doors rolled closed behind me without incident.

I carried the massive pile of books down the hallway and plunked the lot beside my doorway. I searched my pocket for my key and was about to go in when the sound of voices floated down to greet me. By the sounds of things, my classmates were gathered in the common room at the end of the hall. My ears perked up. I grabbed my sandwich, leaving my books and potato salad to be retrieved later. As I made my way to join them, a smile formed on my lips.

It felt good to be back among the people I trusted.

"I don't know how she can hold that harness in the midst of those instructions," Tej marveled.

"I thought those other fellows would burst at the seams when she told them exactly how things would be." Nicolette laughed.

"But she was right. About pretty much everything. It was awesome," Sloane agreed.

They were talking about Lady Rain, I realized.

That bossy, classy lady.

Just what I was hoping for. The time had come to get the dirt.

"I wish I had that kind of talent," Hilde murmured.

"Well, Rick sure doesn't," Greg disagreed.

If he was with them, Rick didn't rise to the occasion.

"You don't know. Maybe he'd like being bossed

around," Marcy suggested. "*You* like when I take control."

"Drives me crazy," Greg teased his girlfriend.

"Yeah, you like your lady in control."

They devolved into kissing noises.

"Oh god. Get a room," Tej ordered.

"Get a clue," Marcy snapped back.

The pitter patter of chatter was so inviting. Nipping at each other over nothing. The whole day had been so serious. Life and death training. I hurried forward, anxious to burst in.

"*Mae* should get a clue," Vince muttered.

I was about to pull the handle and join the collective, but the mention of my name stopped me flat. A couple of the others giggled.

"It's her first day. What more do you want?" That was Beck.

My eyes narrowed. I stepped back against the wall, leaning in and listening. Clearly, Vince wasn't alone in his opinion. But at least Beck had my back.

"Guys, let's not. She might get home at any moment." Sloane tried to move the topic along.

"No way. At her rate of development, they're gonna keep her all night." Greg laughed.

"A dream-cast who can't dream." Vince's voice registered his frown.

"It's not ideal," Nicolette added.

"That's not what she said. She said she had nightmares," Beck disagreed. "Nightmares are still visions."

"She couldn't break the illusion," Tej pointed out.

"Technically, she did," Hilde piped in. "By falling through the chair."

"Technically, *Mauve* did," Greg corrected. "When Ferris caught Mae."

Marcy let out a low whistle. "And ooh boy, Lady Mauve was pissed. Can you imagine going up against that rage train? Ferris is a badass."

"Way tougher than Mae is," Nicolette agreed.

"Even Beck's ex is tougher... and she quit." Vince laughed.

"Maybe." Even Hilde agreed.

For a moment, nobody spoke. I got the feeling that Beck was staring Vince down.

"What do you want?" Vince laughed in his face. "Truth hurts."

"Leave it alone, Vince," Sloane said.

No, I thought to myself, let it all out.

Tell me how you really feel.

"I'll leave off if he admits that it's true. Who's the better witch?" Vince asked.

"He's not gonna—" Nicolette started.

But Beck cut her off. "Shut up, Vince."

"Who's the better witch?" He picked at Beck again. "Just answer."

"Vince..." Sloane's tone threatened him, but the guy was on a roll.

"Who's better, Beck? Who's better?"

"You *know* who's better," Beck snarled.

"I *do*." Vince was delighted he caught Beck up on his hook. "But I wanna hear *you* say it."

"She didn't ask to lead the battle," Beck deflected.

That hurt.

So Beck knew it too.

In fact, they all thought it.

If Josie had competed in the final round of limbo, she would have beat me into the High Council. If she hadn't quit, they all thought she'd be through. I'd be gone, and Josie would be here. The truth stung.

This is the one who got in by default.

"Ugh. This tension's causing stress wrinkles. Stop being so dramatic, boys. I'm gonna get a glass of water." Marcy was bored.

"Just say it," Vince pushed again. Beck didn't answer. "I'm not asking who you'd rather lay." Vince laughed.

I bristled.

"Go to hell!"

It sounded like someone started a scuffle.

"Say it loud and proud!" Vince laughed, shoving back. I could hear the chairs being pushed. "Everybody! Altogether! Mae's a terrible witch!"

"You're a real dick!" Beck told him.

I leaned forward, listening intently. But suddenly, Marcy came out the French doors. Immediately, I straightened, caught fully eavesdropping. There wasn't time to play it off. She looked up, just as surprised.

"Oh, hey girl." At first she smiled, then it dawned on her what I had been hearing.

Beck stormed out the door right after her.

My eyes flit from her to Beck.

"Hey, Marce," I replied.

Beck's mouth dropped open in surprise.

"Guys, it's Mae," Marcy called back over her shoulder to the others. "Back from her training. How long have you been standing here, Mae?"

"Long enough," I admitted, then turned and fled.

TWENTY-THREE

VINCE DOESN'T SPEAK FOR US ALL

I WANTED out of this hall, off this floor, out of this life, just as fast as my legs could carry me. I fled back down the staircase. Somehow, I still clutched my cling-wrapped sandwich. But the books and the platter were long gone. I left them by the door and didn't look back. I couldn't bear to face my classmates. It was all too much.

I was so embarrassed.

So much for friendships.

I could hear them coming, a herd of elephants trampling behind my back, calling my name, asking me to wait up, to listen. But what was the point? They'd only retract what they'd said behind my back. And the worst part was, what they were saying was true.

I wasn't a good witch.

Who would be?

I'd had two days on the job. Six, if you counted all of limbo. And the numbers didn't stop there. I only learned about my magic heritage in the last month. Lived in the town just a few days more than that. Entered the coven at the last possible moment, and I made it to the High Council as a selection by default.

They were right!

I totally sucked!

Even my dreams told me that message.

I didn't practice parsing visions as a child. I mourned my mother. The only other witch in my house was rejected by this clan. That was it! That was me.

Message received.

I hit the next landing on the staircase full-on running.

I knew exactly who I was. And I wasn't good enough. They didn't have to tell me again.

My aunt did her best. Dear, sweet Abeline. But it was clear. I wasn't prepared. The High Council should never have let Josie quit. We should have been forced to battle it out. I would have tried my very hardest, but we all knew the facts. She would have won. She would be here. She should be.

But she wasn't. And that was wrong.

Josie was out, and I was in. And the world sat on my shoulders. The weight of the coven was too much to bear.

"Mae, wait!" Beck shouted. He had tried to protect me, tried to stand up, but his gaze and his pauses and even his silence in key moments gave him away. He still longed for his ex. Whether he admitted it or not, he had always reached out to her in tough moments, and he yearned for her return.

Just another of the many things I couldn't give him.

From the stairs, I fled down the hall into the library, quickly ducking into the stacks. The many rows should give me cover. I wasn't sure how many members of my coven class were following, but I had to get away. Even as I slipped between the columns, I knew the glut of shelves and manuscripts between us wouldn't be enough. I was desperate not to be found.

I heard the others flood into the room.

Quickly, I looked around. What I needed was an exit. But that was what they would assume. My friends would head to the first-floor doors immediately. Try to cut me off. Instead, I dashed to the cartography section. Amongst the study carrels were light tables. The kind you used to illuminate blueprints. They were tucked against a wall. The light boxes hung lower into the legroom beneath the slabs of tables, crowding the space below. If I couldn't exit, this was the best hiding space I could find.

I hurried to the desk, pulled out the chair, and ducked below it, accidentally dropping the plastic-wrapped sandwich as I went. My body barely fit beneath the light box, but I was committed to the pose. My fingers dragged the chair back into the closed position as an extra blockade from unwelcome sight. I propped the chair back in place just in time. Hilde and

Rick's feet appeared in the aisle. The sandwich leaned against the leg of the desk.

"She disappeared," Hilde noted. "That's not a new power, is it?" I could see from her sneakers that she was facing the other direction.

"It is not," Rick's deep baritone replied. Unlike Hilde, his boots faced my way.

I held stock still.

For a moment, they both were silent. Possibly looking for clues.

Why did I hide under a table? My embarrassment was already enough without the others finding me folded up like a fool. Could Rick see my scrunched-up body?

Finally, his feet slowly turned.

"Shall we head in that direction?" he suggested.

Both their feet pointed away from the table.

"Okay. I hope we find her. Vince'll say he's sorry, I think," Hilde noted.

"Perhaps it's her will not to be found," he told her. "We should respect that decision." His foot slid my sandwich further out of the aisle towards my location. With nimble fingers, I reached out and pulled it under with me.

"Let's go," he told her.

Hilde left first, still keen on the hide-and-seek mission.

Rick's boots paused above me in the aisle for one final moment after she'd stepped away. "Vince doesn't speak for us all," he said quietly. Then he was gone.

After that, the room was quiet.

If Beck and the others were still looking for me, I couldn't see them from my spot hiding on the floor. Like a child in a game of hide-and-seek that had dragged on too long, I waited, unsure if the search was still happening, worried if I moved from my secret location I'd immediately be caught.

How long would they look for a girl they'd just spent their night insulting?

I heard the heaters and the furnace kick on, flood the room with warm air, then turn off. Over and over, the temperature regulators churned. But still, I didn't come out. Instead, each time I told myself I'd wait one more cycle. I was just debating the case again when a set of small feet came shuffling along.

"Uh, just so you know, they're all gone. You can come out if you want."

TWENTY-FOUR

TIME STAMPED AND DATED

I SHIMMIED out from under the desk. Lady Blue Moon simply raised an eyebrow and watched.

"How'd you know I was here?" I asked, dusting myself off.

"I saw you come in. Bird's eye view and all that." She motioned to the archives on the second floor. "I told you, it's my favorite spot. Come on." She invited me back to the desk where she was annotating the coven's latest notes. When we arrived, I could see she was busy logging a thousand data points about me and the other three battalion members. How all that data could possibly help, I had no concept.

"You're not doing terribly, you know," she offered with an apologetic smile, moving some notes out of my view, "in the data. But..." She glanced my way again and frowned. "Uh, how to put this delicately... In person, you're looking a little... unhinged. Haggard. Is haggard more complimentary? I suspect a little dinner and a good night's sleep will do a world of good." She pushed my plastic-wrapped sandwich towards me.

I unfolded the wrapping and took a large bite. Mouth full, I sighed. "I just want to go home. You know? See my aunt. Sleep in my own bed." I took another bite.

"Well, why don't you?" Lady Blue Moon asked. "It couldn't hurt."

I was so surprised that I choked on the sandwich. "What? No. I can't. It's not allowed."

"Who told you that?" She looked at me, puzzled.

I tried to think back.

Where had I heard that rule?

But she was right. No one had directly informed me that we weren't allowed any visits. It wasn't in our orientation packet or any of the rules that I'd read. And Lady Blue Moon would know for sure. She was the one who had guided that lesson.

"But Mom never..." I trailed off.

After joining the coven, Sierra became estranged and distant from my aunt. They barely talked. For years.

That was a choice?

Lady Blue Moon pulled her copy of the High Council Rules and Declarations from her canvas work bag. The very same textbook she had given us copies of before the news of the fire. She shoved a bunch of charts and papers that she had stored in its pages out of the way. "I don't know why no one reads this," she muttered. "I don't mean you, specifically. You, I get.

You've been busy," she added. "But the others..." She shook her head. "It's got so much information. I'm sure you'll read it the first chance that you get."

I had shoved the final bite of sandwich in my mouth, so I just nodded yes.

She flipped through the documentation, a clear expert on the material.

"Here. Leaving the grounds." Her finger traced along the words. "Coven members may leave, return, and/or interact with their town and kinship so long as the following conditions are met. One: no details of the High Council or coven are to be relayed. Two: in the presence of non-coven members, the witch's magical abilities are not to be used. Three, four are boilerplate, boilerplate," she said, skimming. "Then five: adherence to these guidelines is subject to and limited under the jurisdiction of the High Council Tribunal." Lady Blue Moon pushed the passage towards me. I leaned in to reread.

"Plenty of witches cut ties," Blue Moon told me. She shrugged. "They find it easier. People in the old world don't always understand these new sorts of rules. I know my family doesn't. But there's nothing here that says that you can't try."

I sat back in my chair. "Huh."

I randomly flipped to other pages in the book. So many answers to the questions I had about the secret society were spelled out in great detail. I just had to look. Lady Blue Moon was right. As soon the Battle of Four was over, I would read this rule book from cover to cover. The previous generations had thought of everything. Not just the best way forward over geographical disputes, but also parabond enforcement, taxation, and a ton of behavior manipulations. The High Council had its own Judicial Tribunal to moderate the group, and their rulings were fast and blunt, like the smashing of a hammer.

We hung out, quiet for a while. Lady Blue Moon working on her data, and me reading the rules. Having had dinner, I already felt better. And there was a lot of information to unpack. I found what I could on the regulations about the Battle of Four and then read up on the Village Victor, the contest my mom had won. It was nice to work comfortably beside someone, happily together, in our own separate worlds, just being pleasant.

"Here. When you're done, shove those back into the book." Lady Blue Moon pushed aside the notes she was making and passed over the spreadsheets she'd tossed out of her text.

"What are all these?" I accepted her papers.

Lady Blue Moon shrugged. "I was annotating prescriptions for the Chemist Society, a club that... Never mind, not important. But when I'm done here, I'll go there next."

"You love your data," I noted.

She smiled. "I really do."

I looked at the spreadsheets with thousands of notations in horrible, doctor-like handwriting. I slid my finger down the chart, ignoring twenty or thirty other unreadable notations, until it came to a rest down two-thirds of the page.

I leaned forward.

Three more 4-12s of mithridate required. Patient unresponsive. SK (Lady Haze). Recommend up carry dose from six to thirteen.

I had no idea what any of it meant, but I stopped on the initials.

SK (Lady Haze).

Patient. Unresponsive.

Sierra Kingsley? When Mom had died, she was marked unresponsive as well. Was that my mom on the sheet? I had a weird feeling it was.

"Who's Lady Haze?" I looked up.

Blue Moon shrugged. "No clue. Why?"

"She has the same initials as my mother... and she passed away in a hospital."

"Patient unresponsive..." Lady Blue Moon looked over my shoulder. "Do you know when she died?"

The notation was time-stamped and dated just like all the others.

I shook my head. "I was six. The month and year are correct..."

She took the paperwork back. "Unfortunately, these things are confidential," she told me, but still she couldn't help herself. "I wonder what mithridate is."

I took a pen and scribbled the word on my arm. I added a big question mark in blue ink.

"I've never heard it before," she admitted.

"Me neither," I agreed. "But there's someone we could ask. Someone very good with words... Aunt Abeline."

TWENTY-FIVE

GOOD TO BE HOME

"YOU REMEMBER THE RULES?" Lady Blue Moon asked me.

I nodded. The guidelines were clear.

As Lady Blue Moon pulled in the lake house driveway, I saw the telltale swoosh of the kitchen curtain at the window. Just a lost vacation house renter passing through, my aunt must have thought. But we didn't reverse out of the driveway.

Lady Blue Moon cut the engine.

The fingers on the curtain returned, this time actually shuffling the fabric aside to get a better view. Aunt Abeline never had visitors. I could see her face through the windowpane. First, she squinted with concern, then I popped out of the car. I stood on the gravel and waved. It took only a moment to recognize me. A mix of joy and worry washed over her.

I smiled.

She dropped the curtain and hurried to the screened-in porch entrance.

"What a surprise." She burst out of the entryway.

I hurried straight to her and fell into her arms. We'd never been much for hugging, but this time she embraced me wholly, and she rocked me like a child. It felt so good to be home. I breathed deeply, inhaling the scent of cinnamon, sugar cookies, and aloe. Every inch of her was familiar and known. In these arms, it was the opposite of the High Council. Here, I was me, and I was home. Every ugly, lumpy, bumpy inch. In an instant, I felt my whole body relax.

"Is everything alright?" She pulled her head back to get a look at my cheeks, worry lines creasing her forehead.

"Everything's fine," I said.

It wasn't true, but it had to be said.

I would have liked another hug, but I knew a second embrace would probably increase my aunt's worries, so I settled for an empathetic smile instead.

She frowned. "You look..." She searched for the right word.

"Haggard is how I described it," Lady Blue Moon suggested from her car door. She'd let us have our reunion moment and now waited awkwardly in the wings.

I spun.

"Oh, sorry. Aunt Abeline, this is my friend..." Suddenly, I blanked. I had no idea what to call her. Lady Blue Moon wasn't her real name, obviously, and I wasn't allowed to mention the coven secrets. Did a nickname count as a secret? I looked to her for help.

"Bonnie Main." She stepped forward and offered a handshake. Her eyes flashed in my direction, but I didn't say a word. Not surprisingly, her real name really suited her. She looked just like a Bonnie Main.

"Nice to meet you, Bonnie." My aunt graciously shook her fingers. "Well, come in. Don't just stand there, my goodness. It's getting dark." She ushered us both in. "Tell me everything," Aunt Abeline gushed, flicking on a kettle and preparing a teapot.

Lady Blue Moon and I shared a glance.

Aunt Abeline caught the look and shuddered. I could see it viscerally took her back. A look she'd seen between two witches before.

"What you can, of course," she tapered herself.

We all sat down.

Lady Blue Moon gave a small nod. The conversation was up to me. I knew the rules.

"Things are good... I'm learning a lot. It's a lot to take in." I nodded. Subconsciously, both Aunt Abeline and Lady Blue Moon nodded right back.

Not talking about the specifics of the High Council when the coven had become your whole world was a lot harder than I thought.

"Tried some new skills, made some new friends." I smiled at Lady Blue Moon. She was my instructor, but I hoped it was alright to consider her a friend. She grinned back.

"That's great." Aunt Abeline tried to maintain her

excitement, but we could all hear the enthusiasm start to ring a bit false. Such vague recollections and general pleasantries didn't give either of us much to build on. Aunt Abeline leaned on the counter and forced a big smile our way, but I could see the worry creeping in behind her eyes. She wasn't sure what to ask next. And she must have been through all this before, I realized, with Sierra.

The things we couldn't say.

The stuff we couldn't do.

But I was determined not to make things hard. I turned the focus of the conversation back on my aunt. "How have things been here?"

"Oh, you know. Same old, same old."

My eyes floated to the Scrabble game. I couldn't be sure, but I thought I'd seen some of the words on the board in their positions before.

"Have you not been playing?" I looked closer.

Lady Blue Moon toyed with an empty rack.

"Oh, of course." Aunt Abeline jumped in beside me and swept the board clean.

I was shocked. That wasn't right. Every game board was sacred until the final tile had been played. Sometimes, we had the same sheet of letters on display for weeks while the vowels and consonants battled it out, and Aunt Abeline cherished every minute of it. I narrowed my eyes, watching her thin fingers pick up and flip each tile. That act was very weird. Something was off.

"We could play," Lady Blue Moon suggested.

My aunt's face lit up. She started to check with me, but just then, the kettle boiled. "That's the tea."

I leaned forward. "She's really good," I warned. "Like really, really."

"I can hold my own." Lady Blue Moon shrugged.

"I'm telling you, you can't."

Blue Moon just cocked her head and wiggled her eyebrows.

"Alright, you asked for it. Bring it on... Ms. Bonnie Main." I grinned. "Here, let me help you with that," I called over my shoulder to my aunt.

She and I flitted around the kitchen, grabbing accoutrements for tea in a comfortable rhythm. I was relieved to see I still knew where everything was, and the patterns between us still fit like a glove. We settled around a fresh game board with hot beverages at the ready.

"Bonnie, why don't you start?" my aunt offered graciously.

"Are you sure? I don't mind going third, or even fourth," she joked.

"Go ahead," I agreed.

Lady Blue Moon looked down at her rack. She kicked around her tiles for a minute or so, then ventured her letters onto the board.

Etaerio.

She used all seven letters. A bingo. A double word score bingo. On the very first word.

"What the heck is etaerio?" I asked.

"A collection of fruit." Lady Blue Moon shrugged.

"Usually raspberries," Aunt Abeline added. The women nodded, impressed with each other. "Oh, this is going to be fun."

"Well, okay." I laughed. "Welcome to the lake house, Ms. Bonnie Main."

For me and my Scrabble rack, this was going to be a long night.

In the end, Lady Blue Moon put up a good fight, but my aunt still beat us both.

"What a pleasure," Aunt Abeline purred as we looked down at the final tiles.

"For some," I complained. My final score was more than a hundred points below the other two. But I didn't really mind.

"Bested by a mighty word warrior," Lady Blue Moon agreed, half yawning to herself. "Very good. But we should probably hit the metaphorical hay."

"Is it alright if we stay the night?" I checked with my aunt.

"Of course." Her face lit up again.

"I'll show you the guest room." I nodded to Blue Moon.

"I'll put out fresh towels in the bath for you both." My aunt fell back into hostess mode.

"Thank you so much, Abeline. We do have to leave pretty early in the morning." Lady Blue Moon eyed me.

I nodded, on board.

"If we don't see you, thank you again. You have a lovely home."

Aunt Abeline beamed. "Come back anytime. We'll play! I'm so glad my Mae has found a good friend."

"She says that to all the competitive Scrabble players I bring home," I joked. "Night." One last round of smiles, then we parted. I led Lady Blue Moon to the guest room in the house. Out of my closet, I grabbed some clothing I'd left behind at the cottage. There were several old T-shirts to offer Lady Blue Moon to wear while she slept. She took the top one off the pile.

"It was a risk, you know, to bring you here," she admitted.

"I know," I agreed. But she didn't have to worry. "I'll be ready to go back at first light." Blue Moon didn't say more, but she smiled. I nodded goodnight, then headed to my own room.

My room.

I closed the door and sighed. Still fully dressed, I flopped down on the bed. In the corner, by the window, a mouse deterrent buzzer hummed its sweet song. Yes, even the ugly buzzer sounded sweet in these walls. Here, no one expected me to be anything more than the person I truly was. I didn't have to reach, protect, or defend. I was just me. And I was enough. I closed my eyes. I might have drifted to sleep right then and there had it not been for a gentle knock on the door.

"Come in," I called, sitting up.

Aunt Abeline opened the door. "Would you like me to see you off in the morning?"

I shook my head. "Probably easier if you don't."

We both nodded.

"It'll be quite early," I added, as if the timing had anything to do with the challenge of saying goodbye.

"I'm glad to see you've made a friend." Aunt Abeline smiled.

"And a few more," I agreed. "Maybe," I added, remembering the last words I'd heard them discussing. I paused for a moment, careful to find the right words. "Aunt Abeline, there are things I can't say, and things I can't do, but..."

She nodded. "I know."

I tapped the bed beside me, and she shuffled in. It amplified the intimacy between us, but mostly, I wanted to speak quietly in case Lady Blue Moon didn't approve of what I wanted to ask.

The conversation I'd come to the house to have.

I gathered my nerve.

"Mithridate," I said.

"Mithridate," she repeated.

"What's it mean?" I showed her the term written out on my skin.

"I don't know." She looked puzzled. "Should I?"

"But your vocabulary's so... enormous."

"I know the top played seven letter words of all time, of course, but that's what? Ten letters long? It would never play on the board. Did you try looking it up?"

"Oh my god..." I was embarrassed to say that I hadn't. We had just jumped in the car and come to my aunt. I was so sure she would know what it meant... or maybe I was just looking for a reason to escape the castle.

Either way, I now stood and went to the Scrabble dictionary on my shelf.

"That one won't do. Just hold on." Aunt Abeline left for her room and returned with the giant, dog-eared dictionary from her youth. It had thousands of words and phrases that modern language no longer used. She cracked it open to the letter *M*. Together, we quickly located the mystery word.

"Mithridate," she read. "A confection believed to contain an antidote to poison."

"Poison?"

A flood of thoughts rushed through my head.

"Who was poisoned?" Aunt Abeline asked.

I couldn't meet her eye. The silence hung in the air.

Was this a coven secret, or was it fair game? I wasn't sure. Sierra's death happened years before I joined the High Council, so maybe it was something I could talk about with Aunt Abeline. But did I want her to know I now thought her sister might have been killed?

Poisoned.

Murdered.

Aunt Abeline waited. She let the silence sink in. We had always been quite good at living in the quiet.

I closed the book. "It's nothing," I squeaked.

"Are you being safe?" she asked quietly.

"It's just a word." I shrugged.

Neither of us believed that was true.

When I could see the silence was again taking over, I added, "I'm doing my best."

She considered this. "That's all I can ask," she finally agreed.

"What was your skill set?" I suddenly wondered.

It felt good to change the subject. To shake the tension from the air. I couldn't talk about my witch powers as that was a secret belonging to my coven, but Aunt Abeline had never made it into the Council. As far as I could see, her abilities were fair game.

"Can we... discuss it?" she worried.

"Within reason, yeah," I agreed. "I think."

Aunt Abeline considered being discreet, but that ship had sailed when I first learned my mother had been recruited to a secret witches' coven.

"I could manipulate the wind."

Harness, I almost corrected. But even that term was likely off limits.

"How?" I asked.

"Well, if I concentrated enough, I could generate a big gust of wind, slam a door, move a garden gnome, that sort of thing. Once, when I was really mad, I upended a tree. I never really had it under control." She shrugged.

"Can you still do it now?"

"You know..." She paused, then almost laughed. "I don't care to find out."

I nodded.

Fair enough.

We let the silence resume.

"What about Mom?" I wondered.

"I don't know. Her powers were never revealed. At least not to me."

I flung my arms around my aunt. Her life, her relationships had all been so fraught, so closed and cold and divisive, all through no fault of her own. She accepted the hug but still sat rigid. I didn't know how to tell her, but I didn't want this pattern to continue in her life anymore.

"I'll come back and visit. A lot," I whispered into her hair.

She patted my arm and nodded. "I'd like that," she agreed. "And bring Bonnie. Not for nothing; it was nice to have a little competition on the board."

TWENTY-SIX

YOU'RE NOT ENOUGH

AFTER SUCH A LONG DAY, a tranquil return home, a drubbing at the board game my family loved, and my sweet chat with Aunt Abeline, slipping off to sleep was easy. I peeled back my clothes, dragged a clean T-shirt over my head, and tucked myself under the covers. The bed felt safe and warm. I drifted off almost immediately.

But even wrapped safely in familiarity, my nightmare returned.

"Mae... please help."

I sat straight up in the loft. "No..."

"I don't want to die," Kate said, weeping. "You have to help." She dangled on the wood beam in the barn. Her arms started to slip. Her legs hung over the old farm equipment parked below. "You can't do this on your own."

"Kate, I'm coming."

I slid out on my stomach, across the wooden beam, moving towards her.

"You're not enough."

"No... I am. I—No!"

Kate's body fell through the air.

Her eyes looked up in terror.

Her bones and the farm equipment met.

The crunch was sickeningly alive, then deadening, then final. It all played out again.

"Why didn't you get help?" Brandi snapped. Her frown cut me in half.

"I tried," I objected.

"Not hard enough."

"You should have called me," Josie piped in.

"She's always gonna need our help," Aunt Abeline agreed.

"No, I'm not. I'm good," I tried to correct.

"Not good enough." Spade shrugged.

"That's what I've been trying to tell her." Brandi nodded. "Rejects stick together."

Josie laughed. "See, you need us."

"You definitely do," Aunt Abeline said.

"No," I told them. "I'm a good witch. I'm getting better."

Suddenly, the dream morphed. Some sort of dome came down over my head. A cocoon or a capsule, trapping me inside. Their voices were muted and distant on the other side.

"Wait, what was that?" I asked, but no one could

hear me, and even if they could, they had no control over the morphing dream in my mind. "Stop, please." The cocoon closed in on me. I was trapped in a gooey bubble. There wasn't room to function, but luckily, I could still find air. I grasped the walls. I had no idea what it was made of.

Josie would know. I frowned.

It was safe and secure and kind of sticky.

Suddenly, the bubble shook and shuddered, and just as quickly as it appeared, it fell off the loft where I was standing, taking me with it.

"Oh my god!" I braced for impact, but instead of crashing painfully into the earth, the bubble bounced and ricocheted to soften the collision. It slowed our propulsion with outside friction, dragging me through a cornfield, the vegetation all around me absorbing the blows. My momentum displaced the stalks and dug a deep gash in the ground until the bubble slowed.

Then stopped.

When the wild ride was over, I picked myself up off the ground. I dug my fingers into the goop of the bubble and clawed it open. When the hole was big enough, I crawled my way out. I wiggled. I had to inch-worm, but I broke free of its bonds. I stumbled out onto the farmer's field of burned grass in the same spot I'd knelt in by accident before. Again, there I was, on my knees, looking up from the ground, center stage in the midst of everyone.

The coven.

The strange tribe.

All eyes were on me.
Everything began to get blurry.
Then somebody yelled. Screamed my name.
I sat up.
Wide awake once more.

TWENTY-SEVEN

IT HAPPENED AGAIN

TRUE TO OUR WORD, Lady Blue Moon and I were both up at the crack of dawn to make our way back to the High Council. I had set three alarms just to be sure. I was glad Aunt Abeline had stayed in bed. Leaving the comforts of home was hard enough without the risk of another blubbery goodbye. Besides, now that I knew more about the rules and what I could and couldn't do in and outside of the coven, our lives could be more normal, and we could visit together again soon.

And I wasn't empty-handed.

I'd also gotten answers.

The death certificate date and the date on the annotated doctor's log lined up. I took a picture of the fading document on my phone. My mom was in the hospital the day that the scribbled notation was made. She had died the next day. It seemed really likely that she was SK. She was Lady Haze, and the mithridate was required for her treatment. An antidote to poison. I was almost positive it was her.

My mom was never sick.

She was murdered.

But how? And why? By whom?

The ten-year-old crime would need to be solved, but today, I had more pressing needs. We were headed back for day two of my training.

The whole Council was counting on me and my team.

Last night, I slept long enough for my subconscious to add in new details. After all the usual insults, my dream persona had done a few new things. Maybe this was casting after all.

The thought gave me hope.

After all, if I couldn't see the future in my dreams, was I really a witch? I was no better off than my aunt, than any human. These training days were imperative. If I was going to be any real help in the battle, I needed Lady Mauve to crack the code and get my special talents to work. I had no choice.

When the other battalion members started trickling into the training facility, I'd already been there for hours, hard at work, sewing extra pockets into my pants, trying out scientific skills, working hard to build an arsenal of chemical reactions for every possible scenario. I even climbed the wall. All by myself.

Without the mat, I didn't go high. Instead, I climbed left to right. And what do you know, I was getting better at it.

"Where is everybody?" I asked Ferris as she joined me on the wall.

She shook her head. "Mauve locked them out. Guess you were right. She decided the audience wasn't helping."

I was right?

As Lady Mauve approached, I hopped down off the holds and stood tall, at attention like a soldier.

"I'm ready to resume dream-cast training," I told her.

"Good." She nodded. "We'll start with harnessing." She turned and marched away.

"But what about my dream," I sputtered. "The nightmares, my visions. I'm ready to tell you..."

I was prepared for more waterboarding, or climbing, or even trying to break another illusion, but Lady Mauve simply shrugged. She had a knack for spotting my fear and shoving her thumbs right in it.

"If you can't control, you dismantle," she told me. She nodded at the other girl who had followed her into the room.

My least favorite person in the coven.

"Brandi, wind."

"You got it." A wicked grin pushed up the apples of Brandi's cheeks.

How I had ever thought she was pretty when we first met was beyond me.

She looked positively psycho.

She lowered her palm into a fist near her hips. Breezy gusts blew in from every crack in the room.

The current appeared from nowhere, circling my body.

My hair tossed in my face.

Brandi's black locks rose too, but they floated behind her like a mermaid because all the turbulence and crosswinds were aimed towards me.

At a nearby desk, Lady Blue Moon valiantly strove to hold on to her paperwork.

"Come on, witch bitch," Brandi said menacingly. "Let's see what you got."

"Please, stop. I'm not ready," I complained. I put my hand up to protect my face and tried to walk towards Lady Mauve. Ignoring Brandi only seemed to incite her anger.

"You'll never be ready. Dismantle," Lady Mauve ordered.

Brandi kicked up the intensity.

The winds grew to gusts. Lady Blue Moon clamped down what she could, but the rest of her papers went flying. Sheets of stationary and note cards smacked my knees and elbows. They cut tiny slits in my skin. The room stirred so badly around me I could no longer see where anyone was. I couldn't feel where I was going. It felt like any second my feet might pick up off the floor, but there was nothing to hold on to. I leaned into the wind, battling to remain standing, determined to stay upright. In this tunnel, it was impossible to move towards her, but we both knew Brandi was the source of the wind. Going straight at her seemed to be my only option.

I tried to push forward.

Brandi easily fought back against my efforts, increasing the speed of her imaginary turbines. My skin reverberated with the new power throttled against me.

"Stop her!" Mauve shouted at me.

"I can't," I shouted back.

But nobody heard it. The wind stole my voice.

The words disappeared.

I tried to bear down, but the force was so strong it took all my strength not to keel over, not to be blown away. Right out of my shoes.

Suddenly, Ferris grabbed a pillow off the nearby couch and smacked Brandi, hard, over the back of her shoulders.

Whoomph!

The girl tumbled forward in shock. She'd been so busy watching and gloating over my powerless whimpers she hadn't seen Ferris coming. Hadn't braced for impact. Ferris hit her target square between the blades.

At Brandi's stumble, her harness stalled.

Mid-wind.

I was fighting so hard against the current that at its abrupt disappearance, I nose-dived over my own feet and splattered to the floor.

"What the hell?" Brandi roared, leaping back up to her feet, but Ferris didn't flinch. She cocked the pillow on her hip.

"Mae, you never go straight at a harness," Ferris told me, not taking her eyes off the girl, not backing down. "You surprise, not attack. Then the weak ones collapse."

"I'm not weak," Brandi said.

"And yet, you're disrupted," Ferris pointed out and shrugged.

The two girls glared at each other. Brandi was definitely ratcheting up her next response, but Lady Mauve was unimpressed overall.

"Right. Thank you, Ferris, Brandi, for the demonstration. Moving on."

She didn't bother to smooth things over between the teens. Instead, she ignored their quarrel. Lady Mauve walked away. The implication was clear: I was to follow.

I quickly did.

Behind me, I didn't hear them come to physical blows, so the women obviously parted ways as well. What must it be like to work side by side, day after day with your kidnapper? I shuddered.

"The girl was right. You must dilute a harness's powers. If there's more than one of you, split apart. Divide. Then conquer. Bait and flank," Lady Mauve murmured.

"So I was the bait?" I put myself back together.

"Yes." Mauve nodded. "And Brandi didn't see it coming." A tiny smile tingled on her lips. I could see it. Lady Mauve had known for sure that Ferris would come to help me. The older witch had clocked the opportunity, set it up, and let the drama play out to prove her point.

"What if I'm alone?" I wondered.

"You back away."

"Retreat?"

"Fast as you can. Dilute the space. She's harnessing wind, but she's also controlling the geography. If you enlarge the area, you increase the work it takes for the other person to maintain command. No one has endless energy. Now." We had returned to our couch and chair in the dream-cast salon. "Tell me your dream," she said.

"Are they really all gone?" I looked around at the empty room. Was there really no audience? It was possible she was tricking me again.

"What do you think?"

"Well, I can check my phone." I pulled out my small device and accessed the home screen.

Lady Mauve raised an eyebrow.

"I discovered this when Spade was chasing me in the cornfield... A lie-guard seems to bring technical difficulties." As I looked at the phone, I was pleasantly surprised to see there were notifications for a whole row of messages from Beck sent both last night and this morning.

Mae, where are you? Let's talk about it.

I'd really like to see you, to explain everything.

· · ·

Wanna meet for breakfast?

I guess you're already training...

Good luck today. You'll do great. I'm rooting for you.

There they were, one after another.

With Lady Mauve's watchful eye on me, there wasn't time to really parse each sentence or figure out what exactly he meant by each specific word or phrase. I had no idea how this discovery made me feel. I still hadn't had time to process things with Beck. There were already so many other things on my brain.

But it was clear he was making a gesture.

That was nice.

If that effort was enough... I really wasn't sure.

But I had to test my cell phone.

That was the whole point of this exchange.

I quickly typed a message in return to him. One word that—whether Beck and I were meant to hash things out as a love connection, or our romantic possibility had been completely crushed into bits—I truly meant.

Thanks.

· · ·

The message sent.

I looked up at Lady Mauve. "Okay, we're good," I said. "No illusion."

"No illusion, huh?" She smiled. Was I reading her wrong, or did she actually seem impressed? "What about all this?" She waved to the large training facility.

I frowned. "Oh right. I don't know, maybe the phone thing doesn't really work?"

"No, I think you're on to something. If a lie-guard didn't think of the communicative world, it's shut down," she acknowledged. "That could be right."

Holy cow, had Lady Mauve actually approved of something I said? That was big. Monumental. I was going to ride that approval as long as I could. I tucked the phone away and sat myself down on the lounge, ready to begin. This time, I didn't lean back like a patient on a bed. Instead I sat forward with intensity. Lady Mauve did the same.

"It happened again last night," I told her. "The same nightmare."

"The recurring dream," she corrected.

"Whatever," I agreed, anxious to spew out the details. "I'm there, in the barn, Kate falls, it's a bloody mess, I couldn't stop it, then the others come. They ridicule the way I screwed up with her death."

"What others?"

"Spade, Josie, my aunt."

"Members of your past..." she murmured.

"Yeah, I guess. And Brandi. She was there. They

all say terrible things. That I suck, and I'm not good enough."

"Take your ego out of the equation," she told me. "A vision's not meant to hurt your feelings. It holds relevant information. Content the fates think you need to see..."

"Like an accurate representation of my abilities?"

Ahhhh!

Crack!

Suddenly, a nasty crash reverberated through the room. Lady Mauve and I sat up from our huddled thoughts. Our heads spun towards the sound. Others were already rushing there as well.

Things felt like they were moving in slow motion.

Beside the climbing wall, Lady Rain was crumpled on the ground. Her arm was snapped under her body at an ungodly angle. Someone was crying.

"Oh no." I involuntarily rose.

But Lady Mauve was already halfway across the room. "Rain!"

TWENTY-EIGHT

DOWN TO THREE

"DO you think this was part of my dream?" I said worriedly. "She fell..."

"I don't know. I mean, your vision was Kate, this was Rain. Kate fell in a barn, she fell in this space... Dream-casting is not a direct science. Even if it was, what could you do?" Lady Blue Moon chewed on her nails. She'd gnawed them to stubs.

Over and over, I'd watched a girl fall in my mind. During multiple nights of sleep.

"I could have warned them," I said.

"I did warn them. Last night." Ferris joined our side. "Remember? I told them someone should always be spotting the climb."

"Someone would have caught her, but we lost all our audience because I refused to openly talk," I realized.

"Stop making this about you," Silverfox snapped, arriving at our group. "We're all screwed." He raked his hand through his ruddy hair. "They took her to the hospital, but I saw, like, protruding bone sticking out. You don't come back from that."

"Not right away." Ferris nodded.

We all agreed on that.

Silverfox was right. We were totally screwed.

The whole coven.

The elders thought so too.

Our little group watched as Lady Mauve heatedly discussed our options with several ladies and fellows and one man I definitely recognized, even from the opposite side of the room. Cornelius Child. His fiery orange hair and rotund belly made him stand out in any clan.

They were not happy.

"I wish we knew what they were saying," Ferris murmured.

"They kicked me out like a fish on his back," Silverfox agreed. "To be a fly on the wall... You're pretty good at that," he told Lady Blue Moon.

She looked up, surprised.

"Why don't cha check it out? Report back." He raised an eyebrow.

Ferris and I nodded.

"I'll try," Lady Blue Moon agreed. Like a mouse, she was able to tiptoe her way over and tuck in to listen. They were so used to the little paper master waiting in the wings of discussions, none of the elders even flinched. They just ignored her. She flipped through her random papers as if they were a prop.

The three of us stood staring. Waiting. Impossibly listening.

There was nothing else to be done.

After a few moments, Blue Moon returned. Her face was ashy white.

"You were right. It's bad. Her arm is broken," she conveyed. "In two places."

"Oh god." Ferris closed her eyes.

"We're totally toast. Roasted tomatoes," Silverfox moaned.

The elders were now arguing.

The news seemed to be getting worse.

"Can she be replaced in the battle?" I wondered.

Blue Moon shook her head. "I don't think so. They'll patch her up as best as they can, but the selections were made. She's got to continue."

"I hope she's okay," I murmured.

"She's not. No one is," Silverfox said. "I'm not okay. Are you?"

"No," I agreed. Although snapping about it wouldn't help.

Ferris frowned. "That was her magic hand. Her harnessing fist. There's no way she can make it work. Trying to close her hand into a ball would be incredibly painful. Our foursome is basically down to three."

"And it's actually much worse," Lady Blue Moon admitted. "Every plan the coven made, all the strategy the elders prepared, it's all out the window. Rain's out. She can walk, but she can't... anything else! All the coven's strategy for attack and even our defenses are gone. We're starting from scratch."

"She's just a body on the field." Silverfox nodded.

"But that's not fair," I said.

"There's no fairness in witchcraft," Ferris said bitterly.

"Guess it's back to the drawing board," Silverfox agreed.

Lady Blue Moon just heaved a sigh. "Could this get any worse?"

Just then, huffing and puffing, a fellow burst into the room.

The whole room spun to see him.

"The fires are over!" he exclaimed. "The Battle of Four begins!"

TWENTY-NINE

TWENTY MINUTES 'TIL THE END OF THE WORLD

"ARE YOU READY?" Lady Blue Moon asked.

Silverfox, Ferris, and I all looked at each other.

"Will we ever be?" I wondered.

"No." Brandi walked past on her way to the exit. "We're packing our bags."

"Good," Ferris told her. "Get outta here."

"Make me, witch bitch." Brandi narrowed her eyes. Suddenly, a wind picked up the ends of our hair, like a threatening force. "You don't have some cheap-shot element of surprise now."

"We didn't resort to violence to get our foot in the door," Ferris shot back.

Brandi's eyes flashed in anger, but Ferris held her ground.

"Go on. Things are bad enough already." Silverfox shooed her away. "It's only, like, twenty minutes 'til the end of the world. You can hold your grudge fest 'til then."

Brandi flexed at Ferris one last time, but even she wasn't willing to pick a real fight with one of the coven's three remaining battalion members on the day of the battle. She shrugged and strolled away.

"Twenty minutes?" Lady Blue Moon repeated.

"You think we can hold them off for twenty minutes?" I asked.

"If we're lucky, maybe an hour." Silverfox looked at his watch. We exchanged a wry smile. Things felt pretty bleak.

After the big announcement, many other witches bubbled into the entry of the training room; several were wringing their hands or talking animatedly. Most were lookie-loos trying to pick up the gossip. A few ventured to the elder group with new information. There were plenty of eyes on us all.

Silverfox shrugged. "Bet they wanna talk strategy away from the riffraff." He glanced around.

Ferris nodded. "Whatever plans they have left."

We looked over at the elder clump. They had started to move towards the door. They distinctly nodded in our direction, intent for us to follow.

More and more witches flooded in.

Silverfox was right. If there was any chance for a quiet word, we'd have to relocate somewhere private.

"This is gonna be rough." He put on a brave face and bounced away, following the elders.

Lady Blue Moon nodded, doubling back to gather more paperwork, and Ferris moved on with the new group before being forcibly stopped to chat with some ladies and fellows intent on giving her their two cents.

Unadulterated advice was the last thing I wanted.

I put my head down and followed Silverfox's path, but someone put a hand on my arm. Their grip pulled me back.

I turned.

"Hey," Beck said.

Relief filled my face. "Hey."

He looked very concerned. "Got your text."

"Yeah."

For a moment, I felt so relieved to see him: that tall, sturdy body, his caring expression, the way his hand was still on my skin. I wanted to collapse into his arms. Let him hold me. But last night's memories stopped me.

"The battle's coming," I told him, like he didn't already know.

Like the air wasn't already thick with anticipation.

Beck nodded. "You feel ready?" He ran his hand through his hair.

I glanced around.

How many people were pretending not to listen, distinctly watching me?

"No," I admitted. I looked away.

"Yeah," he agreed. "About last night..."

I gave a small shake of the head. It wouldn't help to rehash it.

Not now.

Not here.

Not today.

He seemed to understand. "I'm on your side," he told me. He left it at that.

I held very still for a moment, not sure what to say, how much to believe, but I couldn't stop myself from giving in.

I needed those words.

That was where I needed him to be. On my side.

I looked around again.

A thousand eyes were on us. Some offered forced smiles, but most just bored holes into my being, as if this whole thing was my fault.

As if I was the one who'd called for the battle.

As if hating me would somehow help.

Brandi's vicious glare was the worst of all.

"Come on." I grabbed Beck's hand and pulled him into an empty room in the hallway. As soon as we were alone, the words tumbled out of my mouth. "This is bad. I don't know what we're gonna do. The whole coven is counting on us. And Rain just fell. She's basically done. Her arm is broken. In two places. I haven't read, like, any of the books Mauve gave to me. The opposing team of witches has years of experience over us... What have I learned in mere days? Beck, what have I learned? We're screwed."

In the hallway behind us, I could still catch various witches' eyes as they passed. The halls swirled in madness. Fear and uncertainty were on everyone's minds. Was this our last day in the castle? If the coven was kicked out, had anyone planned where we'd go?

Beck stepped between me and the offending stares, blocking the door, guiding my eyeline back to his face.

"It's not your fault," he said. "None of this is." He stepped closer.

I didn't flinch from him.

"You'll do the best that you can. Come here." He reached out his arms.

I didn't want to give in, to hug him, to hold him, but the embrace called me in. He slid his arms around my frame. I buried my face in his chest. I longed to disappear, but also, I breathed him in. He felt so warm and smelled so good. This was what I wanted. We had fought so hard to be parabonded, and now, every day since, I had been isolated from him. We hadn't been alone since this whole thing started.

"Vince was right," I admitted into his chest. "I'm not an amazing witch. I don't have skills like... you know."

"Josie?"

I weakly nodded.

I thought he might retreat at her name, maybe take a step back, maybe undo his grip, but he didn't blanch. Instead, he brought a finger to my cheek and cleaned up an errant tear that had tumbled on my face.

"Vince was dumb to compare. A dream-cast and a chemist? You aren't better or worse. You're *different*. And thank god for that," he whispered. "She quit. She gave up. You won't."

"How do you know?"

"Because I know you. Mae, you'll give it your all."

I looked deep in his eyes. "What if it's not enough?"

"It will be." He seemed so confident. "I'm sure," he added. His eyes looked so deep, so blue. I found myself swimming in them.

Beck believed in me. A smile played on my lips, and I toyed with the idea of believing in myself.

Brandi was correct.

I was the default witch.

I was in a spot I never would have chosen for myself. I was seriously outmatched. But I wouldn't give up. I would fight 'til the end. I would give it my all.

He reached out and smoothed a strand of flyaway hair. His fingers grazed the tender curve of my ear, sending waves of desire flooding over my skin. I shivered in anticipation, but we both stayed very still. His eyes locked on mine.

"You got this, parabond," he whispered.

"Thanks."

"I'm rooting for you." His lips opened. Plump and soft. They cracked a smile, just for me. I returned his grin. His hand floated from my ear to the side of my face and neck, deliciously cupping me in.

His hand teased in my hair, massaged my neck.

We were locked in each other's orbit, the gravitational force pulling us in.

He leaned forward, angled towards me, eyes closing.

My own face tilted up to receive him, ready to drink in those lips.

"Mae." Ferris's stern voice interrupted. "There you are."

Embarrassed, I fell away from Beck and looked over.

Ferris stood in the doorway, frowning.

Suddenly, all the people careening through the hallway, all the noise, the cries, the chaos, it all rushed back to my ears. The corridor throbbed with fear. I blushed bright red.

"Sorry." She nodded at Beck, apologizing for her timing. "They're starting," she told me. "Cornelius wants to begin."

Grimly, I nodded. "I have to go," I told him. I pushed back from Beck's body.

He nodded, the magnetism of the moment completely over.

"Wish me luck," I told him.

"You don't need it."

I nodded and let Ferris lead me away.

THIRTY

THE SHADOW COUNCIL

QUICKLY, we took our seats for the final debrief.

The group of elders had taken over a small, empty classroom. Only those with a need to know were allowed to enter in. But of course, Ferris and I were both on the list. Lady Rain was back from the hospital, her arm in a cast and a sling. She and Fellow Silverfox both wore the same serious expressions that Ferris and I had put on as we waited to hear the last-minute developments in the plan.

Lady Mauve and Cornelius Child stood in hushed discussion, listening to the other experienced men and women. There were several adults who I didn't know, but that was to be expected. I was the lowest seniority rank in the whole room. If I hadn't been a competitor, there was no way I would ever be allowed in this chair. In the corner of the classroom, Lady Blue Moon rifled through papers, her data sets ready and waiting if needed. Fellow Stone and two others were organizing little packets of chemicals, no doubt selections of spells and reactions we'd carry with us to use in the afternoon's terrible clash.

Although Ferris had hurried us over to the meeting, the leaders let their four battalion members stew. They continued to whisper quietly without us. We waited in silence, fearful of the news. With such a heavy task on our shoulders, I was happy to let the leaders have the final discussion. Finally, Cornelius nodded to the others, and their small group broke free.

"Hello." Cornelius made eye contact with each of us individually. He took his time. He gathered the room. "I want to start this conversation by offering my personal thanks to each of you. Being chosen for the Battle of Four is not easy. We know that. Thank you for training to the best of your abilities." He checked in with each of us as he spoke. I could barely hold his gaze. His voice was the same in strength and tenor as it had been in the field. In such a small room, it boomed.

The others also wiggled in their chairs, no doubt equally aware of the importance of this moment.

"I know I don't have to tell you the weight of the contest ahead, but I will. For some of you, this home is quite new, but we have called this land home to the High Council for over one hundred years. Its resources must be protected. Its legacy must be preserved. Generations of witches have walked these hallowed halls. On the field today, you will guard and protect not only the coven's rare plants and species and plentiful resources, but also the unspoken treaties we've built with the neighboring towns. You defend not things, but a way of life, the community we hold, the essence of our clan."

"So don't screw it up," added Lady Mauve.

I smiled. Whether she meant to or not, Mauve's crass interruption had pressed a release valve in the room. The tension broke.

"Enough with the motivational rah-rah, Cornelius. Tell us the plan," Silverfox said. He shifted in his chair.

The rest of us nodded.

"Right." He glanced at his crew.

The ladies and fellows took over. For more than an hour, they outlined the details of their decisions. Since Lady Rain could not cast, her best use would be on orb detail. Her focus would be knowledge. The Evil Eye would be hidden by Lady Rain alone. That way, only one member of our battalion would know where it truly was, and the rest of us would defend dummy locations in hopes of wasting the Damocles coven's resources and draw out the other team. Our battalion would divide into two factions, offense and defenders, with Rain and myself on defense. Ferris and Silverfox would hunt their Eye down. And, as I suspected, we were to line our pockets with all sorts of special chemicals to assist us in our tasks, including a sleeping powder made just for me, in case mid-conflict I needed to dream.

"Just a pinch," Fellow Stone warned, tugging the

lapels of his white coat. "Take too much, you might never wake up."

Great. I nodded.

Another thing to be worried about.

"I'll wake you," Ferris told me with a nudge. "Or Brandi's little brother will," she whispered.

"Who's Bran—" I started to ask, then the realization hit me. "Beck?"

Ferris nodded.

I stared at her, dumbfounded.

Beck was Brandi's brother?

I shook my head. "But she's so gross..."

She shrugged. "Actually, now it kinda makes sense. I mean, she's always hated me for no reason, but you... you've been messing with her clan."

My mind reeled.

No wonder Brandi called me the default. She didn't think I was good enough to partner with her brother... and that was why on the first morning, he'd hugged her and all her friends... He'd grown up with those witches. He had a kidnapper in his family.

"Head in the game, Mae," Lady Mauve snapped.

I looked up, surprised, realizing all eyes were on me. I nodded.

"What did I just tell them?" she asked. Her frown could cut glass.

"I-I..."

"The horses are ready." A lady I had never met before burst into the room, interrupting the gathering. I let out a breath in relief as eyes flicked from me to her face. Ferris stood as Ethan and two other riders appeared in the doorway as well.

"We're all set." Ethan nodded. "If we leave now, we should be at the northern edge of town by the start of the battle."

Ferris joined his side.

Cornelius nodded.

"What are they doing?" With Ferris temporarily gone, I had to whisper my questions to Rain.

"Sweetie, do you not understand anything?" she asked, unimpressed.

I wanted to clap back, but she was right. I didn't understand. I just shrugged and shook my head no.

"They're setting precautions. Like, building an outsider base camp in case the Council needs to evacuate quickly," Silverfox told me.

Rain nodded. "The assets need to be protected. Without my help to win here today, the chance of taking home a victory is frankly very slim. Everybody knows it but you."

Cornelius held up his hand. "We are simply protecting what belongs to the tribe. We have propagated the Valdeez plants and others. These brave riders will take them to safety. An alternative location will be situated as a safety measure, but we are not giving up. We have full faith. We intend to win."

"Even if we do win, it's possible the other coven doesn't care. They still might try to destroy our land," Ethan added. "Remember the story?" He asked me. I nodded. Furtively, I snuck a glance at Lady Mauve. She stared daggers back at me.

"The point *is*, our resources will be safe," Cornelius told me. The others nodded.

I sat back in my chair.

Rain was right.

Much as they tried to sugarcoat it, the elders were preparing for a loss. All this bravado, the pump-up speech... It was gas on a fire without a flame. Nobody thought we would come out victorious.

In a sick way, it was kind of freeing.

I'd felt so much pressure to win, to carry the whole coven on my back, to pull off the impossible, but the leaders were already assuming the worst. My emotions were torn.

Across the room, Ferris hugged her parabond.

"Off you go," Cornelius told them. The elders nodded.

Ethan looked to Ferris. "I'll see you soon," he said.

"Not if I see you first," she agreed.

They knew the whole room was watching, but neither of them cared. They were like soldiers headed off to war. Who knew what might come next? He bent in for a long, slow goodbye kiss. Deep, with urgency.

Wishing for a more private moment for them both, I looked away.

Cornelius's remarks made Ethan and the other riders sound like simple delivery men and women, checking perfunctory boxes, covering the bases. They made our battalion sound like sports competitors, running our races, completing our tasks. But it was clear that Ferris and Ethan as a couple understood the inherent danger in both their tasks. He was essentially creating a shadow High Council somewhere out in the forest as a safety valve in case the real High Council went to hell. And she was one of only four faces with the ability to stop the other coven from running us right out of town.

Finally, the teens broke apart. Love in their eyes, tight smiles on their faces. He looked up to the rest of the room and nodded, then slipped out into the halls.

Ferris retook her seat. She didn't glance in my direction. She looked shaken to the core.

"We'll finish the battle quick as a bunny. He'll be safe before you know it, mark my words." Silverfox made promises that none of us could guarantee.

Ferris simply nodded.

"We leave in ten," Cornelius said.

THIRTY-ONE

IT ISN'T PERFECT, BUT IT'S SOMETHING

SO MANY THOUGHTS whirled through my mind as our group dispersed to the hallway. Most headed straight for the main gates. After Cornelius's discharge, no one felt like chatting. No one stuck around. We'd already said all there was to say. The hallways were no longer crowded. The initial panic over, most witches were off, talking with loved ones or packing their belongings.

Before I could catch her attention, Ferris went running.

She must have had a lot to think about, sending her man on his way. From their own personal recounting, even at year three in the coven, they had been through several trying, desperate situations. I could tell they loved and trusted each other deeply. About my own parabond, I had a lot of conflicting feelings.

Beck.

Brandi's brother.

This bit of news had shocked me. What else didn't I know about him?

At the start of a relationship, I knew people were always on their very best behavior. Even so, with Beck, there were already several red flags waving in my face. He acted sweet, saying all the right things today just before the meeting. But after last night, hearing what was said behind my back, I had some doubts. He cuddled and comforted me in the back of Greg's car after the selections for the battalion, but at the thought of seeing Josie, his head had swiveled on a stick...

"Mae, over here!" Hilde had camped out outside the classroom and leaned against the wall, waiting for me and the other battalion members to exit.

"Hi." I was always happy to see Hilde. As the youngest member of our group, her innocence and enthusiasm were a sweet pleasure. But I wasn't sure why she was here in the hallway, waiting for me now. "I can't stay," I warned her. "They're expecting that I'm coming."

"I know. We'll be quick. We have a surprise. Come here." She tried to lead me back to a second empty classroom, but I didn't fall into step.

"I've really got to..." I looked down the hallway.

"Mae!" She rolled her eyes. "Sloane said you might say that. Marcy said our class holds bad juju for you now." She nodded sagely, although I wasn't sure if she understood what "bad juju" meant. "But you wanna see this. Promise." She pulled me by the hand. Hesitant, I followed. "Ta-da!"

As we entered, all my fellow parabond classmates hopped up from their chairs with big, hopeful smiles. My eyes trailed through all of them.

"Hi," Sloane spoke first, as the others crowded around.

"Hi." I eyed them warily.

Sloane cleared her throat. "We know today's the battle."

"But before you go, we wanted to say that we're sorry," Hilde jumped in.

I could tell they'd practiced this apology routine quite a bit.

"We were giving you a hard time, criticizing you, for something that could have happened to any one of us," Tej added.

"We broke the rules, and you got caught. But you never ratted us out," Marcy said.

Greg solemnly nodded. "Thanks for not being a rat."

"You literally saved our butts," Nicolette added.

"Except for Rick and my butt, because we did what we were told and didn't go to the Orson Bell," Hilde added, going off script. "But you can save our butts now!"

"Anyway, we're proud of you and the effort you've put in to try and improve and represent the coven... and we wanted to do something to help." Sloane brought the apology back on message.

"So... we made notes." Nicolette held out a stack of

notecards with point form scribbles in various hand-writing.

"On all your books," Hilde blurted out.

The others nodded.

I took some of the papers Nicolette offered. "How did you—"

The group stepped back, revealing my pile of textbooks.

"You left these in the hall by your bedroom before you left in a huff last night." Vince shrugged. He had clearly been dragged into this apology.

"So... we divided and conquered. We each took a few chapters, sped-read, and made notes to help," Tej clarified.

"It isn't perfect," Sloane admitted. "But it's something."

"To help," Nicolette added.

"Honestly, it was the most reading I've done in years," Greg admitted. The others chuckled.

"It was Beck's idea," Hilde added. She beamed at the tall boy.

My eyes searched him out in the group. He stood at the very back of the pack, beside Rick. On the table, the stack of books between them was almost as tall as the guys.

He nodded. "You said you didn't have time to read them yourself."

I smiled at him. "This is..." I looked from the papers to each of their smiling faces. "Really great, guys. Thanks."

They burst into big grins.

"Does this mean you forgive us for being total jerks?" Marcy asked.

"For once, I didn't say anything bad about anyone," Greg said.

Nicolette shoved an elbow in Vince's ribs.

"We all know you'll do your best," he muttered.

She nodded, proud as punch at this begrudging admittance. They all looked at me, expectant.

"Yes. Of course. Totally forgiven." I nodded. I looked down at all the paperwork they'd provided. "I guess... wish me luck," I said.

"Good luck!" They all laughed.

I caught Beck's eye. He smiled at me. I smiled right back.

One by one, my classmates came forward and gave me a hug and handed me their notations. Their kind words stood as both an apology for last night and a send-off in today's battle.

"You'll be awesome," Nicolette told me.

"I just joined this clique; try not to destroy it," Tej added.

I grinned. "I'll do my best."

"You're gonna do great," Sloane assured me. She hugged me.

"You got this," Marcy agreed.

"Try not to get dead," Greg told me. They each patted half my back.

I nodded.

Even Vince had something to say. "Remember, climb with your legs."

"I will."

"You got this," he added, then ducked away.

That left just Hilde, Rick, and Beck.

"Good luck." Rick nodded, still formal. Instead of a hug, he offered me his handshake. I shook it firmly.

"I'll do my best."

"You're gonna be awesome, I just know it." Hilde told me, collapsing her arms around me.

"Thanks, Lady Jane." I squeezed her back.

"My name's Hilde." She giggled.

"I know, it's just a saying. A term of endearment." I nodded. "I'll see you when it's over."

"Hilde, help me with these," Rick instructed. He carried ninety percent of the books, Hilde the final ten. It still seemed a lot of paper for her little arms, but she managed to close the gap. She scampered off to our rooms. Rick nodded to Beck and myself and also left, but Beck stayed put.

"This was really sweet," I told him, tucking the notes into a pocket in my pants. I knew it was time to go, but I wanted to stay put. Maybe fall back into his arms, let Beck tell me everything would be okay. But we both knew I couldn't dawdle. They were already waiting for me by the cars. Waiting to start the battle.

"Thanks for organizing."

"It didn't take much." He nodded. "Everyone wanted to help."

"Which is good, because I seriously need it."

"Because we want to support our friend," he corrected, coming closer.

A flood of emotions fell over me. Hesitant, I took a step back.

"It's getting late." I nodded. "They're waiting."

"You're gonna do great," he told me in the doorway.

His blue eyes took me in. He stopped for a moment, I think maybe wondering if he should make a romantic gesture to close the gap between us. But there wasn't time. I had to go.

I floated a hand to his bicep.

"Thanks, parabond." I had meant it to signal good-bye, but the husky whisper of my voice told him I wasn't ready to walk away. He didn't flinch.

I should have let go.

Hurried out into the hall.

But his skin was warm under my hand.

My fingers radiated heat. And I didn't release my palm. We both looked down at the contact between us, then up into each other's eyes. His body was so still, receptive to whatever I would offer. His eyes searched mine and mine his, only inches between us in the small, narrow doorway. He so easily could have closed that space, smashed our bodies into one another. But he didn't. He was patient. Full of longing.

I could do it too.

Pull him in.

Drag him back.

Shut the door.

Touch every muscle.

But there wasn't time. Everyone was waiting.

He made it clear, standing here, humming with anticipation. The choice was totally mine.

I wanted him beside me.

I wanted the passion and the oblivion.

I wanted his warm hands around me, touching me.

I'd wanted them there from the first moment I'd met him. Back, way back, when those hands weren't something I was allowed to want, because they didn't belong to me then. I had always wanted Beck.

But this wasn't the moment.

We weren't nearly ready.

My chest heaved. With each ragged breath, Beck and I breathed together.

I'd already made a mess with Spade. I'd let our physical needs and desires trump our emotional states, and while our sexual chemistry had always been fantastic, our trust in each other was completely destroyed.

Chemistry aside, I hadn't worked out how I really felt about Beck. And Beck hadn't figured me out either. That wasn't something we could unearth today, in this minute, moments before the battle. I needed to concentrate on more pressing events. More pressing than his waiting pink mouth.

I looked at his eyes, so deep and observant. My glance ventured down to his grin, soft and waiting. Proximity brought new intoxicating smells to meet me.

A waft of cinnamon, deep and earthy. Beck smelled so good. I breathed him in.

He stood so still, so tall, so patient.

He waited for even the smallest invitation.

I wanted to give him the signal.

His head turned towards me, those lips swerving deliciously close, but still he waited.

Just give in, my body told me.

Just hold on, my brain reclaimed.

We hung there in that delicious moment, buzzing with anticipation for what felt like ages, until finally, my hand slipped off his skin.

I managed to step back. My legs didn't give way.

"I'll see you when it's over," I told him. My voice was hoarse and throaty.

His gaze was a little sad, but he understood.

"I'll see you when you win," he agreed.

THIRTY-TWO

THE GAME WITH ALL THE MARBLES

THE NOTES WERE INCREDIBLE.

On the car ride to the Orson Bell, I read as many as I could. A shorthand recap of entire books of knowledge, handwritten just for me. Even reading Tej's chicken scratch, I found myself poring over every word.

It was hard to believe my situation was real. I was one of four people charged with protecting a hundred witches from being cast out of their homes.

Witches just like Sierra.

My mom thrived in this environment. That picture of her standing atop the Orson Bell, proudly victorious in her day, gave me hope. She had entered a witches contest and won.

I could do the same.

I didn't have her powers or her range of skill, whatever it was (how was it I still didn't know?), and I didn't have her years of experience, but Beck had been right about one fact: I had her will. I would never quit.

"I will fight for your home," I told her memory quietly. "Our home," I added.

This wasn't just her world. The High Council was mine too. And to protect this otherworldly kingdom, I would give everything that I had.

I went back to my reading.

As we neared the field, the destruction of the fires lined the road. Entire sections of trees were charred with ash. The cornfield where I'd hid was now black and barren. The fires had destroyed everything in their path. Luckily, the town of Alderton was spared. Although I was sure the farmer's who owned these fields didn't feel as lucky. We drove straight through and back, towards the tower. The Orson Bell and its ruins were a public destination with tourist rope stanchions set up to help guide their tours. We drove right by and down to the field where the other coven was waiting.

The battlefield was packed.

I expected nothing less.

Everyone was there. The entire covens had come to watch.

It was strange to arrive at the same burnt-out cornfield and roll into the same crowded meadow far beneath the bell tower and this time have my arrival met with fanfare.

We champions arrived in a cavalcade of cars. Although the mood in the private meeting only moments ago had been dark and desperate, as we entered the battlefield, the entire coven put on a brave face. The High Council did everything it could to give the appearance of confidence and strength.

I looked around for my classmates.

In the chaos, I didn't see Beck or any of my other friends, but I knew they were out there, cheering me on. It seemed every lady and fellow had turned up in their bright whites, while the invading coven had dripped themselves in blood red. There were more of us on the field, but our extra numbers in spectators wouldn't matter. It was an equal playing ground of four competitors per coven. And truly, compared with the group of nomads who had stumbled into our town and tried to take over, in this battle, we were the ones with everything to lose.

Lady Blue Moon brought our car to a stop. "Well, this is it, the game with all the marbles. You ready?"

"No," I admitted. "But that won't stop me." I climbed out of the car and took in the mood.

Excitement and anticipation hung in the air.

Lady Blue Moon felt it too. She came around the car to join me on the farmland. "Don't forget that saying: 'everybody poops.'"

I raised an eyebrow.

"What I mean is, they're only human," she said. "Well, they're witches, but they're human. You know what I mean."

We looked over at the other coven just in time to see one member of their faction create a tiny windstorm in their hands. The woman held it out for just a moment, then quickly snuffed the cyclone. She used her magic as a nervous habit, like someone else might crack their knuckles. Lady Blue Moon frowned.

"Well, that was exceptionally bad timing," she admitted. "But they all have flaws. Weaknesses. Like you and I. They can be exploited..." She could see her pep talk was falling flatter and flatter. "Point is—"

"Run along, Blue." Lady Mauve brushed her away. Surprised, we both looked up.

"Where there's a will, there's a way," Lady Blue Moon blurted. "You got this!" Then she scampered away.

My trainer eyed me. "You look like you're cracking."

"Accurate," I said. We both took that in. I didn't look over. "I never finished telling you about my dream. Kate dies, and then everyone tells me I'm not good enough to succeed."

"So prove them wrong." She shrugged. "You want some special pep talk from me? What do I know, Mae? I'm the one who made Rain break her arm. I thought it was a good idea to train without a net. Look how that turned out. You don't need me to pat you on the back, tell you the meaning of your dreams, tell you every-thing's alright. Maybe it's not." We stood in silence, watching the other coven's players. They looked so capable and strong. "It's alright to have doubts," she said. "Fear doesn't mean you don't belong. Chest out, shoulders back. Show them how it's done. You were trained by the best."

I followed her suggestion, bringing my posture ramrod straight. Immediately, I felt a boost in spirit. I projected more capability as well.

"Better," she said. "Don't screw this up."

End of inspiring pep talk.

After that, without anyone's instruction, Silverfox, Rain, and Ferris gathered by my side. To avoid tipping our hand, Rain wore long sleeves that covered her cast. She left her arm out of her sling. She would string her shoulder up again when the battle had begun. We wanted to appear at full strength. Our foursome detached from the clan. The other coven members fell away. On the other side of the field, the other players found themselves isolated as well. We affixed our opponents with a steady stare.

Suddenly, Cornelius Child and the Damocles' blonde leader stepped forward. Their very presence parted the covens. The witches melted back, creating a circle of respect and power around both the leaders. I admired the strength of the woman in red and her tight jawline. While Cornelius's bravado came across as big and barrel-chested, her version of authority was compact and secure.

No one would doubt her rule for even a second.

Her subjects hung on every carefully selected word.

The two leaders gestured behind them, and the covens parted, bringing forth between them the two

Evil Eyes being paraded into the ceremony space. I had never seen an Eye before. The fiery balls glowed hot pink, carried on large cloths by chosen coven members acting like pallbearers. The orbs were too powerful to touch with the human hand. They had to be carted. The covens did so now with all the pomp and circumstance they could muster.

The balls themselves were only slightly larger than a soccer ball. The light emitted from the center of the stones shone on everyone nearby. It would be hard to hide their glowing nature. I wondered if they were heavy to carry around.

With the procession over, the leaders regained the group's attention.

"Welcome, everyone, to the Battle of Four. As agreed, at the start of the contest, both teams will have seven minutes to secure and disperse their own Eyes into hiding," Cornelius announced to the crowd. "The High Council to the south, the Damocles coven to the north."

The other battle members and I adjusted the weight on our heels.

"At the sound of the horns, the battle begins," the woman added next.

All eyes flickered to the two trumpet players, one from each side of the battle. The musicians stood at the ready with their instruments held in their hands.

"The first to retrieve the other coven's Eye and return it here to the farmer's field before us will be declared the victor," she continued.

"We will respect the final result," Cornelius said.

The woman nodded.

Both sides rustled, uneasy. That was simple to say if you were the winning team. Not so easy if you found yourself to be the loser. Even with a safety backup plan. But that was the tenuous agreement.

"Now for the rules," Cornelius droned on. "The Battle of Four commits to the use of each team's four witch contenders, selected by the rival coven. Eight witches total. No other coven member may aid, cast, or guide in the task."

"There will be no grave bodily injury. No murder. No gross injury or mutilation. Respect each other. Respect the value of nature," the red leader added. "The battle has no pause and only one finish. When one team returns with the other's Eye, they will be declared the winner."

"Upon recovery, the results are immediate and final," Cornelius warned. "The winning coven will remain. The losers shall depart. Immediately."

Both leaders nodded.

"I introduce to you," the woman said, changing her tone and holding up an arm to her Damocles team, "Bodhana, Kristoff, Petregaard, and Myrta." Each member of their team stood at attention and at their name waved an enthusiastic greeting. It was clear they were used to being called on as soldiers, part of the red coven's rank and file.

"Representing the High Council," Cornelius

followed. "We have Lady Rain, Fellow Silverfox, and students Mae Kingsley and Ferris Bean."

I was glad to be called near the end of our list, as the others gave a model of how we should behave at our introduction. We each waved at the gathered witches by way of announcing ourselves, although I would have bet big money there wasn't a person in the crowd who didn't know exactly who we were.

"The teams are ready." Cornelius checked with the Damocles leader.

"Ready," she agreed. "It's time to…"

"Begin!" Their voices boomed in tandem.

We had been standing stoically for so long, the sudden invitation into action felt manic. All eight of us rushed forward to pick up the Evil Eyes from the center of the collective, and we immediately headed out in opposite directions, looking to hide ourselves from the view of our competitors. Neither team ventured into the burned-out cornfield on the left. It was imperative to disappear into the safety of the provided forest, work quickly, and get the orb protected. We each grabbed a corner of the fabric carrier and ran through the crowd. The witches parted, and we jogged into the woods behind the living, breathing throng. As soon as we made it into the cover of trees, Ferris threw up a temporary illusion to further hide where we were going. If they didn't know where we started, they wouldn't know where we finished.

"Oh my god, my arm." Rain immediately dropped her corner of the curtain and got the sling she was hiding out of her pocket and threaded it back on her neck. "You don't know this pain," she complained.

"So this is it." Silverfox breathed heavily, tossing his head as he shot back his hair, his usual antics amplified by the stress. "The whole shebang set in motion."

"Quick, give us the real thing," Ferris instructed.

We let go of the four corners and wrapped up the orb in the fabric. Next, we passed off the Evil Eye to her hands. Silverfox pulled his backpack off his shoulders, and we pulled out several decoy balls of fabric and clothing and pink bulbed flashlights. I clicked on the lights. The illuminated source of light we purposefully lit inside. I handed one off to Rain. She cupped it in her good arm.

"Five minutes and counting," Rain warned. "You need to hurry."

But our other decoys weren't yet ready.

"Are you sure you know what you're doing?" she asked us.

"Alright, chill. Stressing won't help anybody." Silverfox tossed his hair again.

"No, she's right," Ferris realized. "Time is slipping away."

"You go, hide the real one. We'll catch up and be fine," I encouraged, still trying to set the second light up correctly in the new clothing swath.

"You might as well. We're not supposed to know where the real orb is at," Silverfox agreed. "Only Rain."

The women exchanged a glance.

"Well, alright." Ferris traded packets with Rain. "Here."

The real orb transferred into the injured woman's hands.

"It's heavy," she complained.

"You have our numbers," Ferris checked.

Rain nodded.

"Keep us posted." I nodded at Rain, trying to give a reassuring smile.

"Fine," she agreed. "Try not to screw things up now I'm gone."

"Go, Ferris," Silverfox encouraged.

"No, I'll stay. Maintain the lie-guard. You two plant your lures. I'll finish here." Ferris took over shoving the final light source into its ball and handed her finished one to me. "When the horn sounds, we meet at the edge of the trees," she told Silverfox.

"Right. Let's move, Mae." He nodded.

Silverfox and I broke off running. We headed in generally the opposite direction from the route Rain took. The idea of the faulty orbs was to draw the other coven away, pull them apart, drag them around. It was a time-buying tactic. Each phony pink orb needed to be spaced far apart.

"Here's good. What do you think?" I asked him, pulling aside a thick bramble. "This looks like a spot."

"Fine. Drop it down," he agreed. "I should have gone with the real eye," he complained, helping me set up the first decoy.

"The Council said the fewer with real knowledge,

the better. That way we can't accidentally lead them to the winning spot. It's a lot of ground to cover."

"I'm on the offensive," he complained. "I won't lead them to squat."

"Okay, but we have to have someone back here who knows where it is," I countered.

"And you're fine with Rain?"

"More than fine."

"Don't you want it to be you?"

"Not even a little," I admitted. I was glad not to know where our Evil Eye truly was. "One less thing to screw up."

He finished setting up the first prop. It looked real, hidden in thick bushes. If the other team saw its warm glow, I felt sure they'd come running.

And when they did, we'd be ready.

I cracked open one of the pouches the chemists had provided and shook it into a wide circle in the path around the decoy ball. Luckily, the granules were a camouflaged shade of brown. The powder would turn the dirt of the nearby forest into a sand trap sinkhole. When the powder evolved, it didn't look like anything was wrong with the natural surroundings, but put one foot on the chemically adapted dirt and you would drop into six feet of sludge in the earth.

Trap number one was complete.

Next, we ran farther to the west.

"We should have synchronized our watches," I murmured. I wasn't sure how exact timing would help us. I was just unable to shake the feeling there was more we could have done.

"That's, like, movie stuff that happens at the cinema." He laughed. "Not witchy-stuff."

"Well, I don't have very much experience with either," I complained. "We don't even know how much time is left."

"Very little," he admitted. "I've got to get back soon. The horn's about to blow, I reckon. This looks good enough for the last front, don't cha think?"

He was right. We'd run far enough. It was a fine decoy spot. The brush here was thick and scratchy, not the kind of thing you'd walk through voluntarily. The trees grew thick around two stumps, making lots of natural cover for hiding out.

We dug a small spot in the thicket beside the first stump and dropped our second fake package in the hole. I propped up the pink flashlight at the right angle to create a soft glow barely seen from outside the bush. Then, I tucked fallen leaves in on all sides.

"Looks good," Silverfox complimented. "Better than the first."

You could see the glow from a short distance but only if you knew what you were looking for.

"Should I make it a little clearer?" I asked.

"Maybe. Just a wee pinch," he agreed.

I slid one more leaf out of the way.

"Stop. Right there. Perfect." He grinned. "Now, set the trap."

Like in the other location, we backed our way out

of the brambles and checked out our work from afar. It was the perfect mix of hidden and plain sight. Any battalion member who spotted it was sure to come running.

But that was what we wanted.

I shook a second potion packet out of my pockets and sprinkled it out in a circle around the decoy's perimeter. Immediately, up sprung a wild and tangly vine on the forest floor.

"These snap ribbons are nasty." Silverfox whistled.

The tentacles immediately snapped and twisted in anticipation. The wild green ribbons were ready to engulf anyone who tried to cross their path. From another pocket, I pulled out a third potion packet. I sprinkled a healthy dose of plant superfood to encourage the thorny, twisty plant to become even more active. Silverfox picked up a dead twig and tossed it across our perimeter. As the thin wood stick passed, several vines sprung up and wrapped their thorny arms around the bark. The ribbons snapped the wood in half. The twigs fell to the ground, ensnared in its leafy grasp.

"You better watch the other side for booby traps," I warned him. "You and Ferris both."

"We'll be fine. Just cover your own butt. Lead the bad guys astray. Don't worry about us." He grinned. Having planted both fake orbs, Silverfox started to relax. He tossed his auburn, wavy hair.

I wished I had his confidence.

"See you at the finish," he told me with a wink.

"Good luck," I agreed. "To both of us."

Just then, above the trees, we heard the trumpets sound. The two musicians battled for musical supremacy. For almost a minute, their instruments belted out a two-part harmony, then silence filled the forest.

The duet signal was over.

The battle had begun.

"Wish us luck," Silverfox said. "Not that we need it."

I glanced at my peer. He didn't notice he was repeating a request for something I'd already given him moments before. Maybe he wasn't as confident as he appeared.

"Good luck, Silverfox."

"We got this!" he told me, shaking both fists in the air.

THIRTY-THREE

ANY SECOND NOW...

SILVERFOX TURNED on his heels and ran north to find Ferris. With no better plan for myself, I watched his exit. As he first departed, his footsteps crashed loudly through the forest, rumbling like an elephant, until the distance between us grew fainter. Then, he traversed softer like an antelope, making his way through the thicket until I could no longer see his bopping, shaggy-haired head. At that point, his footing crackled in the distance, echoing like a warning, mimicking the weight of a woodland creature. Finally, the sounds of his journey disappeared altogether. I was alone with the wind.

The silence was unnerving.

Here I was, entrusted with guarding this forest. I had no idea what I was doing.

In my pant compartments, I fingered my other weapons. I'd set two traps already, but my pockets were still full. I had a sleeping potion, knockout gas, truth serum, and fresh packages of both the sinkhole powder and snap ribbon plants. The last elixir at my disposal was super glue. I decided to walk farther away from the last decoy, not sure exactly what the best plan might be if confronted in the forest, but intent to lead the other coven astray.

The wind in the branches whispered my name. Brandi and other dream voices echoed in my ear.

Mae, you're not enough.

This is what happens when they let losers in.

You're always gonna need our help.

The one who got in by default.

Default. That one wasn't a dream. That girl said it right to my face.

How could someone as sweet and gentle as Beck be related to someone as cruel and ugly as Brandi? If there was ever a time to prove an older girl wrong, this was it. Only trouble was, I had no idea how to do that. My training didn't prepare me for an empty forest full of whispering trees. The landscape groaned in the wind.

I searched the grounds for signs that the Damocles coven might burst in on me at any moment. I knew that wasn't practical; I was already quite far from the open grounds where we started. They'd have to come tearing over the hillside to cover this much ground that quickly. For sure, I would hear a person coming at that speed, running.

For now, it was just me and the trees.

I thought about setting up more random traps in hopes of lucking out and stopping their coven, but the battlegrounds were massive, and the routes through the forest were plentiful. I was better off holding on to my weapons and trying to implement them in live action. At least, that was what I told myself. That was the elders' plan. Still, as I walked alone through the forest, things seemed very different than the strategies developed in the classroom.

I was happy to make use of some of the survival training.

I could easily identify compass directions, using plants as guideposts. I felt pretty confident about where I was in the forest compared to approximately where we'd set up the dummy orbs, and I could even figure out Rain's initial direction. I wondered how she was making out in the forest. With one arm to fight.

On defense, we had several tasks.

The first was to slow the other team down, and if we could, lead them out of the way, never letting them find even the decoys. The second plan was to utilize our set up misdirections, and if they did go after our fake orbs, entrap them in our booby trap snares. Somewhere in the forest, Ferris had set up a third decoy, and Rain had the real Evil Eye safely confined. Her pockets were likely empty. Around the real orb, I knew she would have layered as many traps as she could.

I kept moving.

As a solitary person, I could move pretty quietly through the greenery. The goal to catch and distract the other coven seemed pretty clear in classroom discussion, but now in practice, the land we had to cover seemed overwhelmingly vast. How was I supposed to defend all of it? It was an impossible task. In fact, the field was so big it felt possible I could spend this whole battle simply roaming around, waiting to come across some others, never setting foot into the fray.

The strategy to leave our Evil Eye alone and unguarded in the forest was a bold choice. It could really pay off if the hiding spot was good enough. I hoped Rain's hiding skills would make the others proud.

My feet crunched the dead leaves of the forest. I walked for what felt like forever. Still, nothing crossed my path. I was beginning to fear that maybe I'd ventured too close to the neutral fields, and maybe they'd gotten by me. I was quite far from the decoy orbs. Was it possible the Damocles coven had passed me?

Crack!

A single tree branch snapped in the forest.

I dove behind the closest tree, blood pumping in my ears.

What was that? Did I hear right?

Crack, crack.

Something was moving on my left. Through the forest. I held still and listened.

Crack, crack.

Footsteps. They were coming.

So this was how it felt, to be the hunter. Or the prey.

Crack.

My back scratched against the tree bark. I tried to slow my huffing and puffing.

They were coming.

Had they seen me?

I was pretty sure it was another single person.

Crunching steady in the forest, the Damocles battalion member wasn't even trying to hide their journey. They were coming to get me.

Crack, crack.

They snapped their way through the trees. Their footsteps quickened. I didn't have long to ready myself. I dug into my pockets. Which spell to use?

The High Council should have been clearer in their directions.

It was hard to evaluate the situation with all the adrenaline pumping in my veins. Was it better to attack with a sleeping potion? Or try to stick my foe in place with a glue mixture? Knock them out? Or strike them down? Or, far as we were from any other witches or item of value, was it best to just let them pass?

I was nowhere near an orb, real or decoy.

I could maybe wait and follow them? If they didn't attack me in this hiding place. If they didn't know to pounce.

Crack, crack.

The footsteps grew louder.

No. They were definitely coming. I leaned further

into the tree, trying to hide more of my body. Trying to regulate my breathing. I decided I would let the Fates guide my choice. I closed my eyes and dug my hand into my pocket without looking and felt around for the pouch that felt the most like it was divine intervention. I pulled it out of my pocket and opened my squinted eyes.

Knockout potion.

Well, alright.

I would hit them with unconsciousness. Then, while they slept, I could sprinkle the ground with the sinkhole sludge to further slow them in the trap.

A two-pronged approach.

I felt ready. Ready as I'd ever be.

They shuffled closer.

I closed my eyes, trying to catch my breath, which I suddenly realized was heaving in my chest. Any second now, they'd be on top of me.

I gripped the potion.

Any second and I'd attack...

THIRTY-FOUR

PLEASE FORGIVE ME

THIRTY PACES.

I could hear them coming.

Twenty.

I listened to the steady footsteps of the person hunting me down.

They must have seen me when they first entered the forest. I'd dropped down too late, and they'd pinned me to this trunk. But they weren't expecting that I'd be ready. A weird calm came over me.

Bring it on, I thought.

Fifteen paces.

I undid the tie from the top of the pouch of knockout potion, opened the chemicals, and readied the bomb in my hands.

Ten paces.

I twisted the package, ready to throw it.

Five paces.

This was it. This was the moment.

Four.

Three.

Two.

One.

I leapt to my feet and spun out into the open, hurling my package. My combatant countered, immediately launching a package towards me also. I tried to jump out of the way, but the bundle burst at my feet. Almost immediately, a sludge developed around me. The ground grew muddy and slick.

"Mae, what the hell!" Rain shouted. She was covered in knockout powder. Coughing, she dragged the granules out of her eyes and shook them onto the ground.

"Rain?" I tried to move towards her but slipped and fell in the slop.

In response, she let out more coughing.

The ground was too wet. This consistency was wrong. It wasn't natural. Definitely caused by a spell.

"Rain, what did you throw?" I asked.

But my teammate couldn't answer. Instead, her eyes rolled back in her head. She keeled over backward, landing heavily in a face-up heap on the ground.

"Rain! Oh god." I tried to run towards her, but the mud under my feet was slick like molasses. Thick and stubborn. It sucked me back in, pulling my feet deeper. "Rain, I'm coming." I tried to reach her, but every inch I hastened forward only furthered my descent into the sludge. "What is this? Quicksand?"

I didn't have any quicksand potions in my pockets.

A sinkhole package, but the High Council leaders must have given us different potions to use on the land. And all without a single antidote. They never imagined we'd use them on each other.

"Rain!" I tried to use my voice to revive her. "Rain, wake up!"

She was totally out cold.

I could feel my ankles sinking deeper. I needed to move forward. I had to get out of the muck. The deeper I sank, the less I'd be mobile. I reached out and snapped off a nearby dead branch.

"Rain," I called, poking her with the end of the stick. I wiggled her clothes, tapped her forehead, jabbed at her leg, but nothing stirred her.

With or without my movement, the ground beneath me continued to sink. Soon, I was up to my calves.

"Come on, Rain. Wakey-wakey." I poked and prodded, but the stick wasn't big enough to really move her limbs.

I looked around.

Behind me was a bigger, leafier branch. Maybe I could tickle her with it and wake her up with that. I'd seen that work when other people were sleeping. Making them itch or making them laugh. I twisted around in my muddy restraints and reached out to grab the plant. In my fingertips, I grasped it. I yanked it towards me, hoping to strip the leaves as well as a branch. The tree was still living, and its bark was far more forgiving. The leaves bowed in my direction, but the branch wouldn't rip. It simply bent. I tugged the tree towards me, but the branch held firm. I needed to yank it. I'd have to pull it from its roots if I was to use it to wake her up.

I gathered myself and redoubled my efforts, jerking on the fresh limb as hard as I could.

Rip!

The branch sliced away from its tree roots, snapping back in my grasp. I couldn't hold its sudden release in my momentum, and together, branch and body, we both fell back in the muck.

Splat.

"No!" I immediately yanked one arm free of the quicksand. But that squirm made my position much worse. I'd fallen on my side, with one hand catching the weight of my body. That palm and my waist were now totally submerged. The mud hole tugged me further. My legs were totally suctioned in. The pressure dragging them deeper was almost more than I could bear. Only one hand and arm were still free to move around above captivity. The other arm was sunk in deep in the mud with my legs.

There was no pulling them out again.

"Rain!" I called again, now more frantically than before.

I could feel my body sinking.

If she didn't wake up soon, I just wouldn't be found. I'd be buried in this muddy concoction beside my unconscious teammate. I didn't want to go out like that.

"Rain, wake up."

The lady didn't stir.

I looked around. "Rain, come on."

The leafy branch I'd fought so hard to free had been sucked into the quagmire with the rest of my limbs. The only thing still at my disposal was the thin, dead tree branch I started with. I picked it back up.

"Rain." I poked at her body, raising the intensity of my prodding.

The mud was almost up to my breasts.

"You've got to wake up, Rain. Open your eyes," I told her. "Open up. You've got to see me."

My pokes became thrusts as I jabbed the stick into her side, but still nothing budged her.

The mud inched towards my chin. It was nearing my clavicle. Sucking me under.

"Rain," I begged.

How to awaken the woman I'd drugged to unconsciousness?

I looked at her slinged-up shoulder. Her broken arm had fallen face up, sitting atop her listless body, all safely tucked inside its cast.

People sometimes woke at the shock of great injury...

I'm sure the bones in her arm were quite tender. It might be the only chance I had left.

"I'm sorry to do this," I murmured. "I'm so sorry."

I mustered all my energy, staring intently at her cast. If I didn't do it now, I would be trapped in the sludge forever. There wasn't another way out. I reeled the jagged tree branch back.

"Rain." I frowned. "Please forgive me."

Then, I pelted the wooden stick down on her broken arm.

Thwack!

THIRTY-FIVE

THEY'RE COMING

"AHHHHHHH!"

Rain's scream was so loud, flocks of nearby birds left their perches and took flight. The agony echoed through the trees.

If the Damocles coven didn't know where we were before, they did now.

"Oh my god, oh my god." Rain curled up and tucked her throbbing arm to her body.

"Rain! You're back." I threw the branch to the side.

"Mae, what the hell?!" Rain hunched over in pain. "What the hell did you do? Ow. Oh, my arm."

"Rain, I need your help."

The mud was up to my shoulders now. I'd managed to keep one arm free, but soon the sludge would suck me in completely. My head perched dangerously above the muck. I couldn't hold on for much longer.

"I can't believe you hit me. In my arm. My bad arm!" She rocked in the fetal position.

"Rain, please, look up. Please, look at me."

Finally, she did, wiping the tears from her face.

"Oh my gosh, Mae. What are you doing?"

"You hit me with some sort of sludge magic," I told her, jarring her memory. My face was dangerously close to submersion. "It's like quicksand."

"It's a mud sandwich." She nodded, calling it the colloquial term given by chemists. For a moment, her bad arm was forgotten, and she got to her feet. She quickly found a thick felled tree limb, much larger than my poking stick, and held it out to me. "Hold on to this."

I did my best with my free hand to grab the branch she was offering me, keeping my face above the dirt.

"Come on." With her one good arm and my one free hand, Rain pulled the branch back, inching me forward, out of the ground. "Come on," she muttered. The simple refrain urged her again. "Come on," she said. Inch by inch, she dragged me out, unglued my body, and yanked me free of the dirt. "Come on." She gave one final effort, mooring my body on the side of the quicksand hole. Then, with my weight safely back on solid ground, I was able to pull my legs and feet out by myself. My shoes made a final smacking sound as I pulled them out of their trap.

Rain and I collapsed, exhausted, on the leafy ground.

"Thanks," I said.

"You're welcome."

For a moment, we lay side by side, breathing together.

"How's your arm?" I checked in after my heart rate had slowed.

"It hurts. A lot."

"I'm sorry I hit you."

"I guess since you almost died, it's fine." She frowned. "But it hurts. And not a little. It shouldn't cause me pain just to save your life," she admonished.

I nodded and let her have that.

"Did I break through the cast?"

"No." She showed me her arm. "It's still good. But a little cracked."

"Ouch," I agreed, looking closer.

Rain's whole forearm was wrapped up in white plaster; the cast's reach came down over her fingers. She rotated it slightly, the only mobility left in her hand. On the underside, I could see the plaster also wrapped under her fingers, cutting a path between her thumb and her palm.

"I can't harness," she told me. She tried to wiggle her appendages and barely made them flicker. Her face registered the pain the inflection could cause.

I nodded. "Does it hurt?"

"Of course it hurts. Mae, it's broken." She rolled her eyes. "In two places."

"Right, of course. What was I thinking?"

"Well, you weren't. That's the issue."

Crack. Crack.

My ears perked up. Something was coming. Still at a distance. Like woodland creature.

"Did you hear that?"

Crack.

Someone was coming.

Crack, crack. Crack.

Someones were coming.

Moving very fast.

"We've got to go," I said. "Can you move it?"

"It's my arm, Mae. Not my legs."

Crack, crack. Crack.

"Good. Cuz they're coming."

We got up to our feet.

There they were, running straight at us. Two curly blonde-haired, blue-eyed competitors. They had clearly heard Rain's shouts and decided the best offense was to come right out and attack.

Both Rain and I started running.

"How'd they know where to find us?" Rain wondered. I didn't bother to tell her that in her anguish, she'd let out a howl. Pushing blame wouldn't help us escape.

I glanced over my shoulder and saw a man and woman. Both quite a bit older. They were lithe and quick in the forest. Clearly, they'd made their way through vegetation before. They were gaining on our momentum.

"What should we do?" I checked my pockets as we ran.

Waiting 'til the last minute and attempting a

surprise bombing had resulted in a specific form of mutual destruction, but, with the other team upon us, what else could we do?

I could hear them coming closer.

"What spells do you still have to use?" Rain asked.

"I could dribble out my sinkhole powder," I realized.

"Do it."

Not slowing, I dug out the package. I struggled to open the sealed tie as we ran. Then I dribbled the chemicals behind me, sprinkling them in my rear view like breadcrumbs.

I could hear the others breathing heavily as they came for us.

"It's working!" I realized when, for a moment, the heavy breathing drifted away.

I peeked over my shoulder. I was right.

The others had stopped in their tracks to avoid the slick and messy crevice I'd created. Instead, a Damocles coven member dropped an arm and balled his fist.

"Oh no. Incoming!" I shouted to warn Rain.

Suddenly, the ground shuddered, letting out an awful stutter as it split open and shot across the tree-rooted path. A dramatic fissure opened, splitting the earth, slicing the forest in half.

"Watch out!" I shouted.

Rain and I both dodged to opposite sides of the crevice.

"He's a ground harness." Rain pointed out the obvious. "Sloppy earthquake. If I didn't have this broken paw, I'd show him how it's really done."

I didn't have the energy to warn her; he was doing pretty well all on his own.

"Split up!" I instructed. Lady Mauve's words stuck in my brain. In the event of an attack, divide and conquer. Make the spread between you and the other as large as you can.

I threaded myself through the trees, holding my breath, wondering when the ground beneath my feet would open up and swallow me whole. But the killer fissure didn't come.

I ducked behind a tree, huffing and puffing.

The Damocles harness could only focus his attack on one person, and I wasn't it. He'd locked on to Rain. She was racing forward, desperate to keep ahead of the earthquake's splitting ground. The earth rocked and rolled us.

"No, you don't," I murmured, working hard to stay on my feet, doubling back the way I'd come.

The tremors shook the vegetation, but they were loud and cumbersome. Over the seismic division he was making in the forest, the sound of my coming footsteps was totally lost.

I couldn't see the second Damocles competitor, but it didn't matter. Stopping the harness was priority one. Rain couldn't run from his tremors forever, and if she fell in a crevasse, she'd break more than her arm. He had to be stopped.

I grew closer to the earth-empath.

He was completely involved in his cat and mouse game with Rain.

I picked up a nearby tree branch, loaded it over my shoulder, and swung it like a bat.

Thwack!

I hit him across the back. The earth-harness man fell forward like a sack of bricks, his energy immediately undone. Rain jumped to safety.

I dug my hand into my bag. I grabbed a sock full of chemicals, intent to dump it on their man, when something whistled up in the trees.

I looked up, surprised.

The second Damocles player was perched just above me, waiting. "Bout time you saved her." She motioned to Rain. The earth-harness looked up from his spot on his hands and knees and grinned.

I realized all too late I had fallen into a trap.

"No, wait." I yanked a pouch out of my pocket. I still had a chemical bomb to unfurl but could only launch it off at one of their players. Who to hurl it at? Already, the tree-top girl was sprinkling a spell on top of me. I aimed to throw it in her direction, but her spell had already begun to work.

"You can't do this," I warned them. "No. I won't let you."

The world grew hazy.

I tumbled, then pitched forward.

The rough forest floor came up to meet me, and my face smashed into the ground.

THIRTY-SIX

FACE THE TRUTH

THE DREAM WORLD TOOK OVER.

I opened my eyes to find myself high off the ground. A breeze whipped my hair. The tendrils dragged across my face, but I pulled my cheeks free from the wind. The sunset around me glowed a stunning shade of pink. I was above the trees and the fields. Here, there was nothing to obstruct the view or the wind. I looked out over the field. I'd seen this view before. Where was it? I was so high up. The angle made me nervous.

"I'm coming down!" I shouted.

"You'd be no use," Josie told me from the ground, shaking her head.

"She's no use up there," Greg countered. He laughed, and it echoed through a large witchy crowd.

The faceless coven murmured. I could see them off in the distance.

Judging me.

Judging my skills.

Greg's voice was loud and clear, but he was miles from where I stood.

"You need help," Josie stated.

"A lot of it," Aunt Abeline agreed.

"Aunt Abeline, you too?"

"You're not a great witch." My aunt shrugged. "It's a family affair."

"My mom was a champion," I told them. They circled underneath my feet like sharks.

"Your mother is dead," Josie said.

The wind whipped my hair. New danger was approaching. I felt it. It seemed to slither in my hair. But that was just the wind. Tickling my shoulders.

"I'm doing my best," I told them.

"It's not good enough," Josie said.

"You're not a great witch, Mae," Aunt Abeline repeated. "You can't do it alone."

"Face the truth," Josie said.

A loud bell chimed in my head, ringing to my core. I tried to shield my ears.

"You're not a good witch."

"Face the truth."

Their refrains drifted away on the wind.

"Mae, wake up."

THIRTY-SEVEN

ALONE IN THE FOREST AGAIN

"MAE." Ferris patted my face with water. "Wake up. You're alright."

My eyes fluttered open, and I sat up from the forest floor.

My head pounded in a chemical-induced haze. Everything felt fuzzy. I touched my forehead and looked down at the muddy residue still covering my arms and legs. "What happened?"

"You tell me." Ferris looked concerned. "You and the other coven seemed to have some sort of run-in. They knocked you out with something."

Suddenly, it all came back.

Rain.

The quicksand.

Their earth-harness. The Damocles trap.

"Lady Rain," I said worriedly.

"You were together?" Ferris pulled me to my feet.

I nodded. "Where is she? And Silverfox?" I looked around for our other partners.

"I haven't seen her. He's hot on her path." She motioned to the trees and the route the others might have taken. That was the last direction I'd seen her in before the world came crashing to silent surrender. I could still see the cracks in the earth.

"They might have caught her, I—They knocked me out." I felt afraid, suddenly wanting to go in several directions. The hair on my arms stood up. I had a grave desire to start moving. My whole body felt anxious.

"Slow down. You're okay where you are," Ferris assured me.

"We should call her. We've got to find her. Help her to safety." I patted my pockets. "Oh my god. All my stuff!"

It was all gone.

Of course.

When I'd fallen unconscious, the Damocles witches had stripped me of all my potions and belongings. They could use them now against us if they could figure out what each of them was. I was seriously glad I hadn't labeled them. But maybe they wouldn't bother to worry about it, they'd just attack and see what happened.

"They took them. They took everything."

Ferris didn't seem that worried. "I'd expect nothing less," she agreed. "It's what I would have done."

"Why aren't you more upset about this? Think of

Ethan. Rain is out there," I shouted. "We have to see that she'll be safe."

"She is. Relax. She will be."

"What if she tells them the spot?"

"The spot?"

"You know, the location of... the orb." I felt weird even saying it.

"She won't. I told you, Silverfox is tracking her." She tried to calm me.

"I didn't know he could do that."

"Me neither, but I guess he can." Ferris chuckled. Without speaking, we started walking. It felt better to be moving.

"We should still call her. Call them both," I instructed. "Meet all together. The other team is fighting in patterns; we should use our numbers to our advantage as well. Where's your cell?"

Ferris reached down behind me. "What the... Look." She stooped and dug into the leafy ground. "Look what's been left!" She picked up my cell phone. "In their haste, they must have dropped it."

"Oh, thank god." I grabbed it from her and opened the lock.

"Okay," Ferris nodded. "You call Rain. We'll all meet up. That's a smart plan."Strange. The signal was dead.

For sure I charged my phone this morning.

There was no way I would have come to the battle without it, and I distinctly remembered entering in all the other battalion members' contact information to a full charge. It was working perfectly then.

But now, nothing responded?

"Shoot," I murmured. "My battery is dead."

There was only one other time when I'd had trouble with signals performing.

It was out in a cornfield.

In the midst of Spade's lie-guard.

"Oh, rats." She seemed disappointed.

I flashed the phone her way as if trying to show her proof, but the screen was just black. My mind was reeling. Where was the lie-guard illusion? There was something very off about this conversation. I couldn't put my finger on it, but...

"You can still call," I offered. "Right? We programmed our numbers this morning."

"No, I lost it. My cell phone. Damn thing slipped out of my pocket as I was running." Ferris shook her head.

"So the two of us are lost in the forest, and there's not a working phone between us."

"Yeah. What are the chances? What a bunch of bad luck," she agreed. "It's the kind of thing they warn hikers to be wary of."

"Such a bad break when we only have to save the whole tribe."

"Heh, that's funny."

An awkward silence grew between us. In quiet, we marched through the forest. This whole conversation with Ferris was weird. She wasn't the type of girl to just lose something and ignore it. She was a woman of action. And she wasn't acting here... Was it possible that...

The hair on my arms stood on end.

Suddenly, I felt certain. *Ferris* was the lie-guard. The girl by my side wasn't really my friend. I'd seen this before, someone masquerading as another person. Using a lie-guard. Creating the illusion. It almost always fell flat in minutes. And this one had gone on for too long to stay convincing.

I bristled.

The smart play here would be to extend the con, use this knowledge to my advantage. But I just couldn't hold my reaction in check. Already, my face was twisting to anger. How dare they try to manipulate me with my friends.

"Everything alright?" the fake Ferris wondered.

"Everything's great." I shoved the girl into the stagnant pond we were passing and took off running the opposite way.

"Stop!" she shouted.

But I didn't stop running.

Argh!

She grunted as she hurled a sack of potion at me, but it only nicked my fingers and knocked my cell phone out of my hands. The little device went flying.

"Damn it." I raced onwards.

There was no time to go back and grab it.

Her next attack would be coming momentarily. There was no more use pretending she and I were

High Council friends. Over my shoulder, I saw the illusion evaporate. The fake Ferris transformed back into the blonde Damocles player as she rose from the pond.

I raced forward.

"She's escaping." Her partner jumped out from nowhere, pumping his hand into a fist at his side to start another earthquake, but the woman stopped him.

"Petregaard, don't bother." She stopped him.

Two other coven members stepped out of hiding as well. They watched me run.

"Save your strength for a real battle," their leader told them. "She's a dream-cast without any weapons. We're looking for the other one. They call her Rain." The woman spit on the ground as if she didn't even like the taste of the name.

"You sure?" a third coven member asked her.

The fake Ferris nodded. "Mud-girl gave it away."

"Well, *she* went that way." The last coven member pointed in the other direction.

"Let's go."

The four Damocles coven members ran off the way Rain had gone.

I crashed through several more branches. But soon it was clear, they had meant what they said. They weren't coming to get me.

And why would they? They had already gleaned all my information.

I didn't know more.

I didn't *have* more.

It was Rain they needed to find.

I kept running blindly, not sure where I was headed.

My foot caught in a root, and it kicked out beneath me. My body splattered onto the dirt. A dust cloud coughed up. I spun around, ready for anything, but it was just me and the tree-rooted path.

I was alone in the forest again.

THIRTY-EIGHT

TOO LITTLE TOO LATE

FOR A MOMENT, I stayed down, ducking my head for cover, listening to the blood pump in my ears. My breath heaved in my chest.

They let me go.

Let me escape them.

I'd already given them all I could offer. I was no use.

Damn.

Their lie-guard hadn't worked for long. I'd figured out their manipulation, but too late. Not before divulging our only secret.

They didn't need to hunt the forest to find our Eye.

They could simply find Rain.

Trick her into divulging the truth.

Or force her.

I shuddered.

I'd put a huge target on her back. And Lady Rain had no clue that they were coming her way.

It might only take minutes.

I had to warn the others...

My phone.

It hadn't worked during their illusion, but now that it was over, I bet the signal would connect again. Perhaps I could get out word.

If the Damocles witches didn't take it.

The fake Ferris's potion bomb had smashed my device out of my fingers. I had run too far too fast to see where it landed, but I could go back and retrace my steps.

I picked myself up and jogged the same route I'd just escaped through. It was easy to spot the pond I'd shoved the girl into. There was still a woman-sized imprint of hands and a butt in the sludge. After that, I had run in this direction. I turned and retraced. It was about here when fake Ferris had smacked the phone out of my hand, I noted.

I looked around.

There was no way that they'd left it.

Was there?

They'd run fairly quickly. Was it possible they believed what I'd said? That in fact it was a dead cell phone, the battery depleted?

A dead phone wouldn't be of help to anyone out here.

Please, god, let it be here.

I kicked at the leaves on the ground.

Silently, I wished I'd been more girly and dressed up my phone in a safety cover of vibrant, pastel colors. Or anything, really, to help it stick out from the ground.

At first glance, I couldn't see anything.

But it didn't matter. I would search all night if I had to.

I dug through the leaves and detritus, searching for the phone I feared was already gone.

THIRTY-NINE
AN UNINTENDED CONSEQUENCE

SUDDENLY, I saw it.

A metallic corner.

Its man-made edges were almost completely hidden in the organic matter it currently called home. I shoved my hand into the decaying slop but instead of brushing away, the leaves snapped back.

A vicious plant tried to snatch me.

Its thorns left several ugly red slices on the back of my hand.

I pulled my fingers back just in time.

The potion they'd thrown. It was the snap ribbon plant spell.

My phone had been covered in it. An unintended consequence that would serve the other coven well. The device was guarded by the tendrils of a green, angry foe. But the roots were still forming. It hadn't had a chance to really dig in the ground. Still, I couldn't reach through it. The plant would attack and destroy.

I tried to remember back to what my training had taught me.

Snap ribbons clamped on whatever moved above them, twisted and snapped until they cut cleanly through. I dropped a twig above them and watched as the talons came out. In seconds it had wrapped its thorny tendrils around the wood tester. The green claws pinched so tightly they snapped the thin wood in half.

They could do that to a human too.

That was why the other coven hadn't bothered to pick it up.

To rescue a dead phone from the snap ribbon plant didn't seem worth the effort. Only I knew the device wasn't actually dead. The battery would work fine if I could just get it back in my hands.

I surveyed the area.

There was a nearby splintered tree whose trunk had been split apart in bad weather. I ran over and yanked off a thick chunk of bark.

If the snap ribbons attached to anything above them, I would have to go under them. I used the heavy bark to dig like a shovel and burrowed into the ground. I made a good-sized hole beside the ribbons, then levered the bark at the edge of the plot. I put the tip of the tree husk at the root of the plant. With a flicking motion, I launched the green growth off of the ground.

I jerked the snap ribbons away from their new home, flinging them in the opposite direction, shoveling the whole bunch together, roots and all. Once clear, I dug my hand in the leaves below and pulled out my phone. The case was scratched and muddy, but the device itself survived the bounce and fall. I threw open the home screen.

Success.

The service reconnected.

I dialed Rain's number and watched my service provider respond.

Come on.

The Damocles coven had a large lead now.

Leaving this phone behind was their first big mistake. I had to make them pay.

Come on, Rain. Pick up.

The phone rang and rang. Then her slightly robotic voice came through.

"This is Rain's voicemail. Please text. No one calls." Her judgy voice hung up the line.

No.

I immediately hung up and dialed again.

Come on, Rain. Come on.

Without even realizing, I'd started marching forward, headed to join the battle, following the other coven. Desperate to help my own battalion.

Come on, Rain. Pick up.

"This is Rain's—"

"Damn it!" I hung up the call.

· · ·

Trouble's coming. CALL ME.

I texted in all caps.

Then I flipped through my contacts to call Ferris. I smashed my finger on her contact. The phone started to ring.

Come on. Pick up, I willed the second girl.

"Mae, what is it? Are you alright?" Ferris answered, immediately on high alert. A wave of relief washed through me, but I wouldn't be fooled again.

"Who is this?"

"What do you mean? It's Ferris."

"Prove it," I instructed.

"Mae, you called me—"

"Prove it!" I shouted.

"Fine. My boyfriend is Ethan. We both hate Brandi."

I shook my head. "Be more specific."

"I saved you in the training with a mat just when you needed it," she said.

"The mat was blue. Then you told me about your introduction to the High Council," I replied back to prove my own identity as well. "Don't trust anyone you see or hear. They impersonate with their illusions. They're all together. And," I said, trying to get out as many details as possible, "they're headed after Rain."

"What? All of them?"

"Yes. I think." I didn't want to say for sure. That

was what I'd heard. It looked that way. But it could be another lie-guard manipulation, I realized. "Enough of them," I guessed.

"It's Mae," Ferris told Silverfox on their end.

"What? Why? What's going on?" I heard him ask over her shoulder.

"Mae, Silverfox is here, you're on speaker," Ferris clarified. "How do you know they're chasing her?"

"I said she knows where it is. The orb. I didn't mean to. They tricked me." I wanted to offer more of an apology, but the others jumped in.

"What?!" Silverfox fumed.

"They tricked me," I repeated.

"Well, try and stop them, girl. Use whatever you got."

"It's all gone," I admitted. "They knocked me out and took everything. All my spells. My potions. They took it all. I tried calling, but she's not answering." Admitting one stupid act after another, I felt worse and worse. "She's not with you?"

"No, she's not with us!" Silverfox roared.

"We're on our way," Ferris said.

I could hear them both start running. Like elephants, they crashed through the trees.

"What should I do? Come to you? Call her name? Shout out loud?"

The phone shifted and sidled, jostling with their rhythm, but suddenly, Silverfox's voice came through very clearly. "Do nothing, Mae. Absolutely nothing. You've already done plenty. More than your share."

Click.

The phone went dead.

FORTY

YOU'VE ALREADY DONE PLENTY

"THIS IS RAIN'S VOICEMAIL. PLEASE—"

"Damn it." I hung up again. She still wasn't answering, although now I was sure that both Ferris and Silverfox would also be calling her line. Somewhere in the forest, they were crashing through the branches, trying to get to our teammate before the other coven members could tear her apart.

And they didn't want me coming.

I'd already done enough.

More than my share.

Those were Silverfox's words. And he was right.

I called her again.

"This is Rain's—"

"Argh!" I shouted into the air.

To Rain, I wrote the clearest text warning I could think of just in case she could see her device but couldn't answer. That way she would clearly know what was happening and either text me back or call.

. . .

Don't trust anyone.

They can use lie-guards to mimic our team.

They know you have the orb.

The message sent.

I thought that would make me feel better, but it didn't.

This was always my fear. I was a terrible witch. And a terrible battalion member. Brandi was right. I was a default selection. I had defaulted my way right onto the field. This was Josie's place. It was she who should have been here today. Josie would know what to do.

"Rain!" I shouted to the treetops.

But even that felt wrong.

You've already done plenty.

Silverfox's words rattled in my brain.

I stopped in my tracks. What if my yelling somehow made things a little worse? Or... I couldn't say how, but what if staying silent created some new terrible thing for the coven? The not knowing was unbearable. Should I act? Or stay immobile? Either way there could be payment and cost. I felt totally lost.

Some witch I'd become.

When my mom graced the ranks of the High Council, she was at the top of the coven, winning championships, leading the charge, and here I was... lost in the woods.

Alone in a forest without any powers or plans.

Even my dreams told me to be ashamed of what I'd become. Over and over. I was a dream-cast who repeated a nightly mantra of shortcomings.

Face the truth, my dreams told me.

I wasn't a good enough witch, Aunt Abeline told me.

Not on my own, Josie told me.

All of them told me. Again and again. I just couldn't do this on my own.

At this point, our battalion wasn't even looking for the Damocles trophy. Their Evil Eye wasn't at any risk to be found. Ferris and Silverfox had no choice but to come back, try to find Lady Rain, and provide her with safety. To protect what was ours.

I felt so low.

Unmoored.

But to stay completely still would drive me mad.

I began to walk forward. I had no idea where I was going or which way to journey to find the rest of the tribe.

If only I was high up, like I'd been in my vision.

Up in the tower, I could see the whole forest. All the trees. The corn. The covens. I could head towards the town. It was the Orson Bell tower, I realized.

That was the view I'd witnessed in the last vision.

I had never been up there, but I'd seen that very

same angle from someone else, looking out. They'd taken that photo.

Mom.

A view from the top, was the caption.

I was sure of it. In my mind, I'd seen the view from the Orson Bell.

That was odd.

Why had my memory incorporated that landscape into my vision?

I knelt low and felt for moss on an outcropping. Moss grew on the north side of the stones, I remembered. I pointed north to get my bearings. The tower was that way. I couldn't see it through the forest, but I knew it was there. Rising high in the field. Between the two covens.

Had I subconsciously been there? Yes... and also, Greg... and so were the covens. In my dream.

Greg had insulted me, and he was definitely in the field.

I tried to remember exactly what he told me.

Aunt Abeline and Josie were by me, by the tower, but the other witches were farther back, standing out in the field. They were waiting for something to happen, for one of the battalions to appear... with the Eye.

My eyes widened.

Since the battle had started, I'd been having the same nightmares over and over.

"You need help," time and again, dream Josie had stated.

"A lot of it," dream Aunt Abeline agreed. "You're

not a great witch," she'd told me. "You can't do it alone."

Face the truth.

You can't do it alone.

Again and again, they'd made the same awful statements. But what if they weren't indictments of my witch powers? What if my dream friends were telling me instructions? What if the insults were actually telling me what to do?

Face the truth.

You need help.

You can't do it alone.

FORTY-ONE
A NEW PLAN

I MARCHED FORWARD SLOWLY at first, then gained momentum. Next thing I knew, I was jogging, then running full speed. As I raced, I dialed Ferris's number.

"Pick up..." I begged.

But no one answered.

So next, I called Silverfox.

Then Rain.

"This is Rain's voicemail. Please—"

Where they were in the forest and what they were doing was impossible to say.

It could be they were fighting through a lie-guard, and their phones had no signal. It could be they were screening me out because it was easier than hearing what I had to say. Maybe they were too busy battling an earthquake from the Damocles harness. I couldn't wait for their answers.

. . .

Orson Bell. Please come.

To all three, I sent the text.

I had a new plan.

But even if my other partners never answered, I wouldn't have to enact it alone.

I dialed another number from my contact list.

"Hello?"

I almost wept at her answer. *Hello.* It was so simple. So generous. To my ears, it floated like a beautiful melody. I was so tired of being stranded.

"Aunt Abeline, it's me. Mae," I told her, trying to mitigate my huffing and puffing.

"Is everything okay? You sound out of breath."

"Yeah, everything's fine. Or it will be. Just don't ask too many questions. We both know there are things I can't say, but..." I leapt over a fallen tree trunk, landing barely beyond it with a thud.

Even with a plan, I still wasn't graceful.

I took a deep breath and steeled my resolve. "Aunt Abeline, I could really use your help."

For a moment, there was silence.

"Whatever you need," she agreed. "What can I do?"

"Meet me at the Orson Bell. You know where that is?"

"I do."

"Good. Fast as possible. Please." I added the last

word at the last minute, trying and failing to soften the request. Trying and failing not to scare her.

"I'm on my way. You be safe."

"I will." I hung up. And pulled up in the forest. I let my finger scroll the contact list again. There was one more person to call.

Face the truth.

I clicked the number. This time, my call was answered right away.

"This is Josie." Her straightforward delivery caused a lump in my throat.

"I need help," was all I could say.

FORTY-TWO

THE STONE AND MORTAR TOWER

BOTH WOMEN DROVE to the tower while I ran my way through the trees. There was no way to tell how deep in the forest I had gone at the start of the battle. I wasn't even certain the swath I cut now would double back straight to the field. But eventually, it would lead to the bell. I was navigating my route by the growth of mossy outcroppings. Still, I felt confident I was moving in the right general direction. I knew I'd find more guidance and cues as I got closer to the field.

The women would be waiting for me.

I just hoped my interpretation was correct. I'd been having the same awful dreams, over and over. Everyone I met in my mind gave me a similar tune.

Face the truth.

You're not a good witch.

You can't do this on your own.

If they weren't insults, they were instructions. My dreams all said the same things.

Face the truth.

You can't do it alone.

Now I was hearing what they were telling me. I couldn't do it. Not by myself. They were right. Hence, I called in reinforcements. The rules of the Battle of Four said we couldn't have help from members of the High Council, but Josie and Aunt Abeline were never inducted into the clan. They weren't part of the coven. Asking them for help wouldn't break a single rule.

I ran on.

By the time I could see the field through the trees, I was red-faced and wheezing, sputtering for breath. A stitch pulled the muscles in my side.

There, far up the hill, was the stone and mortar tower.

I could see the large gray bell. And the crumbling brick walls. The place had stood the test of time. I checked my phone for the millionth time, hoping for some news or even a text from Rain or the others. I'd reached out to all my battalion members, but still there was silence on the line. The notification panel of my display sat quiet, and my battery was running low.

Maybe that was their problem too.

It was possible not a single teammate had texted back because their phones were out of power. I had to hope it wasn't because they'd decided my best use as a teammate was to be left, rotting and silent, in a forest. Cold, unmoving, alone. But until they called back or even texted, I wouldn't know what they were thinking. And of course, that wasn't where they'd find me. I was already in action, moving forward on my own.

Through the trees, I could see both the covens waiting near the edge of the forest, hoping for news. The electricity of our send-off had dampened to a mildly curious hum. It had been hours, I guessed, since any of them had even seen a competitor, and their enthusiasm for staring into the empty forest had drained fairly low.

That would all change if anyone spotted me.

I crouched down in the shrubbery and made my way around the edge of the forest. I traveled just out of view of the landscaped opening and snuck my way up the hill towards the bell. As I moved deep in the thicket, I saw my friends. Beck, Sloane, little Hilde, and the others all waiting together. They were chatting, clearly giving opinions. At this point in the mission, were they still loyal? Or had they descended back into gossip, critiquing all of my skills? Probably a little of both, I surmised. With a fair share of flip-flopping in between. Who could blame them? Just wait until they heard about today. Beck wore a worried frown that none of the others could shake.

"This will be over soon," I whispered.

I moved farther west through the brush until the crowd grew small and distant. They were waiting for something to burst out of the forest. No one was focused on the old Orson Bell. Now that I was closer to the tower, I could see my hunch had been right. The tiniest tones of pink protruded from the top of the column. The Damocles' Evil Eye was in the top of the belfry, maybe stuffed inside the bell.

What a genius hiding spot for their Eye.

Keeping it here, visible to the field, meant the other team didn't have to concern themselves with keeping watch on their package. They didn't need both offense and defense. The coven members in the field could clearly see any potential attack as they arose. In code, they could warn their battalion members in the forest, texting some unbreakable message, acting like total innocents, without interfering with the battle rules.

It was a smart play.

I would have to work extra hard not to get caught.

I hunched low, took a deep breath, and emerged from the forest. Small as I could stoop, I scampered across the grassy field. Beside the bell were other old building ruins, like the broken-down walls and foundations of an old church and a manse. Tourists sometimes came to take pictures of the time-tested architecture. Hence all the stanchions. But today, there was nobody there. I hid myself behind the history-drenched stones. I stayed out of the view of the field. The structures had eroded, but the foundations were mostly intact. The only things still fully sound were the tower and the bell. The Orson Bell was still freestanding. The outer stonework was empty of blemishes, but the interior stairwell was no longer safe to climb. The doorway and most of the inside hallway of the tower had long since collapsed.

A car revved its engine as it drove up the gravel

driveway to the ruins, the second vehicle right on its tail. Aunt Abeline and Josie had arrived. So much for keeping a low profile.

"Mae!" My aunt was out of her car first. She clocked Josie in her peripheral but ran to my side. I hunched up against the tower.

"You're here as a tourist," I warned, holding up a hand to slow her down. "And you don't see me. Please, don't approach," I added. I nodded over my shoulder.

My aunt looked down the valley. "What's going on?" She narrowed her eyes.

"We're being watched," I whispered.

"Do you mean by Josie?" Aunt Abeline was confused. My other friend had joined our ranks.

"No, I—" I looked over my shoulder down into the field. Aunt Abeline should have been able to see them, a hundred white-and-red witches. There they all stood, straight out in the field. Was it possible all she saw was cow pies and corn? They must have built a lie-guard to protect the covens from outside observers, I realized. But explaining that fact to my aunt would be breaking the rules. I couldn't explain any magic. "Just trust me when I say we're not alone. You're being observed. Please, act like a tourist. Just start taking photos."

Josie nodded. "Take her at her word."

Aunt Abeline still looked uncertain, but she played along, framing the impressive tower into a tourist's camera frame.

"Did you bring it?" I whispered to Josie. "Everything I asked for?"

"Mm-hmm." She nodded. "I got it all." She doubled back to her car. "A bucket of sticky putty—my own special recipe—a rope to climb up, and a blanket to hold. Just like you requested. Finally, a knife..." Josie raised an eyebrow.

"To cut clothing," I assured her. She didn't have to worry, I wouldn't be stabbing anyone. Josie handed the pieces over. She had used the same sticky putty when we were all trapped in limbo together. I had seen how it worked then, and I felt confident it would hold.

"Thanks. Keep looking touristy," I warned them.

Josie watched me arranging the items. Then she looked more closely at my hand.

"Mithridate?" she read off my arm. I had forgotten all about the key ingredient of my mom's fruitless prescription. I looked down. The word was almost washed from my arm. "I've heard that somewhere," she mused.

"Yeah?"

"In a book or something. I don't know, I'd have to go back."

"What about me, Mae? What's my plan?" Aunt Abeline asked. She had been doing her best to pretend she was a tourist, but seeing Josie's list of items, she frowned. "I didn't bring anything." Unable to see the crowd she was performing for, Aunt Abeline was losing excitement for the ruse.

"That's alright," I assured her. "This will hold?" I asked Josie.

"Only one way to find out." She shrugged.

"Mae, what's going on?" Aunt Abeline's patience had worn thin.

I looked back down the field. The crowd had started to murmur. Witches from both covens had noticed there were visitors at the bell. Whether they'd seen me or not, I didn't know. But the other two were looking less and less like regular tourists.

"Okay, here it is. Aunt Abeline, I need your help. There's something I need to do. But I can't do it myself."

Josie dutifully took up her tourist role, snapping her photos.

Aunt Abeline came closer. "What do you need?"

"You know I can't say... much." My aunt nodded. "But there's something I need you to do. It's kind of a big ask."

"Whatever you want. I can drive you wherever we need to go. We can hop in the car and—"

"It's not that." I took a deep breath. This was it. "Aunt Abeline, I need your powers. I need you to blow the Orson Bell out of the tower and down onto the field below."

Aunt Abeline's eyes bugged out of her head.

But I hadn't told her the worst part. "With me in it."

"Mae, I can't."

"Yes, you can. I believe it."

"I'm not that strong."

"Are you kidding? You and I are cut from the same

cloth," I told her. "A lineage of mighty, kick-ass women."

But Aunt Abeline shook her head. "No, I—"

"It's okay. I know how you feel. All this week, I didn't think I could do it. And I was right. None of us can on our own. But together... we can."

"How do you know?"

I bit my tongue. To tell her the truth would be breaking a law of the coven. "I just know."

"Mae wouldn't ask if she wasn't sure it could be done," Josie told her.

I smiled. It was nice to know there was one person in Plumpkin who really believed in my abilities. I looked over my shoulder and frowned. The time for chatter was over. The gig was up. The women's continued presence at the tower had gone on too long not to be noticed. Some of the coven members were walking over. If we were going to enact the rest of my mission, it was now or never. The warning text to the Damocles coven had likely already been sent.

"I've gotta go. But you can do it." I ran over and hugged my aunt. "Drive out of sight, behind the tree line. Wait for my signal, then... away we go."

"Mae, I—" My aunt stumbled, but Josie took her shoulders.

"You've got this. We've got this," she told the older woman. She led her back to her car. Josie nodded back over her shoulder to me. "Good luck," she mouthed in my direction.

"Thanks," I mouthed back to my friend.

With that, the women went back to their vehicles, and I looked up at my task.

Climbing the tower.

The women drove off. My coven's interest in the Orson Bell might have faltered at their departure, but if I was in the Damocles coven, I'd still send the troops over just to be sure. I didn't have time to waste. I took the rope provided by Josie and tied one end around the bucket. The other I tied around my waist. I'd haul it up once I climbed to the landing. I placed the blanket on the top of the sticky goop in the bucket and tucked the knife in an empty pocket.

It was now or never.

In my dream, I had been at the top of the wall, a breeze blowing my hair. I looked up above me now. The jutting bricks were even smaller than the plastic holds I'd climbed on the rock wall in training, but they were the only grips I had as options, so they would have to do. I tried not to think about the lack of a safety mat.

Climb with your legs, Vince's voice reminded me. *Keep your butt tucked,* he said in my head.

You can do this, I told myself. The view's from the top. You have to get there.

I tested the knot around my waist to be sure. It held strong.

Two Damocles coven members had started to jog up the field.

Time to move.

I kicked off my shoes and socks to get a better grip

on the brickwork, took a deep breath, and put my feet on the wall. Nice and low, I found my first foothold. I put my toes on the ledge and started to climb.

The first few handholds went pretty well. I was able to move quickly. Bend and straighten, I reminded myself over and over again. But two lessons alone were not enough to help me confidently climb the tower.

In the distance, people started yelling. I heard cheering and clapping. The secret was out. Everyone knew I was here. They could see I was climbing. Some witches were torn between whether to cross the grassy knoll to see me up close in action or to stay where they were for a finish line view.

But I couldn't worry about the crowd.

It was the other battalion contestants who had my concern. Any moment, they would return through the forest. Although my team may never have received any of my messages, the other coven members and their field contacts surely did.

I gripped the next foothold on the wall. My fingers were shaking, but still I kept climbing.

Halfway.

Then two-thirds.

Then three-quarters.

I was going to make it! Holy crap. I couldn't believe it.

Vince was right. Leading with my feet and gripping the bricks in bare feet, I was actually climbing. I kept my eyes trained on the ledge above me. It was my goal. My purpose. My salvation.

Until...
It moved.
I looked again. What the hell?
There was definitely something up there moving.
Something almost... slithering.
Oh no.

HISS.

The thing I'd seen, or sort of seen, the something that was undulating, pushed its body over the shoulder of the ledge with a thick, slithery skin. The beady eyes in its diamond head slipped over the edge of the stone platform and looked me right in the face.

Oh no.

It was a snake.

Not just any snake.

A giant serpent. With a slippery belly, a forked tongue, and two titan, sharp fangs. It seethed in my direction, its slithering torso twisting its body up and over layer upon layer of its own awful, scaly, slick skin. Every inch was alive. Undulating. It seemed to be moving in every direction. My knees started to shake.

I clung to the wall.

The whole tower above me was now in motion.

The serpent was so big, its body took up the entire residence.

I looked down.

The field was a good fifteen or twenty feet below me.

I clung to the stones. I wasn't strong enough to climb back down. My only option was to go up, or I guessed I could fall from this level and hope I only broke bones. The crack of Rain's arm crunching as she hit the concrete echoed inside me. But that was better than the reverberating sound of Kate's shattered body in my dreams. My nightmares. My visions.

I couldn't go down.

I had to keep climbing.

I didn't look up. I tried to ignore the sound of the slithering and the sight of the snake's unfolding. For a moment, I did alright. Head down, I found a new foothold and pushed up towards it. Then the snake changed momentum. Instead of slithering back and forth, it turned right towards me. The snake lowered down the side of the tower, rearing up its ugly head. It was coming right for me.

Paralyzed, I breathed shallowly.

It hovered for a moment, its diamond skull floating above me, sizing up my body, then deciding when to strike.

I was trapped.

Its black, beady eyes trained on my skin.

Teeth ready to snap.

FORTY-FOUR
BRACE YOURSELF

"IT'S NOT REAL," I said. "It's not real," my tiny voice whimpered. I lowered my head and glanced at the trees below as the snake let out a hiss. Suddenly, two Damocles battalion members breached the forest. One had her hand clenched in a ball at his side. She was casting the illusion.

"See?" I told myself. "It isn't real. If you don't believe it, it cannot hurt you." But trapped as I was, already hanging off the side of a tower I could barely climb, focusing on breaking a lie-guard illusion was more than I could control. The snake slithered far too close for my comfort.

"Oh my god," I cried. "It's not real..." I squeezed shut my eyes.

The knife!

It was there, inside my pocket. Perhaps I could stab it? Maybe slit its throat?

The thought was tempting, but it was no use. If I

let go of a handhold for even a second, I would never stay up on the bricks. My arms and legs were jello. I couldn't fight a serpent and climb the tower. I was barely hanging on.

Just keep going, I told myself. Just ignore it. It isn't real. It cannot hurt you.

Hiss.

I pushed up with my legs.

The snake coiled back, showing off its fangs.

Just keep climbing. *Oh my god, oh my god.*

Down in the valley, I wished my aunt wasn't here to see me get attacked by a snake. Or fall to my death.

Why had I called her? Why had I drawn her in?

No wonder she and my mother became estranged. My cynical inner voice almost laughed. Witch life was a nightmare.

The snake might have been a lie-guard. But it didn't matter. I couldn't make it disappear. Or what if it wasn't an illusion, I suddenly realized? Maybe that girl was a harness. She might have called it. Maybe the snake was really, truly here.

This giant serpent.

All rage and poison.

Guarding its tower. And I was forcing my way in. But I didn't have an option.

"This is it," I murmured. I had to push forward. I climbed one more handhold. I raised one more grip.

The snake peeled its head back. There it paused. In the moment, it seemed to relish my fear. Sizing me up. Taking me in.

"It's not real!"

The snake lunged, its mouth of dagger teeth open, desperate to sink in my skin.

Crack!

A bolt of lightning singed through the sky and crashed into the head of the serpent. The flash of electricity fried the snake from the inside out. It splattered against the stones, its charred head flopping to the side. A putrid smell of cooked meat filled the air.

Ahhhh!

From below, a woman cried out.

Rain.

"Mae, you can do it!" she screamed, clutching her broken arm. Her cast was destroyed. She had called the lightning strike. Rain had harnessed, despite her injured limb. She had killed the serpent and then collapsed to pieces in the field.

Ferris and Silverfox burst out of the trees!

But they didn't come for me. They ran straight at the Damocles members, intent on stopping their plans. The cavalry had arrived! My text! They all had seen it!

Renewed with vigor, I climbed upwards once more.

I dragged the dead snake off the ledge and pushed myself forward. In three more moves, I slid my shaking torso over the top of the stones.

That was it! I climbed the tower!

Below me, I heard the earth start to rumble. The ground beneath me rocked and rolled. I braced myself and looked down from the ledge of the tower. The

Damocles harness was calling his power. From where he stood, he was harnessing an earthquake, intent on splitting the earth. Ferris and Silverfox went right for him, but what they did next, I didn't have time to watch. On the roof, I dove into action. With the rope around my waist, I pulled up Josie's paste in the bucket. The blanket balanced on top and stayed safe in place. I dragged it up to the top of the tower and turned at once to face the bell. Up here, the Evil Eye shone boldly. The inside of the bell was engulfed in blazing hot pink light.

I turned to shield my eyes and stared out for a moment. A breeze tossed my hair as I took in the view of the town. This was the spot. My mother's view. The place in my dream.

A huge explosion rattled the field.

Whether it was for or against me, I didn't know, but below the battle raged on. Hopefully the others could hold off the Damocles coven long enough for me to complete my mission. I shoved the blanket into the bell and covered the orb. The fabric protected me from its heat and its light. Then, I used the paste to glue the blanket to the bell. Effectively, I sealed the Evil Eye inside. Finally, I used the remaining sludge to paste my own shoes and clothes to the walls of the bell, leaving only one arm free on the side with my pocket, with the knife and my cell phone in grasp.

"Watch your eyes," Silverfox shouted, warning me or possibly others. He let off a huge chemical boom. If he'd created a blinding attack or just deflected someone else's powers, I couldn't be sure, but it was time to signal my aunt.

I called her cell phone. From this viewpoint, I could see them—her and Josie—from their spot over the hill. My aunt picked up, and Josie stood over her shoulder to hear. They put me on speaker.

"Hello? Mae, what's happening?"

"Aunt Abeline. It's time. Do your thing," I whispered, bracing myself for her blast. "Blow the bell."

"I'll try." She handed her phone off to Josie, then stood very still. Her hand balled at her waist.

My hair blew up around my forehead, gusts of wind whipping my tendrils the same way I'd seen in my dreams. Only now, I couldn't brush them away because I'd glued myself down.

"You can do it, Aunt Abeline."

More wind shook the bell and blew around in its insides, but it wasn't strong enough to get the ancient thing to move.

"Get us moving," I encouraged.

"Mae, I told you. I'm not good enough," Aunt Abeline warned me.

Was I wrong? Were my dreams just ugly nightmares? Was there really nothing there? Could it be that the High Council was right about these women? Did Aunt Abeline truly not belong as a witch?

"Mae! Look out. They're coming!" Ferris screamed from below. Whatever techniques she and the others had been trying to implement in the field to keep the other coven from climbing the tower, it was clear they had failed. The Damocles were coming.

"Aunt Abeline... I believe in you." I could hear the others grunt as they scaled up the tower.

Little breezes still trailed around me.

"I'm not enough," my aunt admitted. She was shaking it off.

"Don't say that. Please... oh no." I looked up. Something was coming. "Just hold on."

I saw his eyes first, cold and heartless. Then his body. The first Damocles coven member had climbed the tower. It was a boy I didn't recognize. The blonde guy I'd only seen across the field.

Kristoff, I think they'd called him.

I didn't know his witchy power. And I wasn't keen to learn.

When he saw me, helpless, glued by my own hand, stuck inside the bell tower with only a cell phone in my palm to defend me, a sinister smile appeared.

As he rose to my level, I could see his hand was clenched. He turned over the tower ledge to stand and safely greet me, and a thousand black, hairy spiders followed him over the edge.

"No... It isn't possible. It isn't real," I whispered, clenching my eyes closed.

A million shaggy spider legs pitter-pattered towards me. Ready to crawl up my clothes. In my hair.

"What isn't real?" Aunt Abeline asked me.

My eyes shot open. She was still with me. The cell service wasn't disrupted.

Those things were not a lie-guard!

The boy was an insect-harness. That was ten thousand times worse. He had called thousands of spiders. The creepy crawlers marching forward, skittering across stones, slipping through mortar. I was glued to the bell with nowhere to go.

I put the phone back to my ear. "Aunt Abeline, you *have* to do it."

"Calling for help?" the coven boy snarled. His teeth spread wide in a dark, vicious grin. "You're gonna need it."

"Mae, I can't."

"Believe me, I know how you feel. I feel it too. But it's only fear. Aunt Abeline, I need you. I believe in you. I dreamt you could finish this. I know in my heart that it's possible. I've seen it happen in my brain. If you can't believe in yourself, believe in my talents. Cuz I'm a good witch. And I'm *telling* you, you can do it."

"I don't know…"

The little black monsters swarmed over the bricks. Towards me.

They didn't stop there.

They climbed every surface.

On my legs.

On the bell.

Headed straight for my face.

"Yes, you do. One last push. Are you ready?"

"I'm ready." On the hill across the field, Aunt Abeline steadied herself in her stance.

"Now!"

Suddenly, a huge gust of wind whooshed in from the horizon line.

The bucket with the leftover glue bounced around, driven by the blast of the wind. It kicked up against the stonework and smacked the Damocles coven member in the face. He batted it aside, but the gale toppled him down to his hands and knees. That was just the beginning of the tempest. All around us, the winds picked up speed.

"Brace yourself," I warned him.

The air whirled around until it whipped into a cyclone. The tiny spiders couldn't hold on. They blasted off into the sky. I turned my face and covered my eyes with my one arm still free.

"What the hell is happening?" The Damocles boy fell to the bricks, holding on for dear life, but then he disappeared.

The Orson Bell flew right off of its tower.

Blew clean off!

With me inside!

The giant bell shot across the sky and smashed into the farmer's field below. I held on for dear life, bracing for impact as the metal instrument landed. It bounced across the field. My cell phone went flying. Every impact made Josie's glue start to rip a little. My insides jumbled. The witches scattered in the meadow. The covens raced to safety in both directions.

I hit the ground once... twice... On the third bounce, the bell didn't ricochet back into the air.

Instead, it dug deep into the ground, a cloud of dirt blooming all around.

We had made a giant impact.

Inside, I gritted my teeth as the momentum drove the bell down, until finally, the friction finally brought the whole thing to a halt. We stopped. Motionless.

Me and the bell.

Plopped down on our sides.

For a moment, I was frozen. The incredible impact still bounced in my ears. I couldn't hear above the din. Above all the ringing. The dramatic jolts had already driven most of my arm and legs loose from the sticky putty, but now, at our final destination, I cut the extra material clear. I used Josie's knife to free my clothing. I was dirty, scratched, and shaken, but still in one piece. Behind me, I cut a large circle out of the blanket. The Evil Eye and the remaining fabric fell down, still safely intact at my feet.

We did it.

I crawled forward out of the bell, on hands and knees, dragging the orb out behind me. Stunned, I looked back at the wreckage I'd made of the field. Then I glanced up at the faces of the witches all around me. With one last effort, I dragged the orb forward and left it sitting in front of me. I took a step back and crumpled to my knees.

For a moment, all was quiet.

A hundred eyes stared at me as I hunched over, exhausted. My skin, reflecting off the orb, shone bright pink. Then, suddenly, Cornelius Child's booming voice broke the silence.

"The Battle of Four is over! The High Council Coven is victorious!"

The whole field around me erupted into cheers!

From nowhere, Ferris, the real Ferris, swooped in and enveloped me in a huge embrace. Silverfox and Rain piled on top. Exhausted, I hugged them back and felt the loving encouragement of dozens of other supportive fans.

Rain's arm must have been throbbing, but in that moment, she didn't seem to care. We were all high on the victory.

"You did it!" Ferris said in what felt like a whisper, but in the crazy melee of celebration was probably a shout.

"We all did," I agreed, then I buried my head in their arms.

FORTY-FIVE

YOU SAVED MY LIFE

IT FELT like three thousand people came up to congratulate me or give my shoulders a friendly tap or squeeze. Before my adrenaline wore off, I could barely feel it. I couldn't hear what they said. Not really. The blood still pumped in my ears.

The battle was over.

The High Council was victorious.

After the initial hug, the battalion members were separated and celebrated. My friends and casual onlookers alike gathered around.

"Well done, Mae," Lady Gray and so many others cheered and congratulated. They all sought me out, but there was one face in the crowd that I searched for as well.

"Beck!" It took a while for me to find him, but when I did, it was like a tractor beam called to his arms. I ran straight towards him. His warm arms wrapped

351

around me, but the throng refused to let us stop and enjoy.

"You did it!" he shouted.

"What?!"

"You did it!"

"I can't—" I pointed to my ears.

He laughed and nodded along.

"This is crazy!"

"Drink it in!" he told me.

"Mae, well done!" Fellow Stone patted my arm.

Other random embraces pulled me in. From every direction, people congratulated me, and quick as it had begun, I was dragged out of Beck's arms. His warm smile never left me. The twinkle in his eye buoyed me all through the crowd. Around and around I turned, accepting more and more well-wishes. When my other battalion members found me again in the melee, Silverfox actually picked me up and spun me around.

"Please, enough with the spinning," I said, laughing.

"Gave us quite the scare there in the middle," he told me above the din. "But now I see it was all part of your plan."

"That's one way to look at it," I agreed. "Wish I could say it was intentional."

"All's well that ends well." He grinned, generously letting my poor actions and his bad behavior off the hook at the same time.

"Thanks for coming back for me." I nodded.

"Thanks for being someone to come back for." He grinned.

Next came Rain. I hugged her tightly. "You saved my life," I told her.

"Yes, well, if you had the skills, I'm sure you'd have done the same." She shrugged. Coming from Rain, that felt like a warm embrace. "I don't know why I always have to suffer just to save your boney behind."

"How's your arm?" I asked.

"It hurts." She looked at me like I was an alien. "Mae, it's broken. I've been kind of busy." She shook her head like I was the dumbest girl on the earth, but I didn't care. That woman with the rude, oblivious tone was now one of my favorite people in the world. Her blunt, uncaring manner had seriously come through for me, again and again. She'd saved my life. I'd be forever grateful. I even kind of liked her.

"Whatever was I thinking? How dumb of me to ask." I laughed.

Then Ferris caught my eye.

I hugged my final team member. "I'm so sorry. In the battle, I should have known it wasn't you."

"Lie-guards are meant to deceive you. Believe me, I know. When you called to tell us, I was just stressed and scared and dumb... I guess I started to believe your narrative. That you weren't a good witch. But look at what you did on your own! Where have you been hiding these skills, Mae? You're a great witch!"

I shook my head.

I was about to confess the truth, that I had serious help, when Lady Mauve interrupted our exchange.

"Don't shake her off." Lady Mauve frowned. "Because of you, our coven is safe. The Damocles faction will move on."

"Will they?"

"They'd better." She stared daggers at them. We looked across the field. The witches in red clothing with the eerie blue eyes were already packing up their belongings.

"Where will they go?" I wondered.

Lady Mauve shrugged. "That's a bridge that *they'll* have to cross."

I sighed. That was sad. They couldn't stay, but they also had nowhere to go. I was about to look away when one of the contestants caught my eye. The mean boy, the one with the dark smile. Kristoff and his spiders.

I nodded at him. I formed a tight smile. But he just narrowed his glare. I could feel his revulsion right across the field. It was similar to the look I'd seen in Spade's eyes.

Great.

Another boy in the world who hated my guts.

Well, do what you want, I thought to myself, breaking our connection. That wasn't my problem.

"What you did today was brave and smart," Lady Mauve told me. "But don't let it go to your head." Cornelius Child motioned to my trainer, and she left, ready to move on to some other pressing coven issue. I was surprised he hadn't come to glad-hand the

Battle of Four champion himself. But he didn't. As he waited for Lady Mauve to return to his side, he did catch my eye. He gave a slight nod. I nodded back.

That was all I would get.

He was off with his elder group, and I was once again a lowly first-year student.

"Hold still for a moment," Lady Blue Moon told me. I looked up, surprised, as she snapped her first photo. "Ooh, candid. Nice." She grinned. "But seriously, I need to get one with the champion and the crashed bell. A portrait."

"Let me just get my team," I agreed. "Why not shoot in this direction?" I redirected Blue Moon to aim the frame so the bell was in the foreground, the distant tower in the back. Then I called in the others to join. Rain, Ferris, and Silverfox all huddled beside me. We bunched together, arm in arm, everyone smiling for the shot. Well, not quite everyone... Lady Rain was back to her frown. I guess the natural shot of adrenaline painkiller had worn off.

"Perfect." Lady Blue Moon grinned, checking out her viewfinder. She nodded, so the group dispersed. "Check it out." Lady Blue Moon showed me the photo.

I looked at our smiling clan, arm in arm in celebration. I was pleased to see, deep in the depth of the field, two other shadows stood side by side on the hill. Barely blips on the horizon, Josie and Aunt Abeline stood solemnly. Every member of the team was there. All the battalion champions who'd saved the coven. Together in one shot.

My pose reminded me of the photos I'd discovered of Mom in the archives. It reminded Lady Blue Moon as well. "This win will be listed in the records," she told me.

"I think," I ventured with a smile, "my mom would be proud."

FORTY-SIX
I KNOW WHAT MITHRIDATE IS

NOTHING in the world could bring a person back to earth after an epic, life-altering victory faster than riding in the backseat of Greg's car. He didn't even offer me front seat privilege.

"Those are the rules of shotgun," Marcy told me. "If you wanna sit in the front, get a boyfriend with a car. Just be glad we got your phone."

"Yeah, Mae. Just be grateful," Beck teased me.

I slugged him playfully in the side.

Battered and dirty, they'd found it. My classmates must have searched the whole field. I was grateful for the effort. But it felt like an even trade. I almost died, like, seven times on the journey back to the castle, and every mile that we traveled, my hands turned brighter white from gripping hard to the safety bar in his car.

We did it!

. . .

I stepped away for myself and texted my aunt once I was safe back at the High Council.

You did it!

I knew you could!

I can't wait to see you again.

*We're gonna... well... *not* talk about it. Soon. That's a promise.*

I was about to text Josie next when the phone rang in my hands. Her face popped up in the contact notifications. I put the device to my ear.

"I was just about to text you! We did it! Thank you so much for your help! I still have your knife to return to you, but unfortunately your blanket, rope, and bucket were smashed beyond repair," I started.

"That's all fine, Mae. I know what mithridate is."

"What?" The smile slipped off my face.

"I told you I'd seen it before. I found the reference in my botany textbook. It was suggested in an ancient book of healings." She paused.

"Okay..."

"It's an antidote."

"To poison, I know. That's what the dictionary said."

So I was right. My mother was definitely murdered.

"Not every poison," Josie clarified. "Its most effective use is against one specific plant. *Attrenpo bellavici.* Better known as lover's pall."

"Lover's..."

"It's a very specific attack. The poisonous spell can only be administered if a victim and perpetrator release a matching type of chemical. A set of pheromones that are only found in one place. Deep, mutual love."

Josie waited for the news to hit.

"Wait... I, what? How..."

"Mae, that chemical ritual can only be completed by someone the victim loves," Josie said. "They're the only ones who can activate the poison."

Someone the victim... loved.

There was only one person in the world who could have murdered my mother. I shared half my genetics with him.

My dad.

FORTY-SEVEN
WITH YOU

THE DOORS to the elevator opened slowly. Throughout the battle, I'd had enough exercise to last me a lifetime, so there was no way I was climbing five flights of stairs just to get to my room. But I was ready for time on my own. I was about to get on the lift, but the box wasn't empty. Brandi and a blonde friend were disembarking. I was so distracted by the news of my father, I almost didn't wait for the girls to step off.

Har-hmmm.

Brandi pointedly cleared her throat. I looked up, surprised. I realized I'd been walking in a daze. I'd have to shelve the information about my dad for another day. Rest up, fully rejuvenate. Then I could take in the awful news.

"Hey, congratulations on the Battle of Four," Brandi's friend told me.

"Thanks." I nodded, exhausted.

Brandi looked me up and down but stayed silent. I

got in the car. The silence was nice, a clear improvement, but I just couldn't help it. "Hey, Brandi," I called after her. They turned to see me. "You should know you were wrong," I told her.

"About what?"

I thought for a moment. "About everything."

Her friend laughed, but Brandi just rolled her eyes. I smiled sweetly as the doors started to close, but just before their impact, a hand thrust into the space. The doors dinged and reopened, but it wasn't Brandi, back for more. It was someone far more inviting.

"Hi parabond," Beck told me.

"Hi," I grinned back, so happy to see him. Alone.

"You did it!" He smiled as he boarded the elevator. Without hesitation, he wrapped me up in his arms. My body was encased in his as the elevator doors closed. "I knew you'd kick butt."

"Thanks." I hugged him back. Sure we were safe and alone, I showed him the pocketknife. "But you should know I had help."

He recognized the hilt of the knife immediately. "That's Josie's... How?"

"I called her. It turns out, we don't have to be as isolated from the townspeople as we first thought. People leave them behind because it's easier. There's awkwardness in the things left untold, but it's not forbidden to reach out." I checked in with his face. Already, he'd retreated. "Beck, she really helped me."

He nodded but didn't meet my eye.

"And if you want..." I faltered. I really wanted

what was best for him, even now, even if it meant giving up the safety of his warm arms for good. "If you want, you can reach out to her. Even though one of you is in and one is outside of the High Council, if the love is there, there's no reason to break up."

We'd thought choosing to parabond meant he was required to close the book on that relationship forever, but I could see now that wasn't the case. Beck could be my partner and still be Josie's beloved. If that was what he wanted.

"Is that what you want?" I asked.

Beck dropped our hug completely. He turned to look at me. Really look at me. He dragged a hand through his hair. "Mae, I'm glad that she helped you and that she's good and all the rest of it, but Josie's not my girl. She's in my past. I'm ready to turn that page." There it was. He didn't crouch it or hide it or play it off. He just stood still, his body inches from mine, and looked intently at my face. "With you."

Those final two words built a buzz in my stomach, and a warm glow burst forward from deep within my soul. It vibrated through my organs and sent shivers through my skin. I couldn't help the smile that danced onto my lips.

"Okay," I said.

"Okay?" He raised an eyebrow.

"Okay," I told him.

His lips parted into a grin. "Well, okay!"

We stared into each other's eyes, an internal light within us shining.

Our chests heaved in syncopation. We found each other's rhythm.

I was so happy I could burst, but I didn't know what to do next. Luckily, Beck did.

"Come here," he told me. He slipped a hand into my hair and cupped my face towards him, pulling my body into his frame. He touched my mouth to his soft, pink lips.

He kissed me softly at first.

Slowly.

Building excitement.

He tasted like hot cinnamon hearts, and his lips felt smooth like ChapStick.

I pulled back with a smile. "Oh, Beck," I murmured.

He kissed me firmer now. Deeper. With passionate certainty.

"Mae," he whispered. He moved us back, pressing me against the elevator wall. His strong arms circled around my waist. My hands wove into his hair, pulling him closer. Tighter. Towards me.

Suddenly, the elevator dinged.

We pulled back and straightened up, cognizant as the doors slid open that anyone could be watching, waiting for us. We didn't want to get caught. But we were alone in the hall of the fifth floor. Awkward together, we giggled.

"You should know how much I've wanted that," I told him.

"Me too," he admitted.

"It was better than I imagined."

"Me too." He grinned.

"But there's one thing... Before we go any further... I really have to tell you... I do *not* like your sister."

"Duly noted. And good news, that's not a deal breaker." He laughed and walked me down the hall, hand in hand, ready to see how life in the High Council witch coven would unfold.

EPILOGUE

(FROM THE POV OF FERRIS BEAN)

"WE DID IT!"

"Yes!"

"Three cheers for Ferris!"

"For Silverfox!"

"For Rain!

"Mae came through!"

"Hip, hip, hooray!"

"Hip, hip, hooray!"

The jubilant cries came from every direction. Maybe even my own mouth. It was so chaotic and loud that for a time, I couldn't tell. Even after Blue Moon snapped the photo to commemorate the moment, the coven was still ready to go wild.

"We did it, girl!" Silverfox picked me up off my feet and tossed me up onto his shoulder. My red hair flared out like a firework above our heads as he spun us both around.

In surprise, I cackled and squealed. "Put me down!"

But I'm not sure I really wanted him to.

It felt great to celebrate our infamy.

His energy was contagious. Free and wild.

He unleashed a triumphant holler from deep inside his throat. The primal vigor cut straight through the crowd. It re-amped the celebration. "Ferris, you're a freakin' genius! When that earthquake-boy tried to crack the dirt beneath me, you smacked him clean from the side with - whatever it was."

"A hockey stick," I laughed. "A lie-guard hockey stick. It was all I could think of."

"It was, like, a thing of beauty. Wasn't it? We saved the coven, you and I!" He was kind of joking, but also meant it.

"Put me down," I complained. More in control now. My cheeks hurt from smiling.

The ruddy man did as I asked.

"It was Mae," I reminded him. "It wasn't *us*." We could both see her still surrounded. A new star in her own right.

"Aye, but we definitely helped. We played our part." When I didn't immediately jump on board, he egged me on. "Didn't we, girl?" He turned, opening his body language up, happy to mug for the crowd. "Didn't we, y'all?!" He whooped up the witches around us. They cheered and laughed. Totally on board. I didn't dare contain him. In a second, he was off. Cheering and celebrating with someone else in the mob.

I had a feeling that when Silverfox retold this tale, which he would, over and over, his role in the success of the final battle would grow larger and larger in time. He was right, of course. As fellow battalion-mates, both he and I and even Lady Rain pulled out all the magic we had to help our teammate succeed in retrieving the Damocles' orb. But it was Mae, that little default, first-year witch, who turned out to be smarter and more resilient than all of us combined. I couldn't wait to hear the details of how she'd figured out the Evil Eye was hidden inside the Orson Bell. It was, after all, also a story that *I* would share... over many a slice of delicious pie.

With Ethan.

And my sister.

And the people who mattered most in my world.

It almost made me wish that after she'd messed up, I'd taken her calls. When Mae tipped off the other coven, I'll admit it, I was pissed. I didn't want anymore of her *help,* that's for sure. But of course, fate intervened. And lucky for all of us, it turned out pretty good. Great, even. When she sent me and Silverfox and the enemy tribe on a wild goose chase following Rain deep into the forest, it also opened up the other half of the field for her to explore. We couldn't have had a better ending. Honestly, I never thought we'd get through the battle at all.

"Congratulations!"

I continued to be greeted by a thousand adoring faces. At least that's how it felt.

While Silverfox fell away to chatter with other fellows and ladies from the coven, the smiles and shoulder pats were unending around me. I couldn't really get my bearings in the crowd. It was disordered and wonderful and warm. Even Clint, Brandi's boyfriend engulfed me in a hug. (Although Brandi wasn't beside him, which was fine. I wouldn't have wanted a phony embrace from those spindly, back-stabbing arms.)

This was the thing of legends.

The Battle of Four.

Fought and won!

Now Ethan could come home!

I looked down at my phone. No word from him yet. Did he know the battle was over? I tried to call him. It was so crowded, I wasn't sure he'd be able to hear me if he answered, but it turned out to be a moot worry. His voicemail kicked in. I hung up.

Instead, I left a text message.

BABE, WE DID IT!

I looked up. Searching.

Where was he?

Had anyone else got through to the emissary? Told them the battle was over? It was safe to come home?

I called again, just for good measure.

Still no answer.

Maybe he was riding. Mid-stride. Coming back to our stables, ready to celebrate.

There had been a lot of pressure on us both. When Cornelius picked him, I had thought he might be kidding. Both Ethan and I directly involved in the conflict? Each tasked, in our own way, with saving the clan?

I'd been nervous to hold up my end, but now that we had, I couldn't wait to share my adventure.

Where was he?

I glanced around the busy field. Everywhere were smiling faces. He was so lanky and tall, I could usually spot his black hair, no matter the crowd. I spun around. They should have received word of the victory by now. The field was awash in white wardrobes and witches I recognized from school or my training. Everyone was chatting animatedly, although the outright whoops and cheering had started to slow down. Success had brought a rosy bloom to all our cheeks. Everywhere you looked were big smiles and no frowns.

"How does it feel?" Someone asked from behind me.

I quickly turned. I seemed to have worked my way to the other side of the crowd. Now at the far side of the collective, I stumbled back into the realm of two of my favorite teachers, Lady Gray and Lady Mauve. The latter raised an eyebrow, an amused smiled flirting on her lips. That was a sight in itself. It seemed to me before this moment, all Lady Mauve ever did was look annoyed.

"How does it feel?" Lady Gray asked again.

"I'm relieved," I admitted to these women who knew me well. They had trained both me and Ethan at the castle. They'd watched us grow in our powers and develop our bond. I hoped they were proud of the witches we'd become. "Can I tell you a secret?" I asked.

I glanced down at my phone. Still no message from Ethan.

The women leaned in.

"After Rain hit the ground... in the training. After her bone... and her arm..." I stopped short of the gory details of the account.

They shuddered. They'd seen what I'd seen.

I shrugged. "I wasn't sure we could go on."

"That was no secret," Lady Mauve pointed out.

I faltered. But suddenly, a wry smile broke through on her mouth. She was teasing me. Lady Mauve made a joke.

I tried to chuckle. Self-consciously, I tossed my hair around.

"Ferris, we're proud of you and Ethan both," Lady Gray patted my back. The neighboring smile had disappeared, (one second it was there, then it was gone) but Lady Mauve was still nodding.

I grinned.

These two women had taught me every enchanted thing that I knew. And Lady Mauve's tough love in the training modules had really lit a fire under Mae. The older witch had gotten through to the girl. Her influence helped saved the day. Of course if I tried to say that praise out loud, Lady Mauve would have shrugged it away.

"Thanks." I accepted the compliment. But, I glanced at my phone again.

Still no word.

It was weird that Ethan hadn't texted or called. He still hadn't answered at all. I knew their little trio had to stay incognito and disconnected in the forest, but surely one of them would have been minding the phones. Seeing when it was safe to come home. Who knew. Maybe he was already back here on the field, and not aware of my incoming communications over the collective celebration and noise?

"Have either of you seen Ethan?" I looked around.

Any second he'd be galavanting onto the scene, looking sexy as always on his stallion. I grew up on a farm, sure, but I never thought I'd end up with a cowboy. And boy, could he take control of a magnificent horse.

He'd trot on by, I'd wrap my hand in his grasp and he'd throw me up on the bare back of the animal, or drop me behind him riding high in the saddle. Either way, I'd hold on tight. I couldn't wait to wrap my arms around his chest.

For us to be together and go home.

We would gallop off into the sunset.... I let my imagination run a little bit wilder from there. And what was wrong with that? We could be a bit carefree. The pressure was off our shoulders. What I felt was the sweet rush of freedom. And I couldn't wait to get in those arms.

To touch him.

To be re-united.

I was so intent on finding him in the crowd that I almost missed the little look between the women.

Almost.

Gray glanced in Mauve's direction. The woman bristled.

I stared at them both.

What was that? What was that moment? That hesitation? I waited for one of them to offer something. But neither of them spoke.

That wasn't good enough.

That little look brought a chill to my bones.

"What's going on?" I asked. "Where is he?"

"Ethan's not coming," Mauve said.

"Wait, what?"

"I'm sorry, Ferris." Gray added. "It's not safe to bring him home."

My brows knit down over my eyes. "What do you mean? It's not *safe*."

It was imperative that he and the other emissaries left before the start of the Battle. They were tasked with hiding our most precious resources while we went head-to-head in competition, as a back-up plan, just in case something went wrong.

But the battle was *over*.

We were victorious!

There was no need to hide anymore.

"We just won the Battle of Four," I added, as if they didn't already know. Why did my voice suddenly sound so small?

"Yes..." Gray hesitated. She seemed to be at a loss to say more.

But Mauve always cut to the chase.

"You're right, Ferris, of course. We won the battle," she said, staring out at the witches still in celebration. "But you should know..." Her gaze reached past us, past the jubilant congregation. Further across the field to the red robes and the lowered heads of the Damocles coven, still smarting from the misery of their defeat. Not yet gone home.

For maybe the first time, I saw their angry and disheartened faces.

Why hadn't they gone home?

"It's not over," Mauve admitted. Her tone said so much more than the words that she chose.

Resigned.

Definitive.

"Not even close." She shook her head. She had seen this kind of thing before. "We won the battle..." she told us. "But we might have just started a war..."

Ready for more? Find out what happens next to Mae, Beck, Ferris, and Ethan in Planted Bonds, The High Council Witch Chronicles book four. Available now.

JULIE CATHERINE
PLANTED
BONDS
THE HIGH COUNCIL WITCH CHRONICLES
4

ACKNOWLEDGMENTS

Wow, book three in the High Council Witch Chronicles is in the books! (Get it, books? Books!... okay I'll stop. It just might be that dear sweet Aunt Abeline got her love of word play from me, haha creative license and all that.)

I have had such a wonderful time immersing myself in the coven, testing out their magical skills and fleshing out the whole tribal world. I hope you've enjoyed reading it! There's so much more to discover in future books!

Thank you so much to Allana Giesbrecht, my beta reader - there's nothing more fun then watching your google doc notes rolling in in real time. (Or opening my email provider and seeing 15 suggestions all lined up overnight. It's the best!)

Thank you to Deranged Doctor Design for really catching the vision for these covers, I've had so many compliments on them. And a big thanks to Katie Wolf for editing all of my funky commas and grammar.

For everyone who's left a review for the book or books on whatever store or social media you use, THANK YOU!!! Reviews mean so much to indie authors like me. Other readers use them to find social proof, so if you liked the books, please let everybody know! It doesn't have to be a long and thoughtful paragraph, although those are always nice, even a star rating is very helpful for other readers to find and discover my book. Maybe they'll love it too!

The fourth book to the High Council Witch Chronicles is now in the works, and I can't wait to get it out to you soon!

Xo
   Julie

The High Council Witch Chronicles

Paranormal Bonds

Predetermined Bonds

Poisoned Bonds

Planted Bonds

Paternal Bonds

The High Council Witch Chronicles prequels

Enchanted Bonds (a prequel novella)